I0668455

hymnandme

Barbara Buck

Onesong Publishing
Quincy, Massachusetts

hymnandme

by Barbara Buck

Published by:
Onesong Publishing
550 Adams St. Suite 234
Quincy, MA 02169

FIRST EDITION

Library of Congress Control Number: 2012904771

This is a work of fiction. Names, characters, places, business establishments, and incidents either are the product of the author's imagination or are used fictitiously, and any resemblance to events, locales, or actual persons, living, dead, or cycled-off, is entirely coincidental.
Cover Art © 2012 by Amber Buck

Book Formatted by Ann Miller

ISBN: 978-0-9853346-0-4

Printed in the United States of America

For more information:

www.barbarabuck.com
www.amberbuckphotography.com

for Amber, my reason
and for Marc, who's something else again

hymnandme

Book One

Prologue

Behold, ~~I Come Quickly~~ I'm Here!

So, I gotta tell you first off that I've never much been into any of this religion crap and I've never understood anything of what those Christ guys say on TV. Once my Nana sent this real famous bible-banger a ton of money and all she got back was one of those little packets that usually hold ketchup, but this one said *Holy Water* on it. That really pissed me off.

But Louis told me I should write it all down and get it all out before I forget, which is what I usually do, and how it was real important because "you don't usually spend nine months intimately involved with a deity," which is what Louis said, not me, and unless you were that Virgin Mary lady, I guess he's right.

So you can probably tell I wasn't looking for any religion or Savior or any of that kinda bullcrap and I was pretty much minding my own business, which is pretty much what I always do and is what Louis calls my M.O. (but not "MO" like gay or anything but just the letters), when this guy walks up to me and says something like, "Hey, my name is Jesus."

Well, I know he means "Hay-Zeus," being born and raised in California and all, but I figure *he* doesn't know that and he's like some down-on-his-luck homeless guy who just wants a little bread or wine or something and probably was once a big shot in advertising so he spiffs up the punch line with some holy-moly baloney. When I realized he meant the *real* Jesus—the H. Christ chief enchilada, the BIG JC, the Way, Truth, and Life guy (I always thought it was Light, isn't that better…Way, Truth, and Light?)—I was real curious as to why he was speaking American and dressed all in 21st century stuff, even though he looked fine, in a crazy "superstar" kinda way. He tried to explain it to me once and, of course, I didn't understand, but I think it's along the line of a Star Trek "Universal Translator" sorta thing.

So, this guy, Jesus, shows up and he wants to know what the hell is going on down here and why we're not all loving each other and everything since he thought he'd fixed all that by dying and hanging around on crosses for two thousand years. Well, then I had to tell him that that only made all those guys in dresses get all hot to trot and create the hugest power trip the world had ever seen and then *that* created all these wars and race troubles and political scams. He seemed real surprised when I said that, like he didn't know his little family company had become the world's biggest corporation. Now, I guess, he just wanted to get to know the people and prove he was this regular guy who loved his neighbor as himself and show how it was possible for everybody to do that—but without all the "cover your neighbor's ass" stuff added in.

Anyway, I decided I could give him an afternoon or so since it was kinda obvious he needed some help, being divine in L.A. and all, and I wasn't doing too much anyway, being chronically unemployed (if you know what I mean), and not real interested in spending a lot of energy finding just the right dishwashing job. I mean, he seemed like he just needed somebody to talk to and I'm usually real good at that since I don't talk a lot and I listen even less.

But, you know, I had this spooky feeling right from the start that he was like picking me to help him, kinda like all those fisher guys they tell you about in Sunday School, getting all tangled up in their nets and trying to become Apologies. It almost felt like a prize or some big treat—like if you could jump in a time machine and talk to good old Honest Abe and ask him if he'd changed his mind about going to plays!

Well, this was sorta like that, just in reverse. Maybe this Jesus guy had hitched a ride on some cosmic time-warp and here he was, in Hollyweird, picking *me* to be the first person in the history of the world for him to talk to since…well, since the end of the Bible. Man!

Yeah, that all sounded pretty cool, except I knew it couldn't be for real. But, as long as he didn't try to kill me or make me sell flowers at the airport, I thought it would be kinda interesting to see what he had to say. I had no idea on that first day I was about to go back to school…one I could never, ever get out of until I died.

My Savior's Back and
You're Gonna Be in Trouble

"Feel like a walk?"

Well, he was definitely a messiah "after my own heart," as my Nana always used to say. Walking is like my all time favorite thing to do. And when I think about it, talking and walking is what we mostly did the whole time I knew him, that and stopping to sit on bus stops and curbs. He didn't get the bubbles in Coke and I didn't get how he could really believe all this stuff about being Jesus. I mean, how could it even be possible?

But, true or not, I was starting to feel this great "new adventure" vibe, and I figured that hanging around with a guy who thinks he's The Savior could be kinda entertaining, in an I-hope-he's-not-a-psycho-terrorist sorta way. He didn't seem to have a past, other than the Bible one, but a lot of the homeless folks in L.A. don't have pasts either, except the ones they make up. I was hoping, instead of some Bible guy from a million years ago, that maybe he was some kind of alien (not from another country but like from outer space). How cool would that be? My own private E.T. or Mr. Spock or Cosmic Lassie or something.

So we walked and talked, and he started teaching me, but in this funky sorta way that didn't feel like I was actually learning anything. It was real cool and sometimes I would forget where I was and what time it was and I wished school could of been like that. I mighta stayed.

I told him that, about school, on that first day.

"It *is* very important to get a good education," he said, with a kinda shine in his eyes like he had this great secret he was about to spill. "But education can only teach you what *man* thinks, not what God thinks."

"What about Sunday School?" I knew I had him on that one.

"What's Sunday School?"

He was always saying stuff like that that would just blow my mind. I mean, the real Jesus invented Sunday School, right? This guy sure wasn't a very good imposter.

"You can only know what God thinks by looking at everything very carefully, and with love," he said, real patient-like. I think he was trying to get me back on track.

"You mean like when a baby gets born and you realize it's a pretty amazing thing?" I asked.

"Exactly," he seemed real happy I understood him (he was gonna find out that was pretty rare), "or when you figure something out, right out of the blue, and you feel inspired." He tried to explain to me that "inspired" was just this spirit guy living inside you. I thought that was kinda creepy so I was glad when he moved on.

"To get deep inside the Mind of God, you must find that still, quiet center inside yourself and just listen," he said. "And there isn't anything you can say or chant or pray because the language of God is silence." I think he meant that there just isn't any password to it at all.

"Huh?"

"Your mind has to get out of the way," he smiled, "because the real conversation is between God and your heart and all you have to do is just sit, be quiet, and listen. Then you'll know all you need to know."

Yeah. Big help.

And if that doesn't drive you nuts, try this on: He said that when you get down to it, to the real inside-the-answer stuff, there's no conversation at all because, way down there at the true heart of it all, you and God are One and so you're really just talking to yourself!

Now, I know that sounds like a lot of bull, and it probably is, but I decided to try it once and it took a real long time, but I thought I had a glimpse of what he meant and it felt…well, it felt like home. And most of us know what that feeling is, that *home* feeling, but it's real far away inside from when we were little kids or babies or just sombreros inside our moms and most of the time we try not to remember it because it just hurts too bad to admit we're not there anymore.

Well, here I was, all grown up and all, and here was this feeling again, like from way deep inside and I just knew that what he said was true, even though it was only this glimpse and only lasted a second and was probably just my imagination or something. But then I thought, if it was just my imagination or something, so what if it was and who cares because it felt good anyway and maybe that's what all this was with him and this adventure and all. And then, like he would always do, he sorta read my mind.

"Just experience it," he'd said. "When we start defining it, we lose the truth and the feeling and it starts taking on a shape, and it becomes just a fact."

So, anyway, back to that first day. We'd gotten so wrapped up shootin' the breeze and crap like that, we'd somehow walked right out of the city and suddenly I realized we were in Griffith Park.

"Everything is God!" he practically shouted, all jazzed

and like a little kid seeing stars for the first time. "Every tree, every star, every shell on the beach, every pebble in your shoe, every person and every animal and all the things in-between and all the thoughts, light and dark, good and bad, all of it, from the beginning to the end, every last bit of it is God. It's all One and we are One with it all!" (Or something like that. Just so you know, I used to have this disease called photogenic memory but then I started remembering things that didn't happen instead of all the real useful algehistorometry bull-shine they throw at you in school and then I dropped out and started smoking and stuff like that so now I have a terrible memory and I'm not exactly sure that's what he said, but pretty close.) He could probably tell by my blank face that dropping out of school was actually a smart thing to do.

He kept on talking but I was trying to figure out where the zoo was from where we were, you know, to show him a camel or something, so I missed a lot of what he was yapping about. I mean, it was great that he was so excited about being alive and all but I wasn't feeling "one with" anything, especially not trees and rocks. When I tuned back in, I kinda figured out that the point of it all was to say that you could never be without God. Nothing was without God, not one thing in the world ever was outside of this Everything-All-At-Once God.

Well, I started to think that maybe this wasn't gonna be such a great adventure after all, if all he was ever gonna do was talk about God. I'm just not into that crap, like I told you, and if he was preaching his head off all the time then I thought I'd have to at least make him prove he was really from the Bible. I mean, I'd pretty much be a sucker to just believe some guy who shows up all divine and all and claims he's Jesus, right? He didn't even have a driver's license, for Christ's sake. So, I decided he better give me some proof or I was gonna have to dump him back on Hollywood Boulevard where we met, and let the next poor schmuck take on this year's version of the Messiah.

Anyway, as we headed back down the hill to the city, he went all quiet for a long time and I was hoping he hadn't read my mind again and was gonna suddenly turn into a cereal killer or something. But he just had this kindness about him that made me relax. So, I summed up my courage and told him that, if I was gonna hang out with him I needed some proof of who he really was. He asked what kind of proof I wanted and I said, you know, like a miracle or something, and he said he didn't do parlor tricks, and I said, what the hell's a parlor?

So, when we hit Hollywood Boulevard, he thanks me for all my help and for straightening him out, which really worried me, if you catch my drift. I mean, the help part—well, yeah, of course, and I would of helped him even if he wasn't this back-from-the-Wherever-supreme-being kinda guy. I mean, jeez, he was a human being, for Christ's sake, so it seems to me anybody would help somebody else out if they could, except when you watch the 6:30 news and find out there are a bunch of creeps running around all over the place, but any regular guy, or lady, divine or not, I think I would try to help 'em out.

No, that's not the part that worried me. It was the "straightening him out" part that gave me the willies—I mean, *me?* Why the hell put all that weight-of-the-world pressure on me? And he's about to go off and do God knows what based on my this-is-the-way-the-world-looks-to-me-off-the-top-of-my-head goofball comments that I just spieled off when I didn't know it was some kinda test or anybody was actually listening or anything. And what if I was wrong, which happens a lot, not on purpose, but just on account of not knowing much and so sometimes getting the wrong idea about something, like when all the witnesses to an accident give a completely different story.

Anyway, while I was freaking out about steering this Jesus guy the wrong way in the world, he gets this kinda look on his face like he all of a sudden made some important decision (I was praying it wasn't based on my yammering), and he tells me he wants to go someplace to get clothes. It was so out of the blue that it made me stop worrying and start trying to get my bearings. Since we were already on Hollywood Boulevard, I figured we could just shoot on over to H & V and head on down Vine to the Goodwill.

On the way, I tried to explain the Walk of *Shame* stars to him but he didn't seem very interested, or maybe he just didn't understand. But when we got to the corner he said, "What's that?" I guess he'd noticed that the crappy old stars suddenly changed to this crappy old moon. He was pointing at Tinseltown's big hoopla salute to some space guys who went to the moon.

"It's just some crappy old moon."

Nothing.

"*You* know, for those space guys…the guys that went to the moon about a million years ago."

He looked like I'd hit him with a ton of bricks. Get this— he said he had no idea anybody had ever been to the moon. What a crackup! I knew he must of been pulling my leg when he said that, but I decided to play along.

"So, you didn't know about the moon landing?"

"I can't even imagine anything so remarkable," he said, staring at the dirty, faded circle that absolutely nobody else in the whole world has ever paid any attention to except maybe some tourists from another country who didn't have space either.

"Yeah, well, it happened. Big deal, huh?"

He just kept staring at the sidewalk, so I decided to put things in prospect for him.

"Y'know, it's not as big a deal as…." I kinda did my arms up and down toward him, like that letter lady showing off her vowels—and he was the vowel! Well, he just stared at me like I was having some sorta fit, or a sudden need to be a headliner in Vegas.

"Never mind," I said as I practically dragged him on down Vine toward the Goodwill.

So, one thing I really liked was he was a pretty fast shopper. I mean, I hate shopping and I really appreciate folks who are just in and out and don't make a career out of "does this make my ass look fat?" But even though he could shop fast, he was still in the store for about a year *talking* to people. Most of the time I just hung outside and smoked and wondered if this was really happening. I mean, how in hell could this be Jesus? *That* Jesus…the *Bible* Jesus! Hangin' with me? It just kept bugging me.

Once he got all his stuff, he thanked me again for giving him the LD (that's "lowdown" in L.A. street I'm-too-lazy-to-say-the-whole-word talk), and we sat down on a bus stop and watched folks going by for a while. I wanted to try to get him on over to Grauman's (that's the Chinese Theatre place, in case you've never been here) to see what he thought of all those Marilyn Monroe handprints and Betty Garbo's legprint and crap like that, but he'd gone all quiet again, like when you gotta talk to somebody or ask them something that's gonna blow the roof off their whole day. I was gonna learn about those quiet times with him, but on that first day I didn't really care that much. I mean, I'm all over doing nothin'…it's what I do best.

When he did start talking again, it was way over my head. I knew it was in his funny English and I think it had something to do with his game plan or something, but I could only tell for sure that he was getting all serious and throwing out words and ideas and stuff and that it was all the way out of my league.

So, I decided I better take him home to meet Louis.

The Ark

Where we live there's a huge street with buildings and stores and crap (literally…nobody picks up after their dogs around here), and then there's an alley, like they couldn't wait to get another street in there, and then our building. We live at 64 Wilbur (yeah, like the pig—Jeez, everybody says that!), which is a real old, crumbly four story building with two apartments on each floor. On the first three floors there's these storage rooms, for everybody, across the back of the building, so the apartments on the fourth floor have extra rooms. And, on the roof, there's this kinda failed greenhouse, and that's where Louis lives.

Louis calls our building "The Ark," not because there are two of us or we're like animals or anything but because he says we have a little bit of everything. Before that day when I brought Jesus home, I knew everybody in the building in a not-exactly-friendly-city kinda way and I guess you could say Louis was my only real friend, in a not-exactly-friendly-just-able-to-stomach sorta way.

Louis is this real old Jewish intellectual guy and his place is just one giant room with windows for walls that face south and west and a window-roof that's just about as good as a real roof since it's so dirty. His bathroom is right out there in the room in plain sight, for Christ's sake, with no walls or anything. And our elevator hasn't worked in about a hundred years, so old Louis has to climb up all those stairs every day. So, I guess you can tell that we all live poor, in the sense of a lot of roaches and what Louis calls the "bane of urban dwelling below the 40th attitude" or something like that. I dunno, I usually fall asleep after "bane."

When I say Louis is old, I mean he was born that way. He's probably about 35 or 40 but he acts 80 and has glasses with those extra glass half moons in them, and a ton of real curly black hair that's just starting to get all salt and peppery in spots around the sides. He's always serious and never laughs but since he's all mature and everything, he "frequently chuckles." And he gives those chuckles out like prizes.

Louis is an authority. He knows everything I've ever thought about so whenever I have a question, I just book it on up to Louis'. He's got about a million books and hardly anything else except one of those ancient fridges that used to be called an icebox and then some genius came along and made it electric so it's got this big space where ice used to go that isn't a freezer and isn't very cold. He has a hotplate, and a bed on the floor, and one of those rickety old chairs made out of polished sticks or something, and some wires to hang clothes on, and a helluva lot of roach motels, and that's it. His books are all over the floor, open to a lot of different places and he has a friggin' cow if you touch the open ones. But it's okay to touch the closed ones—like you'd ever wanna touch a book you didn't have to anyway.

Louis has the best sound system in the building, so whenever anybody wants to hear stuff, we just book it on up to Louis'. He also's got a VCR, but no TV. The VCR is the only clock in his whole apartment (I mean he doesn't even wear a watch), but one day it broke and now it only flashes 12:00. Charlie said at least it was right two times a day, but Louis didn't even chuckle at that one.

14

You probably noticed I don't curse. I don't swear, either, and I don't blastfoamy. (At least, I don't think I do. I don't exactly know what blastfoamy means but my Nana always used to say she better not catch me with blastfoamy on my lips.) Well, Louis doesn't swear either. I mean, I usually can't tell what he's talking about, so I'm not sure, but I don't think he does. He said once that the worse word he ever said was defecate, which makes sense because I'm pretty sure he drinks regular coffee.

I don't know how Louis lives…I mean, how he makes his living. I never saw him go to work and once when I asked him about it he just mumbled a lot of stuff that I didn't understand. But I think he said he was some kinda "child prototype" or something like that and somebody else took care of the bills. Not that there are too many bills, considering where we live and all.

Next floor down is Bernard. Now, he'll tell you that that's pronounced Burr-nerd (like a cold dork) with the stress on the Burr, which he'll tell you "rhymes with purr" because he has about a million cats, that he calls his "babies," for Christ's sake. Bernard is gay—like you couldn't tell from that—and old. He calls himself a "silly, old queen" which doesn't make any sense but he never bothers me and it's kinda entertaining when he bothers Louis. I mean, he doesn't bother Louis in a sense like Louis is gay or anything, but he bothers him because he's always kinda flirting with him and batting his eyes at him and crap like that. He keeps saying stuff like he's glad he lives right under Louis because that's the place he's always wanted to be and then he winks and that makes Louis go all shades of practically purple in his face. It's funny because, like I said, Louis is all mature and all and he only chuckles, so it's fun to see him get flustered.

I live on the second floor. I used to live here with Nana but she got so she couldn't walk up stairs anymore so she moved to this little dollhouse-sized place behind somebody's house that used to be for servants, for crying out loud, and so it's just me now. I live right above Mrs. T, and when Nana still lived here I slept on the old red couch in the living room so that meant I could hear Mrs. T's TV all night long and all she ever watched was those TV preacher Christ guys.

Mrs. T didn't always talk in like regular language but was always putting in Bible talk. I don't mean like thee-eth and thou-eth, but more like all of a sudden shouting out a name and a number or two like, "MATHEW SEVEN ONE!" That was her favorite one. And then, if you were real lucky, she'd tell you what that meant, "Judge not less ye (ye...see!) be judged." But mostly I think you were supposed to know.

Louis was always saying that "Conservative Christian" was an ox and a moron and I actually saw one once on a Cat Stevens CD cover (an ox and a moron, that is, not a Conservative Christian) so I guess it was a good thing that Louis lived on the top of the building and Mrs. T and her Christ guys blaring lived on the bottom.

I live right across from Ty, which meant when I slept in the living room I could hear his violin all night long too. So, between Ty's playing and Mrs. T's TV, it was kinda like listening to a real long movie about Jesus that's always about to make you cry with all that sugary movie music telling you how to feel. I think it would of been way cooler if Ty played the saxophone and there was this real long movie about Jesus with jazz as the music, but that's probably the reason Hollywood isn't knocking my door down to produce any current flicks.

Ty has about a million names. I'm not kidding. His whole name is Tiberius John Coltrane Ornette Coleman Charlie

Parker Smith. Really. So, I'm thinking his folks were looking for a sax player too.

Anyway, Louis once said that "we all wear our own kind of uniform" and, if you look at each of us at The Ark, it's obvious he was right. Mrs. T always wears some loose dress with a thin robe kinda thing and her hair in curlers. I mean, her hair is always in curlers and I gotta admit I've wondered if maybe she was bald and the curlers just came with the hair on them already.

Mrs. T thought jewelry was evil so she only wore a "very tasteful cross" necklace, her wedding ring, her high school graduation ring, her mother's gold watch-bracelet-thingy, another gold bracelet that was flat and had some girl's name on it (MIA somebody), and about a million earrings. She wears earrings all the time, even though her hair is always in those curlers. She pretty much always looks like she's just about to get dressed and do her hair and go out on the town—without the makeup, clothes, or date.

The Earth Ladies, Autumn and Raindrop (I kid you not), who live across from Bernard, look like twins until you get up close. They both wear the same "uniform," which is long skirts (probably to hide some real hairy legs) and sandals (even in winter but then with socks, for Christ's sake) and sometimes just buttoned up vests on top so we all get the big thrill of seeing that they don't shave under their arms either. They always wear these long necklaces made out of dead coconuts or something and even longer earrings that hang about down to their waists. The earrings are all spidery looking, with little bits of dead twigs and feathers and crap like that all caught up in the earring's web. I'm not sure, but there might even be some tangled up old dead bugs in there too since they believe in "all life is precious" and other real deep bullcrap like that.

They both have real long hair and they tie it in braids, but right around their faces there's always these little wispy hairs that get away. Autumn's hair is kinda red, in a dark brown sorta way—like autumn, I guess. Raindrop's hair is black as death, with skin so white she looks like she's already died. Charlie says she'd be a Goth if she wasn't a Granola. I don't know what any of that means. I just think she looks scary.

The Earth Ladies are both a little sad around the edges, like one of those corset flowers that's just beginning to die. You can still tell what it was and how beautiful it must of been, but it's fading a bit—from the outside in. Or like some old, broken-down shack that's still all cozy and warm inside. It makes me think that's kinda what happens to all of us as we get old. Nana used to say she still felt 16 inside and was pretty freaked out when she'd look in the mirror every morning and see some old lady looking back.

Autumn works at the Observatory as a guard (like you could steal anything from there... *Yes, Officer, I saw him run away carrying a 50 million pound telescope*) and also some kinda part-time translator, since she can speak Spanish like a first language, which it is for her (but she doesn't go around showing it off by rolling her rrrr's all over the place like those TV talking heads trying to impress everybody with just how "lingual" they can be). Sometimes, on slow days, she lets me sneak in, which is really pretty cool. I love the stars, the ones in the sky, I mean, but it's hard as hell to see any except maybe once a year in L.A. Like you've probably already heard, Los Angeles is the only city I know of with a ceiling.

Autumn has Leonard Cohen lyrics written on all kinds of different colored and shaped paper all over her walls. She sits all day writing out the lyrics by hand and pasting them to the walls but absolutely refuses to listen to the music. She said it would be like if somebody tried to sing you your favorite poem or the Bible or something—you'd get caught up in where *they* thought the meaning was instead of your own sense of it. And, she won't not-listen to anybody but Leonard Cohen.

Sometimes Autumn draws pictures instead of the lyrics, and I guess you're supposed to guess what song it is. Her favorite drawing is something like an egg with a crack in the middle and a kinda sunset in it, inside shining out. There's about a million of those. It reminds me of like when all those people in that UFO movie started trying to make copies of that tower-mountain-thing out of everything they could get their hands on—even mashed potatoes, for Christ's sake. All Autumn's "artworks" are different and some are made out of pieces of magazines she calls "colleges," but she's not very good at keeping the pictures straight and I guess she has seizures or made them while she was blindfolded because all the pictures are kinda pasted on top of each other.

She has this one other drawing, "post JC," as Louis is always saying, of this lady standing on some kinda landfill by a river and there are flowers and kids playing all over the garbage and this lady is bigger than them all and kinda leaning over the water holding a mirror. That one just knocks me out. Way in the back of the drawing is Jesus, or somebody that looks like him, drowning in this still water that if you look close enough has the word "Wisdom" written in it. Autumn always says that he isn't drowning, he's sinking, but I don't see how that would be any better. I guess that drawing is pretty good because other people always do that "Oh, yeah," thing people do when they see something they understand, but I don't even know who Leonard Cohen is, so I'm not sure.

Raindrop is another story. She never talks at all. Charlie

said her mute button was stuck. I used to think maybe she was like that Helen girl who couldn't talk or see or hear or eat food off her own plate or anything. But, I guess not, because Raindrop can whisper.

She's been writing this book called "1000 Things" about how you're not supposed to own more than 1000 things or you become "a lousy capital S" or something like that. Well, me and Charlie were gonna count all her things and catch her having 1001 but we stopped after about 22 because it got boring. The book has about 300 pages already so I told Raindrop she could only have 700 more things, but Autumn told me the book was *one thing* and then she threw one of those brown flower pots at me and it broke, so I guess she's down to 999.

Anyway, where was I….oh yeah, uniforms. Charlie, who lives right above me, is always in this shirt with the name 'Charlie' on it and what Louis calls his gas station pants. Charlie's real name is Tony but everybody calls him Charlie because that's the name on the shirt he found. It's one of those blue cable-guy work shirts and I guess the guy who owned it (Charlie) took it off to work on the roof next door and forgot it. Charlie's real good with hot-wiring stuff so he just took the shirt so he'd look official when he was committing grand theft cable. Charlie works at night as a janitor somewhere, but his true gift is hot-wiring.

Mr. and Mrs. Yin, who live across from Charlie and under the Earth Ladies, are always in real nice clothes that are kinda silky or shiny, but they never wear anything anybody else would ever wear—I mean, they look like they just stepped out of some Chinese movie about people who lived a million years ago and got caught in some fashion time-warp! Louis said they were being traditional, but it just looks like old-fashioned stuff to me. I did see pictures once of some people from the '60s or '70s and they were wearing that same kinda coat with the little standup collar, but they weren't Chinese or anything so I think *that* fashion died with the music, if you know what I mean.

Ty always looks cool, which is part of his job, I think, and he's like the only one who kinda changes between two different uniforms. When he's Ty, the cool musician, he always wears jeans and a plain white shirt and a tie, that's hardly tied at all, and, when he goes out, a jacket. Class. When he's Ty, the cool black guy "lovin' his roots" like he always says, he wears this real colorful super-long shirt thing, or a down-to-the-floor robe, and sometimes a weird little hat. I mean, it doesn't matter what Ty wears because he always looks cool to me, and I'm not saying that because I'm prejudiced or anything. He *is* cool and if I could be black, I'd wanna be Ty. Hell, I'd wanna be Ty, black or not, if I had one musical bone in my body.

Jimmy (his real name is something nobody can pronounce unless you're clearing your throat, so when he said the everyday American way to say his name is "James," we all started calling him Jimmy), is the only person in the whole Ark who has a computer (Charlie "helped" him get internet service, if you catch my drift). He loves books (like Louis does, so maybe it's a Jewish thing) and he can spend the whole day looking at them online but, since he's just as poor as the rest of us, he never buys anything.

Jimmy lives with his mom on the first floor across from Mrs. T. He used to be just this regular guy but he, or his mom, decided he was gonna study to be a Rabbi, so he took to wearing baggy black suits and a black hat because he wanted to study to be a serious Rabbi and someday become an Acidic Jew. He always walks around with that hat on and a bunch of books under his arm (from the library, though, not real bought-online ones) but I never saw him go off anywhere to Rabbi school or anything so I'm not sure if he is just practicing or what.

Jimmy's mom is short and a little rounder on the bottom, like a pear, and she's always, always wearing an apron. She even wears one out to the market and stuff like that. I don't think she wears it to Jewish church or anything, but I'm not sure since I've never seen her without one on. Her and Jimmy both don't wear any jewelry, not even a star of David (I think that's because of that jerk Hitler guy that made everybody in his jerk Nazi land run around all over the place wearing yellow stars that should of been this great symbol of being Jewish but ended up being some kinda bulls-eye mark of death). But, anyway, his mom does wear a wedding ring, except it's on the wrong finger *and* the wrong hand!

Jimmy and his mom are always buying lottery tickets. Every time they go anywhere, that apron comes home stuffed with lottery tickets. Louis calls it "the new soviet of the people" or something like that but it just always made me sad, that kinda hopeless hope.

Bernard is always wearing "rings, rings, rings, my boy" and a little earring in each ear and pretty much always looks like he's about to go to work, without the jacket and tie. He always has on a belt—a belt, for Christ's sake. And his hair always looks like he never slept on it. Ever. Bernard is kinda short with a little belly (which the belt doesn't help hide) and a real small almost completely bald spot right on top of his head. It reminds me of Robin Hood's buddy Fryer Tuck—you know, that old monk guy that's in all those movies with actors who make that old Sherbert Forest sound like the beach at Malibu. Bernard seems a little shy about it, though, and I always thought he should get one of Jimmy's little hats (that he wears *under* the black hat, for Christ's sake), that seem like they're just made for guys with bald spots. But, I've never seen anybody else wear one around here, except Louis once, and Bernard is Catholic so I'm not sure if maybe those hats aren't just for Jewish bald spots.

Louis is harder to pin down and I think he's that way on purpose since he was the one who came up with the idea of uniforms in the first place. But one thing I can say about Louis is that he's always wearing these black-rim glasses and he's always, always wearing short sleeves. Even in winter. I asked him about it once and he said he never noticed, or that heat rises or something, but he's just always in short sleeves. At Louis', I guess it's always summer.

Once Louis said that, about uniforms, I noticed that I pretty much always wear jeans and sneakers and T-shirts and this beat up old green fatigue jacket that supposedly belonged to my dad who I never met so I can't be sure. I don't wear any kinda jewelry at all but I do always wear a rawhide thong around my neck. There's no reason for it—just some girl told me once it was cool and that was enough for me! And I can never find two socks that look the same. Ty says that shows I hear a different drummer. I think I'm just too lazy to check the washer real good at the laundrymat. But, Ty would know, being a musician and all. So, I guess Louis was right about the uniforms...until this Jesus guy arrived.

When I first met him, he was wearing carpenter pants and a white, long-sleeved shirt with no collar and buttons only half way down. But then he asked me to take him to that Goodwill store, like I told you. Now, you gotta understand, when he was in there shopping for his "threads" as Ty would say, this Jesus guy hadn't met any of the folks at The Ark. And he would of had to "shop" from the Goodwill store's Free Bin or whatever it's called, because he didn't have any money. So, here's the freaky part—it wasn't until a long time later that I figured out that he almost always dressed like the person we were gonna visit! That means that out of that Free Bin, he picked a short-sleeve shirt, a crumpled old black suit, jeans and a plain white shirt, a Chinese coat like Mr. Yin's (but just one color), a work shirt (no name, but a place where one had been), a T-shirt and sneakers, and a belt, for Christ's sake. So, except for the ladies, he had got something that kinda copied what each one of the guys in the building wore. But he hadn't met any of them, except me, when he did that. Weird.

But don't feel bad for the ladies—he had something for them, too. He *listened* to them, all of them, and usually agreed with them. I would ask him:

"Do you really believe that cra…stuff?"

"Of course I do! I don't agree with things I don't believe."

Man. He was a hard guy to understand sometimes.

Anyway, I should probably tell you that Autumn didn't buy Louis' idea about the uniforms *at all*. She said it's not uniforms that tell us who people are, it's horoscopes. So, one night when she had this psychic over (I'll tell you about that later), she told us all what our signs were (I guess when she's not busy protecting all the stars from being stolen she has time to figure out how they're screwing up our lives), and showed us pictures of what they meant.

So, Charlie, she said, is Airy and his special animal is a ram. (Charlie likes to think of himself as a ladies' man so I thought it should of been a wolf!) Raindrop, she said, is some kinda bull, which is a load of crap, and is called a Tore-us, like "tore us a new one," which Raindrop is the last person to do.

Bernard and Mrs. T are lions (more like a pussycat for

old Mr. B) and called Leos. Jimmy's a scorpion (not buying it) and his mom is something with scales—I think it was a Librarian—or maybe a Lizard, you know, with the scales and all. Autumn is one of those lizard things too. My Nana's was a picture of some guy hauling a giant bowl of water all over the place but I can't remember what it was called.

Ty is some kinda Sage and his symbol was some guy with a bow and arrow. I really dug that and wished I could be a Sage too. Mrs. Yin is a Captain Corn and her animal's a goat, and Mr. Yin is two fish eating each other. I don't remember what his sign is called either but it sure didn't look very appetizing. I'm a Gem-in-I and my picture was two dorks holding hands, for Christ's sake. But the very best one was Louis. Louis is a VIRGIN! Louis was born on some crust between being a lion and a virgin and Autumn was guessing that he was leaning toward being the virgin! Man, that cracked me up.

Louis said the whole thing "didn't hold water." I don't think he was talking about that Nana guy, though. I think he was just pissed he was on the wrong side of the crust!

Anyway, so I guess I should tell you that before this guy Jesus shows up, I spent most of my time watching all these old movies on some old-time movie channel that Charlie hot-wired into our building. I hate to admit it, and I know this makes me even more of a goof-off than I already know you think I am, but I love those old movies. I love all the dancing and overacting. I love that those guys like Fred Astaire and Humphrey Bogart and Jimmy Cagney and guys like that can look all normal and not perfect and still get the girl. I love that some of them have crooked teeth and kinda do that whistle thing when they talk. And that Clark Gable guy, look at those ears! I mean, none of them would win a Johnny Depp or Brad Pitt look-alike contest but they still win in the end.

And I hate to think I'm old-fashioned or anything, but it knocks me out that the very worst thing they ever say is "damn" and they can still be tough and cool and "emote" (Louis' word) all this feeling crap. They don't ever show any naked boobs or butts and they can still be all sexy as hell (even though I'm glad they show the naked boobs and butts nowadays, you know, to be more real and all!).

Now, I know they were heavy into smoking before everybody made all these great scientific discoveries that it wasn't cool anymore, and I really will quit someday (I promise, Nana). And they were also heavy into drinking, which I know is a drug just in liquid form, but, I dunno, they were just so friggin' cool. And if I had a ton of "bread" (Ty's word), I'd get some of those old suits and hats and wear them all the time. I mean, I guess I was just born way too late for my own good. But, I always feel like I'm in a movie, like somebody's watching me and doing all these cool camera angles, depending on my mood.

Wait…damn, I always do that. I start talking about one thing and end up somewhere else. Or I zone out completely. Sorry. I'll concentrate because this *is* important. I was telling you about that first day when I took Jesus home to meet the folks at 64 Wilbur. I think it's real safe to say that not one of us could of even imagined how that one night would change all our lives forever.

How Do You Solve a Problem Like Messiahs?

"Go to HELL!"

Mrs. T slammed the door so hard the whole building shook. I had begged him not to knock on her door especially because, like I said, she was like an authority on Jesus from watching those Christ guys on TV all day and night, and I knew, I *knew* she wouldn't take kindly to the real JC showing up at her front door. Not that I thought he was the real deal and not that I thought she would think that. I knew she wouldn't think that and since he *did*, there was gonna be some fireworks.

It was pretty late by now, even for me, and I was wondering what to do with him. He didn't seem anxious to go anyplace else so I finally asked if he wanted to stay at my "pad" (Ty's word) and he said, "Sure."

I kinda made up the old red couch for him in a not very good way. I told him I used to sleep on it practically my whole life until Nana left and I moved into the bedroom. I explained it was pretty comfortable (if he could ignore all the violin/TV noise) but he said it didn't matter because he didn't sleep much. That freaked me out—like I was gonna go to sleep and he'd come in and kill me (which was bad) or watch me sleeping (which was worse). I hate the idea of being watched while I'm asleep. So, while I was imagining my sleepless night, he started fiddling with the TV. He actually didn't seem to know how to turn it on.

"You wanna watch some crap on TV?" I can be a very good host if I apply myself.

"Sure." He sounded like a little kid who agreed with what you said even though you knew they didn't have any idea what you were talking about. I found the remote (under the "bed" I'd just made up for him on the couch) and turned on the boob-tube. He jumped, just a little and in a real divine sorta way, and looked like some of the electricity from the remote to the TV had gone right through him.

"What's the matter?" I really didn't want him to be upset or anything. "Haven't you ever seen TV before?" I laughed. I was *not* ready for what he said then.

"No."

"Who can not have ever seen TV before?" I thought he must be pulling my leg. "Where have you been, on the moon?" It was a stupid thing to say. I mean, anybody who could live on the moon would *have* to of seen TV, right?

It didn't matter much because he didn't answer me. He was gone, man! Ex-moon-resident or not, that TV had him hooked and another soul was lost to the "No Thought Zone" (you-know-who said that one, too).

He had plopped down on the big, purple over-stuffed chair that had once been where Nana loved to sit and watch her "stories." Just for a second I had this flash—he looked kinda like a sad, lonely king, being swallowed up by a throne that could feel he was alone and was trying to give him a safe, I-gotcha hug. I would learn about those looks in the months that were ahead, how he would be smiling or laughing most of the time when folks were around and how, when he thought he was alone, he'd look almost…lost.

So, anyway, I put the remote next to his hand and headed to bed. He was so caught up in that stupid "Box," as he would come to call it, that I knew, tonight anyway, he wouldn't be killing me or watching me sleep. I didn't know then that that Box was gonna cause a lot of grief later on.

The next morning I woke up to what Louis calls the "drone" of the TV. I couldn't believe he'd watched it all night. I lay there, trying to remember everything from the day before and how all the folks of The Ark had reacted to meeting "Jesus."

I had started at the top, with Louis. When we got there, it was just sunset, and this Jesus guy plopped himself right down on the floor in front of Louis' window-wall and watched those tired old streaks of purple-yellow light trying like hell to punch a few lines of color through the smog. That's pretty much all we can hope for in an L.A. sunset, but he wouldn't budge or talk until the sun disappeared. That actually gave me a good chance to pull Louis aside and tell him what, and *who*, this guy Jesus was claiming to be.

By the time Jesus turned back to us, Louis pounced. He started asking all these real smart questions. I knew they were smart because I didn't understand one of them. Jesus answered every one, without pausing or sweating or anything. Looking back, I realize he would always answer our questions, or, at least give us a look that kinda answered our questions (you know, like parents or Nanas are always doing), and I thought he was a pretty honest guy. And, after a while I realized he only didn't answer right away when it was about feelings. I was thinking maybe we all should do that, you know, wait a beat or two before blurting out our love or hate for something, or blowin' some poor schmuck's head all to hell because he was going 30 in a 35.

But, after that first few days, I realized that nobody ever

waited as long for anything as Jesus did with sunsets. No matter what we were doing or even if he was about to tell us God's first name or the real lowdown on the Big Bang (which I always thought sounded like some sorta cosmic rape scene) or crap like that, we had to stop everything and watch the sunset. So, right from the beginning, we had to always go to Louis' when day started fading. It was all about sunsets for this Jesus guy but he would never tell us why. I think he was trying to teach us patience or finding beauty through the smog or something but, you know, I never did figure it out.

Anyway, Louis ended his cross-examination with a question in some other language he called "Aromatic" or something like that. Jesus didn't even blink—he had the answer right there and Louis seemed pretty impressed. I was surprised because Louis never, ever believes in anything or anybody. So, Louis being impressed just impressed the hell out of me. I have to admit I was kinda hoping somebody would ask him about Mary Magnavox but I don't think anybody ever did.

Afterward, as we were leaving Louis', Jesus stopped to check out this weird poster on Louis' wall right over his hotplate that some girl made him in college, if you can believe that. It was all flowery and stuff, like something from the '60s and Louis was always saying that was "retro," which I think is really something from the Jetsons. Anyway, in the middle of all these spooky flowers was this saying, "If God is God, He is not good; if God is good, He is not God." Well, of course everybody knows it doesn't make sense, but when Jesus saw it, he stared at it for a long time and I started worrying he was gonna get mad. I mean, we're talking about his Dad here. Even Louis, who never cared what anybody thought about anything, looked a little nervous.

There was this real uncomfortable silence, like when

three people are standing in a room, somebody should be talking. So, I blurted out, "What the hell does that mean, Louis?" Louis looked relieved to break the quiet and he got his Louis-knows-just-about-everything face on and said, "It describes the paradox of theodicy." Theocrappy, if you ask me.

Jesus cracks this huge smile at Louis and says, "Very interesting. I'd like to talk with you again." Well, Louis looked like a girl had just kissed him or something. It was gross the way he gushed all over this guy, and Louis not even believing in him or anything since he was Jewish. I don't know if I noticed it at the time but Louis was never quite the same after that. It was like he got a big shot of gee-ain't-life-grand or something. He was still obnoxious old Louis, "frequently chuckling" and all, but with just a little bit more oomph. You know?

As we walked out the door, Louis grabbed me and whispered, "Make sure you don't tell anybody about this guy claiming to be the *real* Jesus. Just introduce him as a new friend."

"Alright, Louis. Jeez," I kinda yanked my arm away. I was embarrassed that Louis was treating me like a kid, right in front of this, maybe divine, guy.

So, anyway, next I took Jesus down to Bernard and the Earth Ladies. Bernard was "beside himself" just to have some company. He had to "lay out" his tea things, whatever the hell that meant. Now, when *I* walked in, the cats all scattered like I had a cat-fever or something. But, the funny thing was that when this Jesus guy sits down, the cats all snapped back into a kinda half-moon circle around him, like he was a magnet…laced with catnip! Weird.

So, when Bernard comes back with this 12 course spread, for Christ's sake, he starts out by saying, "Now, tell me,

Jesus…" (but he pronounces it Hay-Zeus—see, like I was saying before. Everybody in L.A. knows how to pronounce Jesus).

Jesus actually interrupted Bernard and says, "That's Jesus" (but he says it Geez-Us, like that).

Well, I thought Bernard was gonna have a kitten. He turned all shades of red and I actually thought he was about to throw us out or something—I mean, he is Catholic and they can get real serious about religion sometimes—but all he said was, "Of course. Forgive me…Jesus." And he smiled! I guess since none of us ever pronounced Bernard the way he wanted (except Jesus did) he understood what it was like to want your name said right.

After about a year at Bernard's, we headed across the hall to the Earth Ladies. As we were leaving, Bernard kinda puts his hand up, like a limp Nazi salute, and says, "Dominos Biscuits" or something like that. I guess he was trying to give a cool takeout tip to his new neighbor, but I didn't have the heart to tell him that I thought it was KFC that had the biscuits.

The Earth Ladies didn't care about any of that Catholic or Jewish crap. They didn't have any religion at all so they had to believe in everything.

They had a poster on their wall that said, "The beginning of wisdom is silence." But every single time I was ever in their place, they had some "music" on that sounded kinda like they were torturing a cat. They called it "sitter" music, or something like that, but I was thinking you sure as hell weren't gonna be very wise not listening to silence with that racket going on.

So this is the first time Jesus has heard this music, as far as I know, and all of a sudden he started yammering on about the great and noble culture of the Indians, for Christ's sake (which it didn't sound anything like native music and how would he know anyway).

I was kinda trying to eyeball the poster to get him to talk about *wise silence* and all, but he didn't and the Ladies got all excited and Autumn says she actually has a "sitter" and they all plop on the floor (at least Ty can play music standing up) so I booked it back up to Louis', you know, to ask him what to do. I had been doing just what he'd told me, introducing this Jesus guy as just some regular new friend, but everybody was reacting to him like he was cooler than a slice of bread or whatever that saying is and I kinda felt like this whole don't-tell-the-neighbors-about-the-deity thing was gonna get bigger than I could handle.

There *was* something about him—not how he looked (not a halo or white robe or crap like that)—that made him seem different from most people. You probably wouldn't notice it if you just passed him on the street but when you were talking to him, there was a…I dunno…a kindness that you just don't meet every day. I mean, even the kindest person I ever knew, my Nana, could dish it with the best of 'em. No, this was a kindness that stayed. You know? He didn't have a mean word to say about anybody or what they wore or what they looked like or who they loved. He was all about what was inside, about the true heart of a soul. But, I still didn't believe this guy could be Jesus…the *real* Jesus…the one from the Bible. I mean, how? It just stayed heavy on my mind.

Anyway, Louis acted all pissed that I'd bothered him again—like he was taking a dump or something (which he wasn't)—but then he practically knocked me over getting out the door to head downstairs. Yeah, real mature. So, after a lot of confusion and tortured cat music at the Earth Ladies', Jesus and me and Louis headed on down to the third floor to meet the rest of The Ark folks.

Charlie acted like his prayers had been answered. I mean, he really got kinda weird with everybody calling Jesus, Geez-Us. He kept staring at him, like he was trying to see right through to his brain or something. But it wasn't a crazy, psycho stare...more of an are-you-what-I've-been-waiting-for stare.

The Yins were very polite and since they're Buddhists, I guess it wasn't any problem for them to be around somebody who was supposed to be divine (*I* didn't tell them). I was real surprised that this guy Jesus knew who Buddha was, since he wasn't even in the Bible, I don't think.

So, Ty showed up for his weekly game of chess with Mr. Yin (which always ended in an argument since they couldn't understand each other). Mr. Yin was an expert in TieOneOn or Judo or something so I kinda always thought Ty should be more careful.

Anyway, I introduced Jesus, and Mr. and Mrs. Yin started bobbing up and down and Ty starts acting all cool and slapping everybody on the back and saying "All right, Brother!" every two seconds. Ty's a nice guy and all, but along with that violin that his grandpa left him in his will, he'd also left him with a pretty big stash of some real head-trip dope, and I think he mighta been sampling some of that inheritage!

Louis headed back up home (mumbling something like "I don't want to see this," which I didn't get at the time) and by the time we got downstairs, Jimmy and his mom had just come in from buying even more lottery tickets and while Jesus talked to Jimmy's mom, I had the chance to ask Jimmy about this whole has-the-real-Bible-Jesus-landed-in-L.A.-for-that-second-coming thing and, if he has, is *this* guy *that* guy? I wanted to know if he was—could even in a billion years be—the real deal. Yeah, I know, Louis told me not to but, damn, I just *needed* to ask somebody.

Jimmy said he'd heard of these things called "visitations" and the way you know this whole thing is real and you're not just flippin' out is that, if it's real, some creepy statue starts crying blood or the Pope makes you a saint or something, but since I'm not Catholic he didn't think I have anything to worry about. He said that all crying-blood statues are Catholic, and even plain old statues that just cry regular tears are too, and that's how you can know the religion of great works of art. He said that if a statue doesn't cry, it's probably Protestant and if it's all falling apart, it's a Pagan statue and that Jews don't have statues at all because that would make them "craving images," or something like that. You already know how not-religious I am, but Jimmy's gonna be a Rabbi, so I guess he knows what he's talking about. I was kinda secretly thinking I'd like to see a statue cry, blood or not, but then I just knew this Jesus guy would say it was a parlor trick and that the more important things are inside you and it didn't matter if statues were Catholic or Protestant. I think I agree with that part, and I feel real sorry for all the Jewish people who, I guess, aren't allowed to enjoy art or anything, but, damn, I would really get a kick out of a parlor trick or two once in a while.

Anyway, once Jimmy and his mom went into their apartment, that's when I started trying to get this JC guy upstairs. But, he'd insisted on knocking on old Mrs. T's door (you know how that went) and while the whole building was shaking when she slammed the door, *that's* when I understood what Louis meant about not wanting to "see this."

Now, in the morning light, I was kinda worried that everything would be different. I mean, I didn't think he was the real Jesus. But, he was an interesting guy and since I didn't have too much to do these days, I didn't want this adventure

35

to end before it started. Too many times in my life, something (or some girl) had seemed great and exciting the night before, but morning always makes things real again—and the fairy tale always ends.

So I'm standing in what Charlie calls "the head" and Bernard calls "the powder room" (and so did my Nana so maybe that's the right nickname…except there's no powder in there since Nana left) and I'm brushing my teeth with the water running and all, and this guy Jesus starts going on about something at the top of his lungs. I was jazzed, in a real *man* kinda way, that he was still there. And I could hear him and hear he was talking and I could hear all the ups and downs in his voice but I couldn't understand what he was saying because of the water running and the noise in my head from the toothbrush.

When I was done, I went into the living room. He was still sitting in that same purple chair as the night before and the TV was still blaring away and he was just saying, "And that's what I mean about the Kingdom of God being here, now."

I couldn't believe it. I'm sure my chin was hanging on the floor.

"Who the hell are you talking to?" I was kinda pissed that he was giving out all this great info and *nobody* was there and I'd missed the whole thing.

"You," he answered my "who" question with one of those gotcha smiles.

"You talkin' to me?" (Who was that guy?)

"Yes."

"Then why the crap didn't you wait 'til I was here to hear?"

"You *were* here."

"Yeah, but I couldn't hear you with the water running and all."

"That's just like the Kingdom of God. It's right here, right now but we're all so busy doing things, we don't realize it. We don't stop and listen and just *be*."

"Oh." He kinda waited for more but I didn't have any more to say. I didn't understand what the hell he was talking about and I sure as hell couldn't understand why he couldn't of just waited until I turned off the water.

I guess in the night he'd found a bunch of paper and a pen because there were all these notes on yellow, lined paper everywhere. From that minute on, every night, he'd sit up with The Box blaring and tons of yellow pages around him, just watching and writing. Weird.

While we were eating some toast (he was all amazed at making toast without fire—man, he was one funny guy!) I told him I thought I was an Agnauseous. I didn't know how I could be, I mean, here I am eating breakfast with Jesus, for Christ's sake, but I just wasn't sure about the whole God thing. And I didn't know how I could not believe in God, hang out with Jesus, and still believe in the idea of a spirit that comes in and does all that inspiring stuff. So, here's how I tried to figure it out.

First, how can there be a God if there's death and sickness and meanness and prejudice and poverty and hopelessness and loneliness? How come some people's prayers seem to get answered and some don't? How come some people get healed and most—*most*—don't? How come when you're all alone and scared and praying your head off, not one word comes back to you? Not one sign. Not one hint. Man, it makes you ache with aloneness.

And then, this guy shows up and, well…I was pretty sure he probably wasn't Jesus. The real one, anyway. He was nice and all, and I could already see he had a way with people (except Mrs. T) and a way with how he put things, but that's not all that special nowadays. I mean, we have TV now and almost everybody has a way with people now that we've all been taught how to have these great TV personalities.

And I don't know anybody who doesn't have a camera crew (in their head) following them around every day and night and recording every damn thought for—what? Dunno. But it *does* mean that we're always "on." It's that Candid Camera style of living that makes us not so god-awful-ripping-your-guts-out lonely. And, if you're real lucky, you'll get so mind-numbed you'll forget whose show you're in. Then you know you've arrived.

So, in that way at least, TV is now the all-knowing God. TV has taught us how to act and how to think and how not to feel so damn all-by-ourselves-out-here-in-the-cold-lonesome. Louis says we're in love with TV because it gives us "30-minute resolutions" to all our problems (but then, according to Louis, we get all depressed and suicidal because the world doesn't live *up* to our expectations of those resolutions….I dunno, I just mostly watch it for the girls). Almost everybody I know turns on that boob-tube before they do anything else at all in the morning. And it's always the last one to get kissed goodnight.

So, being Jesus today just ain't all that special. In fact, being *anybody* isn't special anymore. Oh, yeah, we're all "precious in His sight" as my Nana always said, but precious isn't special either. Louis is always saying that a few folks are here to shine but most folks are just here to be regular. Not everybody is supposed to be a genius. Just like reality show stars have taken the specialness out of being a movie or TV star, everybody getting to be *special* takes the special out of specialness, you know?

Anyway, we've all become real good at putting on that Hollywood face and getting what we want and convincing people to believe like us. And everybody, absolutely *everybody* these days, thinks they're JC reincarcerated, for Christ's sake. I mean, that's the way they act. I sometimes wonder if that's just another way of keeping the Lonely Hearts Club membership cards from rollin' in.

So, if this guy's not Jesus, I mean the real Bible Jesus, and if he's just some poor deluded schmuck just trying to be good and kind to everybody, then he's not hurting anybody and well, I didn't really have all that much to do anyway. Maybe he was just lonely too, and man, I could get that.

Which just left that inspiring spirit stuff. I dunno. I might not believe in God or Jesus for sure, but I *do* believe in that spirit crap. There's just been way too many times when I knew it wasn't me being all smart and deep and confounded and all. There's been lots of times I was just scrambling around for some answer to something and *bam!* There it was. Or, if you knew who was calling before you answered the phone, that kinda crazy bull. Everybody has to admit that happens sometimes so I guess there is this spooky spirit thing that comes along and helps out when you're really hanging out there. But, it doesn't *always*, which is like the whole God thing, so I—oh, I dunno. I mean, I do believe in this spirit thing, I think, but I'm still not sure about the Big Guy.

So, I was yammering on about all this crap and this Jesus guy just sat there, listening to me, real patient and all, but once I finish a bunch of hard thinking like that, I get real tired. So, I stopped yakking and just kinda looked at him and he just kinda looked at me, with that big Jesus smile and all, so I figured it was time for us to book it on up to Louis'.

"Everyone *knows*," Louis was getting all squealy and practically pissing himself. He was squeaking about the fact that the whole building, in just those few midnight hours, seemed to be gossiping about this guy Jesus claiming to be the real deal. Damn. How did that happen?

"So, what the hell do we do with him now, Louis?" Jesus was looking at all the books, even the closed ones, when Louis pulled me into the hallway.

"Look, even if he's just some crazed homeless guy, I feel like we need to assist him and play along with his story until we can find out who he is and maybe get him some help."

I couldn't believe Louis was being so nice. I was thinking that maybe he just wanted some brain-game playmate, but I knew he was right that we should try to help this guy and I also thought it might be fun.

"Okay, what's first?"

So Louis started him on a crash course of money handling. Jesus really got into the coins and didn't have any trouble getting the whole concept of different amounts. He liked the different sizes and, since the first coin we showed him was a quarter, he thought old George Washington was Caesar, for crying out loud. What a crackup!

But, he absolutely couldn't handle the paper, which is weird because I always thought that paper money was easier. With bills, somebody else always had to do the math, like giving you change and crap like that. But for some reason, because bills were all the same size, he kinda got it into his head that they were all worth the same, which didn't go over real well with Louis when we caught Jesus handing out a bunch of $20's and $10's.

There's that dead end alley I told you about, right behind Delaney's, where this crazy, old, mostly toothless homeless guy with a real red nose and wild gray hair lives. He was one of those guys who nobody knew but everybody knew *of*. I don't remember who said it first, but we all just started calling him Alley Guy.

But, there's also a lot of bums and stoners and other homeless folks always hanging out in that alley, who sleep or smoke weed or piss on the walls, for Christ's sake, and a few days later we found Jesus in there, completely surrounded, and he's handing out Louis' money like it's going out of style.

"What are you *doing?*" Louis' face looked like he was about to explode, all purple and veiny.

"Hello, Louis. I'm giving this money to these friends. I'm…" He stopped and turned to Alley Guy, who kinda cackled, "Sharing the wealth! Least of the brethren!"

So, this Jesus guy turns back to Louis and says, "I'm sharing the wealth. Would you like to help?"

Louis grabs Jesus by the arm, not rough but fast, and pulls him back to the entrance to the alley. "You can't just give money to…bums," Louis lowered his voice way down when he said "bums."

"Why not?" Jesus really didn't get it.

"Beeecaaaaauuuuusssse," Louis said it sorta long and drawn out, like he was talking to a kid, "if you give them money, they'll only buy booze." He got even quieter. "Or the stoners will just buy drugs."

So, naturally Jesus points to this one just-down-on-his-luck homeless guy all huddled up behind a trash can and asks "What will *he* buy?"

Louis was turning colors again and almost whispered, "He'll probably buy...food."

Well, Jesus cracks this giant smile and walks out of the alley all full of being right and already off to his next good deed just like Robin Hood or that guy with the windmills and we followed behind feeling stupid and a helluva lot poorer.

So, along with not getting paper money, we found out he didn't understand traffic at all. And I couldn't explain it to him because I didn't either. What he couldn't get was why we'd pay all this money and pollute all this air to try to get someplace else that we could walk to faster! That was all okay with me because I love to walk (which is good since I don't have a car). But we did ride in cars sometimes—I mean, Bernard has this giant *pink* car, for crying out loud—and we rode in cabs and on buses.

He seemed to like the bus most of all. He said it reminded him of these carts that were pulled by donkeys or something and all these people would hop on and just catch a ride in the cart with hay and fish and God knows what all. It sounded cool—except for the fish—like some kinda Bible hay ride. He said that on the bus you could get to know people, and I was thinking he'd gone a little crazy since nobody ever talked to anybody on a bus, unless you arrived with them and then only low and whispery, unless you were a teenager who had to make a lot of noise to prove to everybody that you were there or something, which I wasn't anymore. A teenager, I mean. You practically had to be some pirate or explorer or Commander Data to figure out how to get anywhere on a bus in L.A., but he didn't mind just sitting there and talking to people and riding all over the whole of creation and wasting a helluva lot of time. And by the time I'd get my tokens or Golden Dollars out, he'd be heavy into somebody's life story already and I'd have to come to the rescue and bail him out of what could be some real interesting but dangerous conversations.

I know I tried to teach him not to introduce himself because he'd say, "Hey, I'm..." and I'd have to cut him off and quick-like say, "...new in town" or something like that. He never did get that you just can't go around to everybody saying you're the Messiah or Jesus, when it's pronounced Geez-Us, even if you are, which we really weren't sure he was.

But those bus rides weren't all fun and games, especially when some good, self-righting Christians decided to give him a ton of definite grief because he looked very Middle Eastern, which, of course, he is. Using *his* title as *their* badge, those loudmouth bullies threatened to kill him, or at least lock him away in some god-awful prison so he couldn't go turning into a terrorist any time soon. That got him a little freaked out, in an all-knowing-divine sorta way, while I was practically dropping my load in a dumbass-please-don't-beat-the-crap-outta-me sorta way.

So, after about a week of trying to keep him out of trouble and especially not spend all of Louis' money or get ourselves killed, I decided it would be safer (and cheaper) if I took him around to meet some real special friends of mine—the Delaneys. And that meant I had to comb my hair.

I guess I should tell you that I usually forget to comb my hair and it's a hard sell to waste money on getting it cut when, like Bernard says, "hunger grows faster than hair." So, when I get to what Louis calls "shaggy," I just book it on up to Bernard or the Earth Ladies for a trim and the latest gossip from the streets. But, whenever I'm gonna see Angela Delaney, I remember to comb my hair.

Now, to get to Delaney's you gotta walk by that alley I was

telling you about. And somebody, about a million years ago, had written "It's a sad and beautiful world" on the wall at the back of one of the buildings. Every day, from that first day I took Jesus that way, we had to stop and he'd look at those words like it was the very first time he ever saw them. Every time.

And right under that sad and beautiful graffiti is where Alley Guy lives. He was flipped out, for sure, but whenever we walked past the alley that crazy old dude would yell something like, "Witches are only mirrors," or "We are the Dream of God," and Jesus would always stop and listen.

I only asked him once why he stopped every time. He said, "In my day, we sought his visions." That was it. We never talked about it again.

So, anyway, the Delaneys had a store called Delaney's, for Christ's sake, and it had been closed up, with one of those metal doors over the window, ever since Mrs. Delaney committed suicide when their son died in Iraq. I don't know what Mr. Delaney did—for a living, I mean—after that. But besides their son, the Delaneys had two girls, Angela, like I told you, and Zoe. I wanted Jesus to meet them because I had what Louis called a "dilemma" with those two girls and I thought maybe he could help.

You see, they have the same voice. I mean, if you weren't looking, you wouldn't know which one was talking. First, there's Angela. I really like Angela. She's funny and sweet and always has something nice to say about people. She just has this voice. It's kinda squeaky and a little too high to be comfortable, but it just knocks me out. I mean, it makes her even more funny and sweet and I wouldn't change it for the world.

Then there's Zoe. At that time, when I first met Jesus, I

44

couldn't stand Zoe. She was selfish and mean and always complaining. And she had that same voice. It's squeaky too, but in a chalk-on-a-blackboard sorta way and a lot too high…like a dog whistle that you can just almost hear and it sends shivers through you with a nagging kinda doubt that maybe, overnight, you somehow became a dog. Hearing Zoe talk made you wanna run away screaming—anything that would drown it out.

So anyway, I told him about this one day when I hear Angela talking right around the corner and I start getting all excited to see her and see what kind of funny story she has today kinda thing and I turn the corner and—damn if it isn't Zoe. I was completely freaked out. Here, I was half in love with the idea of seeing my friend and somehow it turned into that nasty kinda surprise like when you think you're going for ice cream and it turns out to be the dentist. But I'd been fooled and I didn't understand how that could be. I mean, it was the same voice and still I could have two completely opposite reactions to it, depending on who it belonged to.

So, we went up some back stairs in the alley to the Delaney's apartment, which was over what used to be their store, and after making nice with Mr. D, he calls the girls to come out and meet Jesus. Well, you could hear them coming for about a mile and I shot Jesus this quick look, you know, to see what he's thinking. He gave me this big I-gotcha grin and I was sure he was about to solve this huge "dilemma" thing for me.

Everybody was all polite and all but Zoe wouldn't sit down. She was running back and forth to the kitchen, trying to prove she was "Julia Crocker" or whoever, bringing out these horse's ovaries thingies and, sad to say, *talking* the whole time. She had to tell us all about her "secret" recipe but all I could think was, if it was such a big friggin' secret, why the hell was she yapping about it? I mean, it was painful to listen to her.

Angela didn't say too much, but she did talk enough for him to hear her. She mostly sat on the floor and listened. When she did start to tell us one of her great stories, Zoe interrupted and starts showing off all these crappy pictures she sewed up, *telling* us every freakin' detail about how and why and…man, I wanted to scream.

When Zoe said she was thinking of taking singing lessons, I jumped up and said we had to leave.

When we got back to my place, he sat in his big purple chair and leaned forward, with his hands over his mouth.

"Well?" I almost yelled it but then I sat back and tried to pretend to be calm.

"It has nothing to do with the voice," he said. "And, it has nothing to do with Angela or Zoe."

Okay, now he was way off base….who the hell else did it have to do with? Then, he starts doing that reading my mind thing again.

"It has everything to do with *you.*"

Me? No. That made no sense at all but he wasn't through.

"Angela is like looking in a mirror on a day when you feel good about yourself and Zoe is…."

"A bad hair day?" I tried to help because I didn't think he'd know all the new, trendy sayings yet.

"Yes," he went on. "Your perception of everything in the Universe is a reflection of how you *feel.* For example, when you look at the stars, you might feel excited about the possibility of going there someday. Or, you might see the same stars as distant and cold. They are the same stars, either way. What has changed?"

I was trying hard to remember all this because I thought

it might be important.

"I dunno," I said, "what *has* changed?"

"You! The only thing that has changed is *YOU*. Your feelings. Change how you feel and the whole world will change."

I think he could see I still wasn't getting it. He tried to tell me that all of life was like that—it just really depended on how you saw it, on how you were feeling that day. And why that made it so important to love everything because then everything was your friend and everything loved you back.

He said we could even look up that "love everything" crap, and we tried to find it in Nana's old Bible, but when we started reading, so much had been changed from what he remembered that I think he got kinda depressed…and a little peeved. He didn't say anything about it, though, so, that night, while we were walking home from buying some oranges (I'll tell you about that later), I decided to cheer him up.

"Y'know, Louis says that your *love everything* cra… uh…line is the 'one original concept' in all of Christianness!"

"Really?"

"Yeah. How 'bout that?"

"That's wonderful. That's a good message. It certainly takes the guess work out of it, doesn't it?"

"Huh?"

He just shook his head so I thought it would be a good time to get some stuff off my chest.

"So, if we're supposed to love everything, how come there's still bad guys and poor people and death and—"

He stopped dead in his tracks and looked up at the stars. He did that a lot when I started talking. I couldn't exactly tell if it was one of those "desperate frustration" moments, or if he was gonna break out and start talking to his Dad, or if, maybe, he just really loved looking at the stars a lot.

"Let's have some quiet time," he said.
"Okay."

HYMN
Or, How Do You Explain Church to a Deity?

So, after a pretty intense discussion about names, we decided to call him JC or Jaycee, even though I thought Jaycee was too girly. JC got all professor-y on me and tried to explain that Christ wasn't his name. I told him then he shouldn't of been trying to fool us for 2,000 years because practically everybody in the whole friggin' world knew his last name was Christ. He told me that Christ was a title, not a name, and nobody ever, not once in his entire life ever, called him Christ to his face. He told me that one of his guys said he was the Messiah once and some other folks evidently didn't like that because they all started chanting Messiah and throwing palm trees at him, for Christ's sake. So, long story short, he wanted to just be called Jesus. And then he tries to explain that *that* wasn't his name either! Jeez.

Well, I was getting pretty annoyed and started asking him who the hell he was then if his first name wasn't Jesus and his last name wasn't Christ. He told me his first name and I won't even try to pronounce it here, and you wouldn't believe it anyhow. It didn't even start with a J. He said in our language it was close enough to say Jesus so then *I* had to try to explain— again—how we couldn't call him Jesus because everybody would either think he was some sorta nut or that he was mispronouncing everybody else's name (the whole Hay-Zeus thing I was telling you about before).

Anyway, it had been a few weeks since I met JC and I was already exhausted. I mean, all we ever did was walk and talk and, even though I didn't mind the walking, the talking was making me tireder than death. And even though Bernard or the Earth Ladies were always baking rye or pump-a-nickel bread and making sure we had at least a few loaves each week, I really didn't feel like cooking (slicing). I told JC we needed to take a night off and just chill, so I got some "bread" from Louis and we walked on over to Prizzi's to get a pizza and buy *another* friggin' bag of oranges.

It had become practically a tradition by now that every time we went out for any reason we bought a big bag of oranges. But by the time we got home, there'd be only two left. JC would give all the rest away, tucking them in the arms of the sleeping homeless guys we passed, like he was tucking kids into bed, wishing them sweet dreams. Or some poor old geezer would stick out his hand for some spare change and pull it back with a big, fat ball of Vitamin C. After just a few weeks of this, we became known as the "Orange Men" in all of L.A.'s very best alleys and covered doorways.

So, this time, on the way home, after almost all the oranges were gone, he starts asking me all these questions like where I come from and what my family was like and who I really was and stuff like that. I told him I thought he should know all this stuff if he was some big messiah guy and that he wasn't doing much to advance the idea of him being all-know-ing and all-wise! I said it kinda kidding so he wouldn't get mad and strike me with lightning or something—you know, just in case—but since he didn't laugh or smile or anything, I thought I better pull out my big guns.

I told him the story of when the Earth Ladies had that psychic lady over (like I told you about already, with all the horoscope crap) and invited The Ark folks up to listen to her speak. Her name was Karisma, for Christ's sake. Anyway, Autumn had pulled me and Charlie aside and told us we better behave and not make asses out of ourselves. We said okay, but that didn't set too well with us, being kinda scolded like that. So, when I walked in, I stuck out my hand and said, "Hello, Karisma, how am I?!"

That was my funniest story and I thought it kinda went along with what I'd said about him being all-knowing, but all he did was give me one of those real tolerant smiles he was always giving me and then he settled down on his haunches to explain God, the universe, and everything to me—again. I hated when he did that. We'd just be walking along and shootin' the you-know-what and he'd ask me some question (like I was supposed to know anything), and when I didn't or couldn't answer he'd just settle right down on his haunches, right where we were, *anywhere* we were, and start explaining the whole damn thing to me. Right there. In front of God and everybody. It was so embarrassing.

So, a lot of the time I'd just pretend to understand to get him moving again but most of the time he didn't buy that and I'd have to really *get* what he was talking about or we'd stay there, all hunkered down, right in the middle of who knows where, just talking and trying to understand the nature of damn near everything. I mean, he was sorta nice about the big stuff I couldn't get but when it was something he thought I should get, he could look a little "stern," as Nana used to say. But in a teacher sorta way, not in a preacher sorta way. He never looked scary, not really, except that one time, and that was because of all the "desperate frustration" and all. (I'll tell you about that later.) What he would do was look disappointed, and that just about killed me. I mean, I hate to disappoint anybody, especially some kind of messiah guy.

Anyway, so he asks me where and what and who and all and I tell him he should know and tell him my funny story and he flashes that tolerant face at me and we hunker down in the middle of wherever we are so he can teach me the meaning of life.

"I don't know about you. I don't know about anyone any more than you do. All those things are just facts."

"Whaddaya mean?"

"No one knows anything about facts until someone else tells them."

"Oh, I get it," I didn't. "That's why there's education and crap like that."

"Yes," he smiled. "But, what I *do* know about, what everyone can know about if they're willing to quietly listen to that still small voice within their own hearts, is truth."

"I think I get that," I said and, in a weird way, I *did* get it and it made sense and it made me feel good about things, which is why I think he said almost everything—to make sense and make us feel good.

He knew all about truth and he told me we all did, too, because when somebody speaks the truth, or you hear from that little inside guy, something in you just recognizes it and you feel something and you know that it really is the truth. He called it "resonates" but I didn't have a dictionary handy or anything so I just took his word for it.

So, since I kinda *did* understand, I got him moving again and while we were walking, he asked me who my heroes were. I got kinda excited, and embarrassed, because when I was a little kid I saw this movie about this weird little bald guy wearing a diaper in public, for Christ's sake, and he was a hero because he used to walk around everywhere, and you know I love to walk, and he like got rid of all these bad guys with accents from his country and became king of it or something but wouldn't take the job because he was so regular and probably too skinny. I don't remember his name but I gotta tell you, that guy knocked me out. I mean, he looked all frail and simple and kinda girly but then he chases away all these guys with guns and weapons and all just by walking around with a big stick (which he never even used to hit anybody), and talking his head off. So it makes you think that maybe, sometimes, the little guy can win.

And, like I told you, I also loved those old time movie guys, like Bogie and Cagney. I know they're not real or anything but they made a big impression on me. They're not beautiful. They don't swear. But through all the crooked teeth and hissing when they talk and smoking like fish (which I do too but I know it's bad), they *still* get the girl. They make it possible for us not-as-perfect-as-Keyonyou-Reeves guys to have hope.

Anyway, the exciting part was remembering all that stuff. He was always making me remember things, all this wisdom kinda stuff that I knew when I was just a real little kid but kinda forgot as I got all adult and like that. But the embarrassing part was that he was looking at me, all kind and all, and I realized I hadn't mentioned *him* as a hero. Crap. I tried to add his name in there like he had always been on the list and I'd just forgotten about it. He sorta chuckled, but in a real nice way, not a Louis way, and said that wasn't necessary. He could make me feel terrible and okay with myself at the same time and I was thinking that someday I'd ask him how he did that. It wasn't like he pointed anything out to you. He'd just let you discover what a goofball you were and then look at you like he absolutely loved goofballs! And, in a slow and very real way, he *was* becoming my hero. And I knew he'd hate that.

He never, ever did anything that pointed the spotlight his way. He really got a kick out of walking around and nobody knowing who he really was and seeing how people act and talk when they don't know that this guy they're all praying to and saying they'd do anything for and wanna be exactly like was actually there, right there, listening and watching everything. Just like Santa Claus.

He got a kick out of it right up until he found out somebody with those gold crosses clanging all over his neck blew the brains out of some poor schmuck who was just trying to protect his pitiful little store. Or when somebody, right after coming out of church all moral and godly and crap, goes home and screws his neighbor's wife all to hell. Or when all these folks stand up on TV and shout and yell and fall down all over the place crying for him, and turn around after being all saved and all and don't let black people or gay people or anybody not just exactly like them come into their church. He called them hypocrites and the first time he saw that kinda thing going on was the first time I saw him get a little stormy.

Once we finally got home and we settled in to eat *cold* pizza and oranges, I started thinking how, if this guy was the real Jesus, he would know what heaven was like and what dying was like. He would know everything, right? But I already knew he didn't know everything.

"Are you ever afraid?" I asked with my mouth full of cold pepperonis.

"Sure." He swallowed before he talked.

That was good. I've always thought it was real stupid how we never admit to being afraid. I mean, doesn't it make you feel better when you know somebody else has gone through

54

what you're facing and they survived? And, if some guy's a god and knows everything and knows where he's going when he dies and all, then how the hell is that gonna help the rest of us who don't know? How could he understand what it was like to feel that kind of fear? So, I was glad that *this* Jesus would admit to being afraid. But if he was *that* Jesus, I mean, Him, for Christ's sake, how could he be afraid of anything? And, it was even weirder to find out there were things he didn't like. I don't know why, but somehow I thought that if you were Him, you had to love everything and everybody. He didn't.

He didn't seem to hate anything, well, except maybe ignorance where it was real obvious people could of done a whole lot better. But he really did *not* like when people wouldn't think for themselves. And, I gotta tell you, I was real surprised when he said something about people being sheep and that they *shouldn't* be.

We had started watching The Box, like we almost always did late at night before bed, and there was a news story on about some real crooked politician (big surprise, huh?), who's just spouting all these lies that anybody could look up online and find out they were lies, or they could *tell* were lies if they even just tried to think about it for a second. But all these people are there, cheering and just going right along with that lousy creep, without asking any questions. I usually tune that kinda stuff out and that's pretty much what I was doing but then all of a sudden JC said, "Sheep." Just the one word, and he didn't say it very nice, like he really didn't like sheeple. Then, he just went on eating his pizza.

"But, aren't you the Good Sheepherder?" I was real amazed.

"What?!" He was real amazed.

"You know, like all of us are your sheep and you go

around with that crooked stick and grab all of us up before the Devil gets us. Right?"

He looked kinda confused, like I'd just grown a couple of extra heads and was speaking some strange, alien language. So of course, I had to keep talking.

"*You* know, like you're walking around the earth fishing men outta lakes and herding up little kids and letting old ladies touch your dress and stuff like that, right?"

Nothing. He just popped an orange slice in his mouth, cocked his head like a question, then turned back to The Box.

It was those kinda times when I would doubt he was *the* Jesus and think that maybe he was just a real nice crazy person who didn't like who he really was so decided he should try to be better than everybody else. He didn't seem to know a lot of stuff from the Bible, at least not the new part—the part about him—and I thought that if he was the real deal he should. I mean, he wrote it and all, right?

When I tried to ask the Earth Ladies about it later, they just said that souls—regular ones anyway, once they've "slipped those slurpy bonds" and all—do sometimes go for a rest, some sorta divine you-deserve-a-break-today R & R, while real BIG souls, like JC, do something called "cycling-off." I don't think it has anything to do with that French Lance guy and as I get it (which is *not* usual) they never, ever come back, once they've cycled-off. Not ever. Except maybe for a rare photo-op vision.

The Earth Ladies said this cycle-off thing is like a "joining" with the Universe or God or Great Spirit, and it's supposed to be some big treat to get completely wiped out and soaked up by this all-loving but scary embrace from the "All-That-Is." Instead of getting to hang out and count galaxies or spook folks out on other planets (which is kinda what I always

56

thought dying was), you gotta just get all sponged up into the Holy Hereafter Goop and not even remember you ever were a you (which might explain JC's anemia about the New Tenement).

And—get this—*that's* The Prize! That's the award, the trophy, the number one blue ribbon you-win-it-all-'cause-you're-so-damn-special reward you get just for trying to live a good life and not hurt anybody and walk around ant hills and not laugh at old people and cry when your kids admit in public that they love you. That's what waits for you at the end of *you* and no amount of puttin' on the brakes will change it.

Good news, huh?

The next day we walked into this dark, creepy bookstore and just as JC walked by, some giant old book just popped right off the shelf in a big cloud of dust and landed open right in front of me. I gotta tell you, any doubts I had the night before just disappeared! I mean, it was spooky as hell. JC whipped around to see what the bang was and I crouched down to pick up the book—and try to catch my breath.

"No. Don't touch it." He said it loud and strong and it kinda freaked me out, like it was about to burst into flames and he'd just saved me from a third degree burn. I jumped up and started getting ready to run, but in a manly, I'm-not-really-afraid-just-checking-out-my-leg-muscles kinda way. So he crouched down and all gentle-like turns the book, still on the floor, so he can read it. He closed his eyes and put his finger down on the page, read it, and then looked up to me and cracked a big Jesus smile.

And all he said was, "It's for you."

Now, I'm still kinda freakin' out and making sure it wasn't an earthquake or somebody fighting or walking drunk in the next aisle but everything else in that store was still and quiet. So then I thought, *Cool, here come the parlor tricks* but, no, he was off to check on some ancient "Cab-a-lot" or something like that. I dunno, it sounded like a taxi for God.

When I could breathe again, I crouched back down to check out what he'd pointed at. The book was everything some old geezer named Shakespeare ever wrote or said or even thought about, for Christ's sake—I mean it was huge. It had opened to some stupid play about a dealer down at Venice Beach, I think. Anyway, where JC had pointed it said, "How far that little candle throws his beams! So shines a good deed in a weary world." (I wrote it down on the back of a receipt to make sure I got it right.)

And when I tuned back in from trying to figure *that* out, we were standing out on the street and JC was giving an orange to some lady with a shopping cart and it hits me that I never knew how we got anywhere. We'd just all of a sudden arrive someplace, and it was never anyplace I could identify as here or there—like in a dream or nightmare or when you just realize you're where you're going and you can't remember how you got there. Dazed, I think, is the word of how I felt.

When he finished with the lady I asked him, "What the hell did that book mean? And that 'light on a tired planet' crap? Is this about sunsets again?"

He just smiled and said, "You'll figure it out," and he walked off down the street to his next random act of sense-lessness. Man.

I started following him and decided to drop behind a few beats in an I've-got-your-back kinda way, and you know, there weren't any flowers suddenly growing up out of the sidewalk or rivers parting as he tried to walk through and, a few days before, we got caught in the rain and he definitely got just as wet as me. Drenched. No, even with that eerie bookstore message from some old fossil (Charlie calls old people fossils) named Shakespeare, it wasn't like that with him. There wasn't any God-reincarcerated fairytale bullshine that would of made everything seem real impressive to us poor peons—or "parlor" tricks like he always used to say. Nope, like I told you before, he was just some regular guy walking down that street and there was nothing, absolutely nothing, that would single him out from any other regular guy.

What was different was the way everybody *else* seemed ...like in a trance or something, but not in a zombie way. Just all of a sudden stopping and noticing—like an unexpected cool breeze in summer or getting all knocked out when, without any warning at all, you hear a little kid giggle. It wasn't anything out of this world. There was nothing different about him. But there was a whole lot different about us.

In a way it was kinda cool, nobody knowing who this guy was and where he was from and me and the folks of The Ark being the only "inside traders," as Louis would say. I really liked the days when I felt like that. But then there were days when I thought this guy couldn't be "The Christ," not in the way all those guys on TV talk about him. He was just a guy called Geez-Us, who grew up in a small town and, after a lot of thought and study, came up with some real amazing ideas about the way things are underneath all the bull.

So, anyway, I'm following him down the street and he stops to talk to some guy with no legs who was picking through a trashcan. When I caught up to them, JC was picking day-old lettuce out of the bin for this guy and saying something like, "...yes, and the difference between a weed and a flower is called judgment."

And all of a sudden I got hit by this lightning bolt and I

realized what a dufus I was for not writing down all this cool "spiritual" stuff he kept spouting (instead of me just writing some middle evil dork's jumping-right-off-shelves-giant-book-sayings on the back of a receipt, or bus times and new take-out numbers on somebody's old bank slip they threw on the ground—which is just about all the writing I ever did before JC showed up).

I still wasn't sure what I believed or if I even believed him or *in* him, but these were real interesting stories he was telling and amazing things he was saying (most of which I couldn't understand) and I thought it was a smart idea to make some sorta record of them. I'm a horrible writer and can't take diction or anything, so I decided to start carrying around one of those little cassette recorders and then every time he started spouting all this great spiritual crap I could whip out my handy recorder and not have to worry about remembering anything if I zoned out (which happens a lot).

I have a terrible memory now, like I told you, and the recorder seemed to fix the problem—except all he ever *did* was spout great spiritual crap, so I (really Louis) had to buy about a million of those little cassettes and I started carrying around this beat-up old backpack just to hold them all. I wanted to make sure I had enough—I mean, he was always talking, you know? The backpack was one of those black ones that had some sports store logo on it so I stuck a bumper sticker over it that said, "Very Important Person—Pass With Awe." I got a real kick out of the idea that people would see that but not know just *how* important the person was that they were passing by (but I would know...I mean, if I believed all that crap).

I remember that day (the bookstore day) was on a weekday and all of a sudden I realized we were sitting in this giant, empty church. I think we were there to kinda check out these big buildings spouting his name but not his ideas. Once JC understood that all these giant churches were all for *him*, that was the only time I ever saw his eyes get kinda mad.

"Then why aren't these people living in there, in warmth and love?" he'd asked me, a few days before, as we walked towards some cathedral past about a million homeless folks, lining the sidewalks of L.A. like carpeting.

He had looked sad and mad at the same time. It was the first time I think he realized nothing had changed, and hanging around on that cross for 2000 years had just been a great deal for architects and Mrs. T's Christ guys, but didn't do much for regular folks.

He definitely was what Louis called "bewildered" with all the hoopla. I think he just expected his guys to boogie on out there and keep spreading the "good news" and all, but from where he was standing, in what Louis said was the first century (even though I'm pretty sure there were tons of centuries before that), there was no way he could even imagine seven billion people in the world and that a whole helluva lot of them would wind up praying to *him* as God.

I couldn't tell if he was getting mad or what when I said that—that people were praying to him like he was God. He looked funny though, and not in a laughing way, but in that shadowy way people look when they're up against something you can't understand but they do and you're not sure they like it or not, but probably not.

So, we're sitting in this humongous church and I look down and there's this book called HYMNAL and it's full of songs about being all thrilled that JC got strung up, for Christ's sake. I leaned over and asked him what that meant, HYMNAL. He said it was about getting all excited to know God and wanting to sing about it.

"Make a joyful noise unto the Lord, all the earth," he said. "Serve the Lord with gladness—come before his presence with singing." He said it with a smile, but his eyes were sad.

I just kept staring at the word. HYMN-AL. Then, all of a sudden, I got it! HYMN must of been some old-fashioned way to say "him." It was a "HIM"-NAL. A book to sing about "him." That made all kinds of sense to me and in a weird way, just the word kinda sang. HYMN. So, from then on, whenever I would say, "This is him" or "That's him over there" I would think about HYMN and I'd say it with a little extra hum. I don't think anybody ever noticed, or if they did they just thought that I had some kinda speech impotent or something, but I knew it and I liked it.

From that moment on, he became HYMN to me. And because we were the closest of friends now and because I knew he loved me, in a not back-door kinda way, it was HYMN and me. Hymnandme. That close.

False Profits

Hymn and Louis were talking about false profits and how easy it was for people to believe in somebody else instead of themselves. I wasn't believing in either one of them right then so I switched on my new recorder (Louis thought it was a good idea and had fronted me the bread) and tried to decide if I wanted to take a nap.

"From what I've seen, there are now 'gurus' and 'shamans' who say they can bestow enlightenment," JC paused for just a second, *"but only to those who are wealthy enough to purchase it?"*

He looked a little pissed. It was like he really didn't get that, like Louis always says, "There's a lot of sham in shaman."

"But there were false prophets in your day, too." Louis was getting a real kick out of this real boring discussion. *"Why do you think it hasn't changed?"*

"We are spiritually lazy," JC kinda sighed. *"And we seem to get lazier as we get older. As we age, we lose the ability to believe in ourselves and our own dreams. We have to transfer all that belief-energy to someone else or the whole thing becomes meaningless."*

"Huh?" I wasn't really following because I wasn't really listening.

"When we're little kids, we're all supreme beings," JC smiled at me. *"We understand that we are connected. We live*

our dreams and don't just dream our dreams."

"I get it." Louis was always getting stuff. I was glad I had the recorder on so I could zone out. *"When we start out, we are the hope. And we spend a lot of time and energy putting some emotional flesh on that hope. We personify it ourselves and make it about us."* I started to ask a question here but Louis just went on…and on…

"Then, one day we realize we're past the age of hope. We can't possibly accomplish all our dreams. We've grown older without the promised accumulated wisdom. We're not the elders of aboriginal tribes, honored and revered. We're expendable. The best we can expect is some warmth and comfort. But what about hope? We have to transfer the hope. We have to align that hope with someone younger or stronger, more able to carry it out. And, of course, those younger, stronger gods-in-the-making love this. It buys right into the ego-ification of their belief in themselves as The Hope. And even though it's a false hope, even though they are false prophets, we buy it. Because we don't want to give up on hope. It's a vicious circle. We can't ever escape it. We're all failed gods. And it never ends."

Yep, like he could read my mind. Jeez!

"But not all false prophets today are for the wealthy, JC," Louis turned and kinda winked at me in a real lame, can't-wink-but-looks-like-he-has-a-tick sorta way. *"Right?"*

He *was* right. When they started talking about those false profits, me and Louis immediately thought of Noman. John Noman—like "let no man put us under." He was always saying his name meant he came from "no man," like he was divine or something. Noman was pretty sure he was supposed to be the current messiah and he made no bones about trying to get everybody else to see it the way he did. The fact that nobody else ever *did* see it that way didn't seem to bother him at all. He was his own PR agency and never missed a chance to tell anybody who would listen all about how great he was. As Louis was always saying, when it came to John Noman, "there but for the grace of God, goes God!"

Noman's family had come from Italy or India or some other Middle Eastern country like that, so he played it up big that his family was from the same 'hood as Jesus. He seemed to think he was the *real* Jesus, reincarcerated, for Christ's sake, but he never actually said that, exactly, unless you really pressed him, which nobody did.

But Noman was always *hinting*. He'd rub his palms and stick his hands in his pockets real fast when he walked past the hardware store (you know, in case there was a sudden uprising of 10 penny nails). And, if the sun came out from behind a cloud while he was talking to you, he'd put his hands out wide, like he was on a cross, look up to the sky and say, "Thank you." And he was always telling all the teenybopper girls on the block how he kept "remembering" flashes from his previous life—2,000 years ago!

"It all came back to me when I was hauling my surfboard up the beach at the Santa Monica Pier. All the lights and people suddenly took on the look of an ancient Israeli city on a hill (like they had a lot of neon hanging around back then) and my surfboard became....a cross!"

Really.

He cracked me up but Louis was always saying how guys like John Noman were dangerous because they prayed on innocents. I don't know about that, and I never saw him actually making that cross sign on anybody's chest or anything, but it was true he liked 'em young and stupid. Louis said that was because anybody over the age of 10 could figure

John Noman out for a phony, but I know a few of them were at least 15.

Noman was always telling people how to live their lives, without any kinda clue on how to live his own. He was going on 50, was what Louis called "unemployable…by design," and lived off the good will of whoever the latest schmuck (his dad, brother, old friends, current lovers) was in his life.

There wasn't anybody who believed him, or *in* him, so he had to always find new people to "pass his ego on," as Louis would say. He usually went for teenage girls because they would say he was cute, in a terrorist kinda way, and they didn't know enough to not get pulled into his story—until they heard him talk for a while. Noman was always talking. You couldn't stop him. He'd run right over any other conversation. It was sad in a way, and everybody thought so, except when Louis would get all annoyed at him and tell him he wasn't the Messiah and they'd get in a long argument about it and then Louis would say that *he* (Louis) was the Messiah, just to make Noman crazy. So, you can imagine how interested we were to have him meet my new roommate.

So, me and Louis arranged a meeting between Mr. N and Mr. C for a sorta "Messiah-off!" We didn't tell Noman that this guy was claiming to be the real Jesus. I really didn't care if he was or not, at that point. I didn't like Noman that much and I wanted somebody to shut him up for a change. Noman just thought JC was a friend staying with me who was interested in religion and the Bible and stuff and, of course, as the one and only authority on religion and the Bible, Noman was happy to oblige. I have to admit, in a very weird way, Noman was a lot like Mrs. T's hyper-Christ guys said the Jesus in the Bible was and JC wasn't at all. It made me wonder—but not for too long. Too much wondering leads to thinking and I'm not real happy when that happens.

Noman wore all white (of course), made sure the sun was to his back (the halo effect, dontcha know), and perched himself on some crates outside Delaney's, just to make sure we all had to look up at him. Noman was very loud and he was always checking around to make sure people passing by were noticing how profound he was. JC smiled at him, settled right down on his haunches, and, just about the whole time we were there, almost whispered everything he said. At the end, before it got dangerous, old John Noman had had to move himself down off his throne and onto the ground, just to hear what Jesus was saying. Priceless.

"What would you like to know?" Noman was so full of himself that it was hard to breathe. He was actually sucking the air out of the atmosphere.

"Whatever you'd like to share," JC almost whispered.

"I see."

He didn't.

"Do you have any questions you'd like to ask me?" Noman almost looked panicked. I was starting to realize that he needed things to be a certain way and we didn't know the rules of his game.

"No." JC was calmer than all those still waters Nana used to yap about.

"Well, then, I don't know how I can help you." Noman was getting pissed. He stood up and, believe it or not, it was Louis who jumped in to save the day.

"Why don't we talk about religion, John," Louis said in his very father-knows-best voice, "I know you always enjoy discussing Christianity and the Messiah and how HE might just be around these days." Louis was baiting a trap like an expert hunter of bull.

"Very well." Noman was such a turd. He sat back down on his crate-throne and started yapping for about a week. I zoned out, of course, and at one point realized I didn't have the tape recorder so I ran back into The Ark to get it. I got a little side-tracked talking to Jimmy and Ty and helping Mrs. T change a fuse (we still have fuses at The Ark) and by the time I got back, I realized I must of missed something real good because Noman was turning red and getting louder and louder and Louis was grinning from ear to ear like that cheese-eater cat in those Wonderland books.

"...and, to fulfill my destiny, I realized I was required to truly vanquish my sinful nature." Yep, old John Noman was on a roll.

"Sinful nature?" JC was still just talking in that real soft voice and I had to kinda inch the recorder closer so we could hear hymn. "In what way are you sinful? Because you are human? Is that what you're trying to overcome... being a human? I just don't understand this idea that God makes junk, John. We are talking about the Creator of the Universe, and everything and everyone in it. That means you are part of God. Your nature is divine, and a perfect expression of that divinity." Noman was eating that up, like he was Lana Turnip and had just been discovered at that Swartz's soda fountain. "You may not always behave perfectly, you may doubt or get angry or question. That's okay. I conclude that your nature is a direct expression of God, and therefore, is Perfect." Noman was beaming. At last, somebody who recognized him. Brother.

"Well, yes, you're right," Noman was kinda talking softer now, too. "My nature is divine." He looked off into that dreamy gray-brown sky. "And that's why it's so frustrating to try to talk to these young people. They're always asking *questions but not always accepting what I say.*" That made me kinda sad. It was like he'd finally found somebody who understood how hard it was for him to be the Messiah. It was the only time I ever saw him look real. That was about to change.

I hadn't noticed, but Zoe and Angela had come around the corner from out the back of their Dad's store, and had walked up behind us and were just kinda looking on. But old John Noman had noticed. He went into full performance mode, louder and more obnoxious than ever.

"*I know they are eager,*" he pointed to the girls, "*and that's good, but they don't seem to understand the danger of questioning truth. They doubt the obvious truth—that danger and ignorance stems from Original Sin.*"

"*From what?*" JC truly had no idea what Noman was talking about.

"*Original Sin.*" He waited, but nobody said anything. I don't think anybody except Louis knew what he was yammering about. And the only reason I thought Louis knew was because he had a look on him like a gravedigger just waiting for John Doe's last breath.

"*You know, as in we are all born sinners.*"

Not a peep.

"*We all have inherited Adamic sin. Satan's influence corrupts our natures from the very beginning, from the moment we are born, and exposes us to ignorance, suffering, and death.*" Noman seemed a little smug, as Louis would say, that JC didn't know about this real important Bible idea.

There was a silent beat and then JC busted out laughing. It was a huge laugh and he could barely choke out, "*Preposterous! You think babies are sinners?*" He was laughing so hard he looked like he was about to cry.

"*Yes!*" Noman shouted. "*That is exactly what I mean. We*

are all born with original sin. I know liberal apologists don't want to believe that, but it's all right there in the Holy Book. Look at Genesis. Investigate Galatians. This is the reason we must suffer the little children."

JC was beside hymnself laughing and it took a few seconds for hymn to catch his breath. *"'Allow,' John. I think you mean 'allow' the little children."*

"Allow the little children?" Noman looked all confused and like the air was leaking out of him.

"Yes, I agree. Allow the little children, for the Kingdom is theirs." Man, did Noman look like an idiot. *"Why would we teach precious innocents that they are born with sin and a need for guilt? I believe we can teach them of a loving, joyful spirit instead of a red-horned boogie man they must fear in order to be good. It's all about joy, John."*

Kinda puts a new spin on "What would Jesus do?", huh?

"But the Bible tells us to put away childish things." Noman was real pissed.

"Pardon?"

Everybody did one of those inhale all-together things. *HE* didn't know. I couldn't believe it. Even *I'd* heard that one.

"First Corinthians," Noman barked. JC just kinda shook his head, still trying to recover from his big laughing fit, but it was real clear he didn't know the saying.

Believe it or not, it was old Louis who came to the rescue again. *"John, you were talking about the danger of questioning truth? Was that it?"* Louis winked at me.

"Yes, I...I try to show them the error of questioning God's perfect design. I lead them down the path of righteousness." Noman was still trying to get his bearings back, I think, but it doesn't take an ego like that very long to recover.

"I don't think God is really worried about people with

questions, John. I believe in a Creator who has given me a mind and free will, and intends for me to use them." JC wasn't letting up either, but he was a lot more nicer about it.

"Yes, we were created in God's image, but this 'free will,' as you say we were given, has been used to disobey God's perfect plan for all mankind." Noman was right back to his old self. Jeez. I was finally understanding what my Nana meant when she used to say 'no rest for the weary.' *"So God was forced to judge all of us for our sin of disobedience against His perfect will."*

It didn't make any sense to me, about God having *His* will and then giving us *"free"* will" but then getting pissed when we *used* the *"free will"* that *He* gave us in the first place! But since nobody else seemed to be wondering about it, I decided not to bring it up.

Noman was still yammering away. *"When I look at humanity, I don't see holiness. Do you? No, I see sin, and so did Christ. Therefore, Christ chose to suffer the humiliating death of crucifixion in order to save us all. On that cross, he died for the sins of the world. On that cross, he died for* my *sins."* Old John Noman was starting to rub his palms! *"Christ paid the price for our sins by suffering and dying, so that we might be forgiven by God and not have to face the penalty of our sins, which is death."* Okay, he really lost me there. As far as I know, everybody who has ever lived since the time of Jesus has also died. So, not a great return on that payment, right? *"So, God set us free from the penalty of our* original sin, *because the price has already been paid for by Jesus Christ Himself the day He was crucified!"* I kept thinking, man, if he only knew who he was talking to.

"Christians all agree that humanity is evil and corrupt." You see what I mean about Noman always talking. Jeez. *"God*

is perfect; man is depraved. But, I know God has now called me to minister to the sinful, just as Christ did. I spend my days preaching to others and bringing them to understanding and since I have been saved, I can bring others to know Christ as certainly as they know me. They know Christ through me, so to speak."

"*John, when you say 'know Christ,' are you referring to—*" You could tell JC was just trying to be polite and kinda show some interest in Noman's crap. But Old John Noman was on a roll and he cut JC off, right in the middle of his sentence.

"*Questions just slow the process down,*" Noman snapped, like one of those annoying little dogs that wets all over you if you look at it funny, and I couldn't tell if he was aiming that at JC or everybody. He stopped, just for a second. He looked at each one of us, kinda like a challenge, daring any of us to speak. When he figured we were gonna be a good little audience and know our place, he went on—the jerk.

"*You know, I was 'questioned' when a young drug addict held me at knifepoint...a black man who came here from Amsterdam. We all know him in this neighborhood. He is a corrupt soul with many strange beliefs and many, many questions. He yelled and screamed and flashed his weapon at me. He raged at me to leave him alone. He kept crying out about how horrible his life was. 'Why, God? Why, God?' he whimpered. But I shouted, 'Sinner, repent. Accept the blood of Christ and be saved. Father, I pray that Your Will be magnified and enforced in this sinner and in his spiritually wicked land!'*"

Noman had gotten himself down off his throne to act out this scene for us (and, just so you know, I've heard this story about a million times, any time there's a new sucker to impress).

"That must have been a very frightening experience, John. But it seems to me that what the young man needed was acceptance and tolerance, not preaching." JC was sincere and kind. It made me almost wanna cry.

Noman practically jumped down JC's throat. *"Acceptance? ACCEPTANCE?"*

But JC was calm. *"Acceptance is not agreement, John."* I kinda felt like that was something real important and I was glad I had the tape going. *Acceptance is not agreement.* That made all kinds of sense to me, and judging from the faces of everybody standing around, it made sense to them, too. *Acceptance is not agreement.* I was trying to memorize it. It made me feel calm and connected, but I didn't know to what. But the battle was on and I started trying to pay attention again.

"Obviously, something has hurt him very deeply." JC was still talking about that black guy Noman had tried to "save"— poor schmuck. *"People with that kind of rage don't just suddenly explode. In my experience, souls who act like that are frightened and hurting. I would suggest that, when challenged with an individual who has such rage in him, you find a way to see him as God in disguise. Accept him, just the way he is at the moment."* JC paused for a second and I wasn't sure if he was trying to guess the mood of the scene or what.

"There's a big difference between sin and judgment, John. We all have opinions about right and wrong…" Noman was boiling and he sat back down—not a good sign. I was starting to think maybe this meeting wasn't a good idea after all. *"…and we all make mistakes; errors in judgment that may bring us anguish. I would say that sin can only be judged by the sinless. And, using your definitions, John, there are none who are sinless, save the Creator."* I remembered this one

from Sunday School—don't throw rocks unless you're Jesus Christ! (But, now that I'd gotten to know hymn, I didn't think he'd really throw rocks at anybody so, I guess it was just one of those lessons they try to teach you about how not to be too human.)

"*To approach someone without judgment can be very calming*," JC just kept going, like that energy rabbit. "*Just see him as part of you, as your brother—one who is lost and struggling. You don't even have to say anything to him. If he is that agitated, you probably shouldn't speak at all. Just hold him in that light in your heart. I think that will help him, in ways unseen.*" Noman looked just like that rabbit dog in Old Yeller, all caged and crazy, but JC just kept on.

"*As to the spiritual practices of any land, I believe God is big enough to embrace all the life on this earth. I believe they are praying with the same God you are. They may have another name for God, but the nature, the essence, is the same.*"

"*Are you saying God listens to the prayers of the heathen?*" Noman had all kinds of angry, purple veins popping out of his neck.

"*I'm saying that prayer is not for God to listen to you, John—it is for* you *to listen to God.*"

Noman went all quiet...a creepy kind of quiet. He was that creepy quiet for an uncomfortable amount of time.

Finally, that snake Noman started hissing, low and threatening. "*You seem like a very nice fellow but I'm afraid you are in danger here. What you expound is heresy. When you see and know the truth, then it is your duty to make others see it. That's why I have been called by God Himself. That's why I have returned* [here we go again] *and that's why I will continue to spread this Good News to everyone. Humanity is in error and I'm here to help correct that error. There are no other Gods. No other paths. Only the one true God of Christ. My God.*" Then Noman leaned way far out on his crate-throne and whispered right toward hymn, "*And there is only one true religion.*"

JC didn't even seem ruffled at all. "*You could also say that Hinduism is the one true religion for Hindus, or Buddhism for Buddhists, Islam for Muslims, Judaism for Jews, and on and on.*"

"*And what exactly is* your *religion?*" Noman barked, snarling at hymn.

"*My religion is kindness. My God, compassion.*" JC stopped for a second, and he got this look of love on his face and he gave that look right to Noman. I couldn't believe it. To Noman!

I got this weird feeling of goodness or something running all through me. I thought I could understand what folks in Bible times must of felt like to hear words like that for the first time—strange and comforting words. *My religion is kindness.* Wow.

JC just sat there, looking at his new arched enemy with all the kindness his religion could muster. It seemed like he was done talking and you could tell Noman was ready to pounce. But JC wasn't quite finished. "*The downfall of any belief system, John, is when the* religion *becomes the Deity. Eventually, adherents all worship religion. Not God. The truth is, every individual must come to know the Creator in his or her own way.*" Noman choked but JC went on. "*Everyone must be their own messiah.*"

Noman's eyes practically popped out his head and his leg started bouncing. I kinda thought everybody being their own messiah was about the coolest thing I'd ever heard—and the scariest. It sure took care of all those ego maniacs around today, like Noman, trying to tell everybody else how to live their lives. But, it also put a crapload of responsibility on *us*. I mean, if we're our own messiah, who the hell was gonna tell us how to live our lives?

When I tuned back in, everything was still quiet and Noman's leg was still bouncing. Then, JC went in for the kill. *"That makes for more than seven billion 'true religions' on the planet today."*

Noman was on his feet and shouting, *"No. NO. No, no, no! I've got the one true religion, buddy. These people need to understand who they're dealing with or they're going to burn. You need to understand who you're dealing with. Respect isn't enough. Your New Age, pagan bullshit isn't going to cut it. There's only room for one messiah here. And we all know who it is."*

So much for hinting.

Noman was insane and not in a good way. He'd worked his way down off his crate-throne and was standing right in front of JC, kinda pumping his thumbs at his own chest and spraying each word with a ton of spit. He was definitely acting like a jackass—but a dangerous one.

Well, Noman's King-of-the-Jungle routine sure set off the crowd. Zoe and Angela started laughing, and laughing hard. They ran across the street and were talking with some other girls who'd stopped to listen, and they all started pointing and giggling. The shape of our city makes things like girls laughing at you echo, and Noman's embarrassment echoed all over L.A. The girls left, strutting and laughing on down the street, and taking with them (at least in Noman's eyes), a whole bunch of potential believers.

Noman was practically foaming out his mouth and yelling over his lungs. *"Don't they know who I am? Don't you?*" It was sad—in a real funny way—and I just started cracking up, which just made the whole scene feel real dangerous, real fast. Noman spun around and was glaring at me—ME! He actually looked like he had fire coming out of his eyes, so I stopped laughing and tried hard to swallow. I looked to hymn to calm it all down and save me from the hellfire of Noman's stare.

JC stood up slowly, and very quietly shot Noman right where it hurt the most—his ego. *"John, messiahs aren't here to do the thinking for others. They don't come to be glorified. And any messiah who requires worship, cannot be genuine."*

Man, you could of heard a pin drop. Noman looked like he'd been hit with a sack of Old Tenement profits. JC really nailed the guy, in a not-on-the-cross sorta way. I was practically pissing my pants I was so jazzed. Somebody finally shut Noman's mouth!

Hymnandme and Louis started to walk away and all of a sudden Noman started yelling, *"What do you know about it?"* He yelled it over and over. As we got farther away, his voice sorta boomed and ricocheted through the buildings, *"What do you know about it?"* Louis was humming, and I think he was kinda tickled that, if anybody knew about it, it would be hymn.

But, in a real weird way that I didn't understand, the whole thing was starting to make me sad. And nervous. JC seemed quiet too, in a maybe-it's-not-a-good-idea-to-piss-off-crazy-people kinda way. And, I started to worry that maybe something bad would come of all this.

Louis looked at our faces and practically started singing.

"Don't worry about Noman. It was a very successful encounter."

Yeah, it may have been a "successful encounter" but I was

afraid it wasn't gonna be their last.

We walked home and booked it on up to Louis' for sunset and Chinese. I didn't think it was a good sign that the very first thing out of JC's mouth after sunset was:

"What's Galatians?"

Real Life Ain't For Real

"What happened?" JC looked all wide-eyed and confused. "How did the message get so far away from its meaning?" I guess the meeting with Noman had upset hymn more than we realized.

"Noman's an idiot," I knew how to cheer somebody up.

But, naturally, Louis decided he knew a better answer, so I had to turn on the tape:

"*2,000 years ago, it worked,*" Louis was one damn sure-of-himself professor. "*For that time, everything in your original message was profound, dramatic and powerful. Turn the other cheek was a stance boiling over with empowerment 2,000 years ago. Today, it might just be foolish.*"

JC winced but Louis went on.

"*A small population in Rome and Israel, relatively uneducated and unsophisticated, and raised with unquestioned, authoritarian values, can be stunned, subdued, and ultimately transformed by kindness and passive resistance. Not long ago, another small but militaristic population in England, overeducated and pridefully sophisticated, was persuaded, manipulated, and ultimately transformed by world public opinion and reaction to passive resistance in the form of what the crassest media called 'a little man in a diaper.'*"

Oh, yeah! That India guy I was telling you is kinda my hero.

Louis just kept rollin'. *"Can it work, though, when a large, bored, unmotivated, highly armed population, worshiped for its power in the world, becomes disappointed and disillusioned with its own ideology; when profundity is a mediocre commodity; drama, a false and frail mask for moralizing; and faith, a weapon used to crush individual empowerment?"*

He didn't even take a breath. Jeez.

"2,000 years ago, this transformation from the incurious, mundane mind of 'us or them' to an inclusive, ever-expanding spiritual awareness, abundant with possibilities and opportunities for self-actualization, was simply the care and watering of the bud to bloom. Those seeds were bursting with eager anticipation.

"Today, the task of continuing the ethical evolution of human consciousness is confronted with a rigid, uninterested spirit, devoid of even your 'mustard seed' to nurture. We've seen it all before on TV, in the movies, on our laptops, even in our churches and temples of worship—the sucking of our spirits from the marrow of our souls.

"And when the Beast of greed and lust, masquerading in salvation-clothing, is satisfied, and the mind-numbing comfort of apathy sets in, we are tossed aside, empty and terribly alone, pockets wrong side out, eyes sunken and heavy. Then, the Beast laughs at us, and is on to the rape of yet another spirit, another mass murder of the very souls that provide the food for its growth."

Happy hour at Louis'.

"But, 2,000 years ago, there was no way to know it happened to anyone else. Your message took centuries to reach the masses and, by the time it did, it had been twisted and revised to serve the pulpit politicians in power at the

time. Everyone started looking AT *Christ instead of* THROUGH *Christ. You said 'Love your neighbor as yourself' but the deliberately diluted addendum became 'As long as they're just like me.' "*

JC put a finger up and said, "*Actually, I said…*" But Louis was on fire and just bulldozed right over our sad and all alone messiah.

"*Today, there are borders to God.* Their *god and* our GOD. *The Beast holds the pendulum of emotion that swings from apathy to anger, with little else in between. Apathy breeds separation and separation spawns an ego-blaze of resentment. Souls are cremated in their own frenzied spasm of self-righteous wrath. And suddenly, there's a phoenix of fury in those slain, depleted ashes. It rises again and again, without conscious conscience.*

"*The passion of legitimate grievances then becomes the rage of imagined slights.* They *drive too slow;* they *cut in line;* they *take our jobs;* they *rape our women;* they *defile our hallowed ground.*

"*That phoenix of rage, with its fundamental mores and elementary understanding, then buys a small but deadly symbol of Beast worship—a gun—stuffs down the last memory of the genuine spirit of faith, truth, love, reason, hope, and innocence, and in an orgasm of sudden, irrevocable belonging, hails the Beast for its guidance—and pulls the trigger.*"

Yeah, that was pretty much what I was gonna say. You can see what I mean about Louis, but JC seemed to be following along, nodding his way into Louis' trap.

"*And why all this rage? Because we've been lied to. And we who have been lied to become the lie. The 'message' you treasured has been redesigned, reinterpreted, and reinvented for the purposes of the current authority. And, as you've seen* with Mrs. T, your message is delivered, without mercy, via everyone's favorite best friend…television. And those newly ordained automatons, they point and shout 'sinner' with one hand while holding fast to the head giving the BJ with the other."

I could not believe Louis said that…not to *hymn*.

"*There are no saints today because we have TV. We don't need the drama of saints. No one wants the truth. The doing is nothing today…the telling is everything. What happened 2,000 years ago was radical. You went from a vengeful, militaristic God to a loving Father in one, immeasurably huge step. But you, I'm sorry to say, were the First and Last Christian, my friend. Today, we're back to the beginning. Fear is the religion and the military are its priests. No more Mr. Nice God. According to fundamentalist, born-again believers, God is coming back and He doesn't want any New Age BS. No more choices. Their way or OUT.*"

I felt so sorry for hymn. He looked so sad. But Louis just wouldn't stop.

"*And by the time it's ritual, it's too late. The experience of spirit has died. Mass media is the pulpit and the zeitgeist. Beauty is the beast. And, today, those 2,000 year old whips and chains of forced compliance have been replaced, and everyone is kept in line, by the most vicious inventions ever to cripple mankind—isolation and loneliness.*"

Yeah, how to win friends and influence God.

Louis sat back for a long drink of self-esteem and waited for the applause. I think everybody, including Louis, thinks Louis is so smart because they can't understand a thing he says and would rather call him smart than think of themselves as stupid.

*   *   *

When we got home, I decided to kinda ease into the question that was bugging me.

"You didn't buy all that crap, did you? Did you even understand it?" Well, maybe not ease in.

JC didn't talk for a long time. Then, suddenly, he stood up, said, "Excuse me," and walked out the door. I felt like he must not be feeling too good after what Louis said (if he could even understand it), so I followed hymn downstairs to Mrs. T's.

We must of sat there with her for weeks, watching those Christ guys on The Box. Looking around her living room, I noticed a new kinda sewn up picture on her wall, right over her TV. It was all done in different color threads, with flowers and daisies and stuff and it said 'Christ Died For You.' I leaned over to hymn and pointed.

"Shouldn't that be Christ LIVED for you?" but Mrs. T shushed me so I shut up and tried not to listen to all the Amens.

When a commercial finally came on, JC got up and was real polite to Mrs. T, thanking her for her hostility.

When we got home, I asked hymn what he thought of those guys hollering about sin and repenting and stuff, all in *his* name.

"The sinless, begging for forgiveness..." He kinda shook his head as he said it.

"And what about all that bread they get, just to send you some ketchup packets." I guess I hadn't told him about Nana and the Holy Water.

He looked confused for a second, then all he said was, "Freely you have received, therefore freely give."

Go figure.

He didn't much seem like he wanted to talk (and who

83

could blame hymn after the Louis Lecture), so I said good-night and he flipped on The Box.

He seemed to be having a rough time with real life after the "successful encounter" with Noman and the whole hymn not knowing all these names and sayings and titles from the New Tenement. I think it had gotten to hymn, in a real divine sorta way. So, I waited a few days and thought real hard to come up with a subject as far from all the crap Noman and Louis had laid on hymn as possible. No Bible stuff from me.

"So, is this resurrection stuff real?" I figured that would get hymn going.

Now, I gotta tell you that I've always loved that part of the story. Not so much the resurrection stuff, which I wasn't sure was real and never understood why it was more important than all the years he'd spent running around and healing and making wine and yakking his head off at all the Farrahs and leopards. I mean, it was a cool and spooky part of the whole story but why should being dead for three days count more than three years of trying like hell to set everybody straight? Being dead just ain't all that special, right?

No, the part I liked was the casting. They send this huge multiple of angels and serpents and stuff to announce this guy is getting born, which is pretty much the way all of us get here and not a great accomplishment. And then—and here's the kicker—they send this Mary Magnavox chick, who's got a real bad rep, to announce the most amazing thing that's ever happened in the whole history of forever! A resurrection. That knocks me out. It kinda made JC's story (that was getting all sci-fi and not very believable), well, it made it kinda touchable and close and "if she can do it so can I" like. It brought hymn back down to us. So, I asked hymn if this resurrection stuff was real.

He patted his chest with both hands. "Guess so."

I couldn't believe he said that.

"And how can I get into the gang, man?" I was trying to sound all cool and tough and maybe get hymn to pull some divine strings, but I'm not a very cool or tough person, as you can probably tell. He looked at me and I just knew he was gonna laugh—I mean, it was the kinda thing he always laughed at—*me!*

But he didn't. He got all serious looking and leaned way in to me like he was about to tell me the greatest secret of all time. I leaned in too and all of a sudden my heart was racing and pounding so bad I was sure he could hear it. I was kinda embarrassed, I mean, to be all interested in stuff that was way out there like that, but jeez, if you can't get it from the horse's mouth….

So he leans in and I'm starting to sweat like a pig and now I can hear my heart in my ears and I'm afraid I'm gonna miss what he has to say. I was also mad at myself because the tape recorder was across the room and I didn't wanna come off too dufus-y and uncool and like the jerk I was for forgetting to keep it close so, I just stayed there. When you're about to hear the secret of all time, you know you'll remember.

He looked at me with real intense eyes and I stopped myself from breathing so I wouldn't miss anything.

"I don't know."

I sat there staring into those deep, dark eyes like I hadn't heard hymn. He just kept looking at me and I just kept looking at hymn, and he didn't say another word.

Finally, when I realized he wasn't gonna explain hymnself or even try to, I got some spit back in my mouth and just about screamed at hymn.

"What the HELL do you mean you 'don't know'?"

"I don't know."

"Whaddaya mean, YOU don't know? How can *you* not know? You're HYMN."

"Him?"

"Yeah, you know, you're IT—the big guy, the top cheese, the all-mighty chief kahuna. How can YOU not know everything?" I wasn't quite as upset as I sounded but I was still wondering inside. I mean, shouldn't he....know?

"Why do you think that?" He was all serious and all of a sudden I got this half-sinking feeling that he really didn't know. I wanted hymn to be the real Jesus so bad now. I wanted it like I wanted there to be a God who could really jump in and save me when I had to walk home late at night through a not-too-good part of town.

But, he didn't even know hardly anything that happened in the new part of the Bible, like that Galactica part Noman was talking about. So, we decided I should tell hymn why folks thought he was God, and I started with all the stories I could remember about hymn from Sunday School.

"Okay, so, first there's this whole birth thing," I thought I should start from the beginning.

"Yes."

"Well, this guy Joseph claims he never touched your Mom but she gets pregnant anyway. So, when it's time for you to be born, he starts hauling her all over creation and ends up getting her a place in a barn because he was late getting there and I guess they gave away his reservation and that barn was all they had left." You'd a thought she would of got another husband or something. I mean, hey, big spender!

"Go on."

"Well, then your Mom's all screaming and moaning and

you're all trying to get out and into this world, for some reason…"—I mean, jeez, if he only knew, right?

"Sounds pretty ordinary to me."

"Just wait," I said, "it gets better. So, then all these angels start singing their heads off and they wake up all these sheepherders who are asleep when they're supposed to be watching their sheep and all and they start getting all excited that this baby's being born," (like he's the first one—Jeez). "That's you."

"Right."

"Then, all these wise guys come to visit you and they bring you birthday presents like gold and Frankenstein and mirth—" I was on a roll but he interrupted.

"Mirth?" He said it with one of those smiles like he was about to laugh.

"Yeah. But then this King got mad that you were being born and he took it out on every other little boy baby being born so that Joseph guy decides that then was a real good time to go see the pyramids."

He looked like he was trying not to laugh but I didn't understand why…I mean, I didn't make up this crap.

"So, then nobody wanted to talk to you for a real long time, probably because of all the ruckus, and then you started running away and being a wise-ass in some temple and your parents didn't do a very good job of keeping track of you, so I guess you were a pretty normal kid.

"Then you grew up and decided to go down and beg this guy to shove you under some river and when you got all cleaned up and everything, some dove comes and lands on your head, like the pigeons do sometimes at 6 Flags, and even though it was kind of a drag, you didn't seem to mind because it made you start seeing all your career ops and stuff like that."

"I see."

He didn't.

"So then you started having visions and annoying people so they got all mad and started chopping people's heads off so you decided it's a helluva lot safer to have visions when you're all alone. So you boogied on outta town and got lost in the desert, not living by bread or anything, for 40 days. Or was that the flood?"

"Anyway..."

"Anyway, so this Devil guy traipses all the way out there into the desert to see you and tells you to bow down but you just said 'No,' so you got to go back to the ocean and started running around making people put all these men in fish nets. Or something."

"Or something?"

"Yeah...uh...so, then there were all these miracles, like not getting dunked when you decided to take a stroll on the ocean!"

"Really?"

"Yeah, and all these dead guys just kept popping up out of their graves just because you asked them to."

"Remarkable!"

"Yeah, and then, when you did all that dying on the cross and all, they took you down and stuck you in some cave with a door," (like you've ever heard of a cave with a door), "and all these angels came and tore the door off so I guess you had to get up real early on Easter!" I was just kidding about that part.

"Indeed."

"Then you went around spooking everybody, which was kinda cool, and then you went fishing, for crying out loud, and then you just got all filled with helium or something because you just floated up to heaven to rain on somebody's hand."

Well, I gotta tell you, he looked like he'd been hit by a rock. He looked like *he* didn't even believe a word of it. And then, like he did a lot these days, he just started laughing. It was one of those laughs where you're not sure if it's okay to laugh too, like if you do and it's not a good laugh then he's gonna go all psycho on you.

But, he didn't and when he calmed down he asked me if I remembered learning about anything he *said*. And, of course, in that second, I went completely blank and I just threw out anything I could think of, like, give unto Caesar all the little children and don't take any money to church. This time he didn't look happy at all. Not mad, just kinda sad again and I got worried that I'd been this big disappointment to hymn for about the millionth time. Jeez.

He never talked much about his "before" life, if you know what I mean, and after I told hymn what everybody *thought* the story was, I was pretty sure he never would. I mean, would you? So it really surprised me when he did say something, a few weeks later.

"You remind me of someone…"

He was always saying stuff like that right in the middle of us doing something else. We'd caught the old 217 down to Canter's for some hot pastrami and a side of mom-like scolding from Rosie. It had become like a habit by now that at least once a week hymnandme, and sometimes Louis, would hop the bus down to Fairfax to sit at Rosie's table for some great Kosher and tough love.

Rosie's this real old lady who asks what you wanna eat and then brings you what *she* thinks you need! Man, that knocks me out. You always end up getting what you ordered but you also get some matzo ball or chicken soup and a lecture

on your hair being messy or how you're too skinny. I dunno—
it makes me feel cared about. You know?

So, after we were stuffed out our eyeballs, we spent most
of the rest of the afternoon at the Old Farmer's Market and he
really seemed to love it. He even said it was the closest thing
to home he'd seen. Well, that just made me sad, I mean...
vegetables? Anyway, it was a cold day for the end of October,
too cold for walking all the way home, so we called Bernard
for a pickup and while we waited, we ducked into the most
boring place we could find—that big museum downtown next
to the Tar Pits. I didn't know if they had dinosaurs in Bible
times so I thought he might be interested. But, get this...he'd
never even heard of a dinosaur! I mean, c'mon, Man. Even if
you're not some big science guy you gotta at least of seen the
Flintstones, right?

So, anyway, we're in the museum looking at some real
interesting rocks, for Christ's sake, and he says I remind hymn
of somebody.

"Oh, yeah, who?" I wasn't real interested but then it
occurred to me that it might be somebody famous and that
would be kinda exciting. I mean, I was thinking that the last
time I heard this story, I didn't know I was part of it!

"Someone I knew a long time ago." Yeah, a REAL long
time ago, is my guess.

"Yeah, who?" I was starting to get interested in these
statues across the way and was practically yelling to hymn. I'm
not real good at following along on slow, lazy kinda conversations and so I'd already forgotten to be all interested in being
somebody famous in a before life.

"His name was Cephas." He turned to me, and I could
see he had that kinda smile in his eyes, like he was remembering his best friend. He looked happy to be far away, back

in his time.

But, I only realize that now, looking back. At the time, all I could think was… "See-Fuss? Who the hell is that?"

(Crap, did I say that out loud?) I mean, I'm sure this See-Fuss was nice and all, but I never heard of him and I'd come back around to being interested in being somebody famous after all, because the statues turned out to have clothes on.

"He was my friend. He was impulsive and quick and had the kindest heart I've ever known."

Great.

"I've never heard of him. Was he just some guy you hung out with?"

"Yes, he was a good friend and I miss him. Thank you."

Thank me?

"For what?"

"You remind me of him and that brings him back to me."

"Yeah? Who was he…anybody good?" I can be real stupid sometimes.

"Yes," he laughed. It was a good laugh, sudden and unexpected and it made me relax. He didn't seem to mind me being a jerk all the time. "Yes, he was good. I'll tell you about him sometime."

But he never did.

Does Love Your Neighbor Mean Louis Too?

"Mrs. T? Why do all these faith-healing Christ guys wear glasses?"

I'd spent a big chunk of the day watching those hyper-Christ guys on The Box with Mrs. T and thought that would be a great question to kinda break the silence.

I was feeling a little guilty because the night before, the Earth Ladies had invited the whole Ark and a few neighborhood folks to get together for a Not-Halloween-or-Thanksgiving-and-Something-You-Can't-Pronounce-but-the-Pagans-Did-It-First Party. Jimmy and his mom and Mrs. T had all refused to come, and the Yins had said something about having to burn something, but nobody could understand what, and they didn't answer their door when we knocked on the way up to the Party. I didn't hear the smoke alarm (the Yins, Bernard, and Mrs. T are the only folks at The Ark with working ones), so I guess they just kinda wanted to be left alone.

I was worried Mrs. T mighta felt left out, even though she was the one who never stepped foot outside her apartment and who said she wouldn't be caught dead "dancing with the Devil." I don't think he was invited, and he never showed if he was. And how would we know anyway?

Jimmy and his mom couldn't come, I think, because the party had the word Halloween in it, even though the real

Halloween had already happened a few days before, and Jimmy said they already had their own Jewish Halloween called "Purell" or something like that. It has costumes and candy too, but Jimmy's mom thought trick-or-treating was "just extortion."

Louis, who you know is also Jewish, said that the Torah (Tora, Tora! He gets so pissed when I say that) was always yapping about some guy named Abraham and his tent being open on all four sides and that's why Halloween was okay with him. I didn't know who Abraham was, except Lincoln, and I know he didn't have a tent, except maybe when he was that Rail Splinter, you know, or just out hangin' in the woods.

JC had agreed with Louis about that Abraham "cat" (Ty's word) and about how welcoming strangers was practically holy or something. Then he flashes this look at me and I got one of those spooky feelings, but a good one, like maybe *I* was holy or something since I'd welcomed hymn when he was a stranger. He could do that—make you feel good and holy and like you mattered in the world. (He'd say everybody can feel that way when they "wake up and listen" to that little inside spirit guy.) It was still weird to me, though, that he knew all about this Torah book, but, like I said, he didn't seem to know hardly anything about the new part of the Bible and what it said about hymn.

Anyway, he'd seemed to dig sitting in the window on the real Halloween and watching all the witches and goblins and Lady GaGa's trolling down the street (nobody ever came into The Ark, thank God, since we were pretty notarized for never having candy) and he said he was looking forward to the Party.

When we first arrived, I was real excited to see Angela was already there, and any danger of me being holy went right out the window, if you catch my drift! She was sitting on one of those giant pillows on the floor, listening to the tortured cat music and she gave me one of her best I-think-I-like-you-too smiles. Me and her had been getting closer since hymn, and my heart was doing that flip-floppy beat like maybe tonight would be—*the* night. (It wasn't.)

But, wherever Angela went, Zoe was usually lurking close by, waiting to open her mouth and send anybody within range to the ER for first degree ear assault. Louis said Zoe was always with Angela because she had a "Withered Ghost" syndrome, or something like that, and started yammering on about some chick named Ruth in the Old Tenement, but since Zoe had already started talking I couldn't really hear Louis and I suddenly figured out that this is what they call "a blessing in disguise!"

I won't bore you with all the details of the stupid party except to tell you they had some crazy good food I couldn't pronounce (food is my main reason for ever going to a party—or to see Angela, if I know she's gonna be there). But, since it was at the Earth Ladies' pad, they came up with some loser game we all had to play. They were always doing that, coming up with these real lame games and telling everybody that groaned that it was an "awesome" way to get to know your neighbors better—like anybody would wanna get to know people better that you're freakin' forced to live next to through no fault of your own.

So, *this* party's crappy game was called First Memory and all it was, was having to tell everybody the first thing you could remember. I was kinda glad I'd forgotten the recorder so I won't have to annoy the hell out of you with every mind-numbing detail.

So, Autumn's first memory was looking at stars, lying on

the grass in her backyard with her dad. Thrilling. But, in a way it *was* kinda interesting that she would go on and work at the Observatory and do the whole horoscope thing.

Raindrop still wouldn't speak, even at her own party, but she'd told Autumn that her first memory was her folks putting up a circus tent in the backyard for her first birthday. Yeah, right. But it did kinda explain why she didn't talk—I mean, she was probably scared voiceless by some stupid clown.

Ty remembered the smell of his grandmother's kitchen and some big iron pot boiling over with cholera greens.

Bernard said his first memory was waking up during one of his Aunt Bitsy's "fabulous parties," covered in pink boas. "Explains a lot!" Louis said and Bernard tossed one of those little pillows at him and then threw him a kiss! Louis blushed and I started thinking this party was kinda fun after all.

Charlie said he remembered somebody—either Jesus Christ or The Ant People aliens…and no, I have no idea who The Ant People aliens are—coming into his bedroom at night and turning his revolving zoo-light lamp on and off. Angela kinda giggled at that and Charlie puffed up a bit and I had what I think was my very first stab of jealousy. It was funny though because I was mad at Charlie, not Angela.

Louis told us about how his grandfather had a watch shop and his first memory was trying to open this huge pocket watch. I thought that was real weird since, like I told you, Louis doesn't even own a watch or have a clock and here he practically grew up in a watch shop.

Zoe didn't wanna share—and you could actually *hear* people feeling grateful—but Angela told us that her earliest memory was seeing her mom giving her brother a bath in the kitchen sink. Charlie made one of those "Oooo" noises at that and Angela shot him a dagger look that made me feel much better, so I decided to share next.

My first memory was, I think, that I was standing at the side of a lake and Nana was rowing a boat. I was waving and she was wearing a polka-dot dress with white gloves on. Or, maybe it was my mom. I'm not sure if it was MacArthur Park or Echo or if maybe it was just some place I've always wanted to remember and I just made it all up.

So, everybody was *real* interested in JC's first, I mean, talk about long-term memory, right? He told us the very first thing he could remember was what he called a "snake with legs" running around while his mom was cooking in a pot—outside! Everybody kinda laughed and he laughed the hardest of all so I'm not real sure it was the real truth.

Anyway, the next day I was feeling depressed since I didn't get to hook up with Angela, and maybe a little guilty about Mrs. T, so I spent the day with her and her Christ guys and wound up asking her why, with all that healing going on, those preachers had to wear glasses.

"SHUSH!"

Mrs. T liked silence, especially when she was watching The Box—which was always. I still didn't feel like I'd made up for her not being at the party so I dug in for about another century of yammering about Praise the Lord and End Times until I just couldn't take it anymore.

"Mrs. T," I kinda whispered it so she wouldn't shush me again, "don't you think that maybe we wanna believe these are the Last Days because we don't wanna think about things like life and the world going on without us?"

Charlie and Ty had been talking at the party about this book in the Bible called Reservations and said that if our JC was the real deal, then this might be the Last Days. Last Days sounded more like a shopping opportunity to me, so since her Christ guys were always yammering about Last Days and stuff like that, I decided to ask our local expert, Mrs. T.

She looked at me like I was the Devil himself. But I thought it was a good question. I mean, I don't wanna miss anything, do you? It's like when you're a little kid and you kinda think that when you die, the world dies. That way you don't miss a thing. That way, you never gotta be alone.

"These *are* the Last Days," she really barked it at me.

"What exactly does the Last Days mean then? Is it the Last Days of the whole world or...are you just feeling kinda poorly?" I can be very caring sometimes.

"The Last Days are the Second Coming of Christ." She sure could be grouchy for being the local rep for this all-loving religion.

"Well, I guess it *is* the Last Days then!" I smiled when I said it, and pointed upstairs to my apartment.

"We'll see," she said, and then she shushed me again.

Those Christ guys on The Box were foaming out their mouths about how everybody but those folks in *their* special, we're-the-only-ones-going-to-heaven crowd were gonna go to hell, especially in "these Last Days."

And suddenly I got real worried about Mr. and Mrs. Yin. I mean, they're Buddhists and all, which means they don't believe in God but they gotta have a religion anyway and now these guys on TV were saying the Yins are gonna go to hell because they hadn't *claimed* Jesus—like he was a pawn ticket or something.

I tried to ask Mrs. T about it but now she was all yammering "in tongues," which means goommie gobbie and crap like that, so I booked it on upstairs to talk to the horse's mouth.

JC wasn't home but, since the day was fading, I knew where he'd be. I grabbed the recorder, and by the time I got up to Louis', I had just enough time before the sun set to tell them what had happened at Mrs. T's.

So, I asked hymn if he thought the Yins would go to heaven even if they were Buddhists and looked different and talked different and wore kinda strange clothes and all.

"The Yins will have places of honor."

He said it so fast it was like he already knew what I was gonna ask.

"Everyone, absolutely everyone is a child of the Creator," he went on. *"Differences don't matter at all. Differences are a wonderful example of the endless palette of the Great Artist. What matters is that we perceive rightly with our hearts, not our eyes."*

I really liked it when he said things like that, because I always got these great head-movies about all these people running around with giant eyes right in the middle of their chests.

You-know-who decided to translate, *"He doesn't care how you* look *but how you* see."

I knew that. Louis was always saying those double on tundra kinds of things that sounded real smart but didn't make any sense. And sometimes I kinda resented that he seemed to be taking over everything about hymn. I mean, it was me that first met hymn and me that gave hymn a place to stay when nobody knew hymn from Atom. Now, all of a sudden, Louis became this smarter-than-anybody-and-only-one-who-understands-anything-he-means special interpreter of hymn. Don't get me wrong, I really love Louis—in a guy-loves-guy-without-any-messing-around kinda way. But, I was the first contact and I thought I should have some special place in the high arches of this new world we were always talking about.

But this time, Louis kinda made sense and I was starting to have one of those spooky tumbling stomach feelings like I was gonna learn something without even meaning to.

Right from the start it was easy to understand that JC had no interest in how people looked. You could tell he was one of those guys that just doesn't care if you're dressed in rags or smell or have about a million different colors of hair or teeth or half your face is falling off. I guess it was all that practice with the leopards which you gotta admit must of been kinda creepy. I mean, that 'how are ya' handshake could get pretty uncomfortable if you pull back with an extra hand!

But it took me a whole lot longer to get the "how you see" part. JC was always talking about how we create our own worlds...like basically, what you believe is what you get. He said that was why witnesses of accidents and crime scenes all had different stories, because they were seeing it from their own private world. He said that that was why we all felt lonely so much of the time and that it took somebody real special to be able to see into another person's world and understand what they were seeing. But, then he'd say that's what makes life interesting and it would be real boring if we all saw everything the same. I could get that because, as you know, all the folks at The Ark are as different as you can get and I always thought that was kinda fun. But it took me a real long time to get the "I'm creating my own reality" bit.

So, in honor of the Yins, Louis ordered in Chinese (not the words but the food), but we weren't allowed to eat until after the sunset.

While we were eating, Louis decided to play the Devil's Adjective and started telling hymn that he didn't think there was really any need for God, from a science point of view. You gotta understand, Louis thought of himself as some kinda fizzysist (that's a science guy, I think). So, Louis spent the rest of the night trying to convince hymn there was no need for God. I got one word for that night—TOTALLY BORING.

I kept nodding off and every time I kinda drifted back to this world I'd hear words like quark and photon and crap like that, so I'd just drowse away again. It was weird because I dreamt of elves or something—all these tiny little people buzzing a circle around a sunflower. Finally, a shock of light went right through my lids and I woke up with one of those falling feelings and grabbed the floor so I wouldn't fall through onto Bernard.

Louis was still talking—naturally—and the tape had long since run out. When I was as conscious as I get in the morning, I picked up the very end (praise the Lord, as Mrs. T always says) of his lecture on that Big Bang baloney. Louis was saying something like, "...and that leaves just one electron and one proton."

He sat back for a slow victory stretch. Wow, even I was impressed. Louis had taken the whole of everything there is and brought it down, in one night, to this one electron and one proton—whatever the hell that is. I dunno, but it sounded small. And he did it all without once needing God.

So, we sat there, just staring at hymn. He looked all relaxed and awake and I don't think he meant to destroy Louis, but he said, "Okay, and where did they come from?"

After we made sure Louis wasn't gonna kill himself, hymnandme went back down to our place. Since I practically slept through the whole Great Universe Debate, I wasn't all that tired, even though I can usually almost always sleep if there's nothing good to do. But he hadn't slept at all and he was raring to go. I never understood that. I only saw hymn sleep once. Every night when I went to bed, no matter what time, he was sitting in that purple chair, watching The Box and writing his pages. And every morning he was exactly still there.

Anyway, he started reading but I was wondering how he could follow all that crap Louis was always spouting. And he didn't just follow it, but he put stuff in hymnself. So, I decided to ask hymn about it.

"How can you follow all that crap Louis is always spouting?" He looked up from his book and smiled but didn't say a word. So, I kept going.

"How do you know all the stuff you know?" I was always wondering that since he didn't have public schools or colleges or that kinda stuff when he was, well, here before. I can tell you I wasn't expecting his answer and it blew me away.

"I don't know." He threw me one of those gotcha grins and went right back to his book. He knew I hated it when he said that. *He* doesn't know. Jeez.

So, a few days after the Great Universe Debate, hymnandme were hanging out at Bernard's with Louis and the Earth Ladies and my girlfriend Angela (yep!) and JC made some comment about *Lost* Angeles and we all kinda laughed.

Then Bernard says, "If the United States is a 'melting pot,' then *Lost* Angeles is fondue."

And so I said, "If *Lost* Angeles is fondue, then The Ark is a pizza—loaded." Everybody laughed and it made me feel like we were this crazy little family being born.

For The Ark folks (and Angela and her family), hymn being Jesus was pretty much accepted by now (except for Mrs. T, of course). At least, hymn *thinking* he was Jesus was accepted.

I don't think there was ever a time when everybody believed it completely. But, being "in the know," or with the "in-crowd," was a great feeling for me, one I wasn't used to. The only nagging thought was, what if all this good feeling and family crap is just because we're thinking this guy is something special and we're all kinda gathering around that idea—like a campfire? Or we're just going along with his self-deluding lie because it's entertaining for us. It *was* fun and a helluva lot more interesting than the real world. And I've noticed that a lot of times in life, we feel closest to the folks we have this silent agreement with to go along with each other's lies. Was that what this was?

But, there sure was what Louis called "evidence" that our JC might be *the* JC, and this might be that Second Coming everybody was always yammering about. Bernard said that if this *was* the "Second Coming" then Los Angeles was the best place for JC to land, with all the different folks from all over the world right here in one city.

"All of humanity is right here, right under your nose," he'd said, and everybody laughed. And that's how what Bernard called the "Queen of Angeles Tour" came about.

So this one day in early November, when the air was dry and the sky was trying real hard to be blue, hymnandme and Louis and Autumn and Angela and, of course, Bernard, all packed into Bernard's giant Pink-Mobile convertible, like it was a summer vacation and we were tourists, just seeing the sights and joking around. Bernard, in honor of hymn and the occasion, brought a huge bag of *pink* grapefruit along to give out, instead of oranges. And Autumn brought a picnic basket, for Christ's sake, filled with bread and wine and cheese. We were sailing!

We had a great ride all over the hills and the most of the

city. We started at the top, at the Observatory, and man, the day was just perfect for the view. I just *knew* JC was gonna want to come back up here for a sunset or two. But after about 30 seconds I get bored with a view because it doesn't change or do tricks or anything, so I wanted to get moving.

We drove all over the park, past the zoo and the pony rides and Travel Town (JC'd never seen a train—what a crackup!) and we even stopped at the Merry-go-Round where he insisted we all get out and ride. What a trip that was. All these adults with all these little kids and, unless you could tell by who was tallest, you'd never know which was which.

Next, I wanted to take hymn by the Haunted House (Bernard said it's called the Ennis House—you know how Bernard always wants us to say names right) and Autumn knew all these cool roads through the hills that got us there pretty fast. As we were inching past that huge wall, I was telling hymn how the owners had these attack dogs who had all their vocal cords removed so you wouldn't hear them until right before they ripped your heart out of your chest. Louis said that was an Urban Legend so I was glad he finally agreed with me on something.

I mean, we showed hymn all the sights. We drove past the Hollywood Bowl (or "The Bowl" as native Hollyweird people call it) where a few days before, me and Angela had had our first real date by sneaking into the "nosebleeds" for some wine and, what she told me was, great music.

Louis always says The Bowl is the "most glorious place on earth, because it combines the best inventions of God and man—stars and music." I don't know about that, but after our first kiss there, me and Angela had our second, third, and fourth date—all that same night, if you know what I mean!

We didn't have to take hymn up and down Hollywood

Boulevard since hymnandme walked that whole street practically every day. So we did what Autumn called a "Culture-Run-Slash-Pub-Crawl" and hit every ethical neighborhood we could. We drove to, through, or past Olvera Street, Little Tokyo (and stopped for some killer Sake), Chinatown (where we stopped to see the Yins in their shop and had some of what they called Jew but Louis said is spelt j-i-u), Thai Town, Little Armenia, Koreatown, Little Ethiopia, and Leimert Park to Fifth Street to see where Ty works and have some wipe-up-the-floor Scotch.

And, every chance we got, old Bernard or one of the other of us, would say, "All of humanity is right here, right under your nose," and we'd all laugh hysterically.

And then, as a kinda tribute to our own private messiah, we went down to the beach for sunset. I don't know if it was because of hymn being there or us being drunk or just something that happens out of the blue, but the way it looked was like two suns, right on top of each other, setting together. I'd never seen anything like it. I looked around at everybody's faces and you could tell they were all seeing it too. But what's probably the strangest thing is that nobody said a word. Not even Louis. Nobody moved.

Two suns spreading disco-colored light all over the sand, that lazing humming chant of the ocean, and us, just taking it all in—like a breath.

All of a sudden it was like we all woke up and realized it was getting real dark. So we hit West Hollywood to make Bernard happy and then took a Mr. B's Wild Ride down Barham to Bob's for some double-decker heaven.

Even with the hamburgers and milkshakes we were all still pretty plowed (except Bernard who was our Denigrated Driver) and getting tired and sloppy and silly and wanting to go home. It was a Beatles' Magical Mystery Tour day for sure and I didn't want it to end. It was like the best Christmas morning you ever had but you're kind of afraid of that after-the-presents letdown and then your mom or Nana comes in and says, "Get dressed, we're going to the movies!"

But, there was gonna be one stop we hadn't counted on.

There was a parking space right in front of The Ark, something that hardly ever happens, and Bernard practically squealed when he saw it. You'd of thought it was a naked movie star or something, the way he acted.

So, we all practically fell out of the car, laughing our heads off, when JC says, "One more stop."

He looked at us, each of us, for a long minute. Then he starts walking, and we all follow along after hymn, like the Seven Dwarfs—minus a few. But he stopped almost immediately, right in front of the alley, and we all did one of those Cobblestone Cops routines, all bumping into each other since we weren't paying attention. Everybody was giggling and acting goofy—everybody but hymn.

He looked at that graffiti he liked so much, about how it was "a sad and beautiful world." And then he looked at Alley Guy, sleeping behind his trash can.

"All of humanity is right here, right under your nose," he said. He turned and gave us the kindest smile I think I'd ever seen. And that smile cut like a knife. Then, he just turned and walked into the building. We all just stood there, looking at Alley Guy and each other. Angela and Bernard started to cry. One by one, each of us slowly peeled away and went home—to a warm bed and good food and light.

And Alley Guy dreamed his first good dream in a year.

*   *   *

106

"Creation is the unification of difference."

Here we go again. I mean, it started to seem like JC had just come around to entertain Louis with what Louis called, "intellectual gymnastics." I don't know what kinda brain sport it was supposed to be, but I usually just flipped on the tape and zoned out when they started up. Or I'd try to find a TV with some good "old-fashioned, mind-numbing, commercial-filled, leave-the-thinking-to-us fluff "(what Louis called it).

So, they started up again and when I closed my eyes I was having trouble figuring out which one was talking. They really got a kick out of it, talking and debating, but it started to seem like they were just showing off, each trying to out-God the other. I know that's a real bad thing to say about hymn, and I know I was just probably jealous, but I felt real left out most of the time and like he didn't need me around anymore. I mean, I'm sure you can tell I'm not "intellectual" and I usually couldn't understand a thing they were saying.

Just as I was thinking that, JC turns to me and says, *"How did you learn to speak?"*

Okay, so maybe not so intellectual. I sat straight up, kinda excited to be part of this "Olympic Event!"

"Whaddaya mean?" I couldn't imagine what he was getting at but I had the feeling I was about to learn something.

"How did you learn to speak? What do you think was the process?" JC asked again. Louis was almost smiling at me with that smirky kinda I-already-know-what's-going-on look. Man, I hate that look.

"Well, I guess my mom or Nana or somebody tried to teach me the words."

"That might be true in the beginning. We all need a few success experiences to see how the program works. But, after that, when your 'mom or Nana or somebody' wasn't around

all the time. How did you learn to speak, to put together the words to form a sentence?"

Yeah, I was supposed to learn something here but I still didn't have a clue. After about a year I finally thought I'd come up with a clever answer.

"I listened?"

He smiled so big I thought his cheeks would break. Now, since I thought I was about to become a member of the Smart-Guys Club, and because I thought it would please hymn, I went on.

"I listened. I heard people talking and after a while I figured out how to do that myself. Right?"

He just kept grinning like that cheese-eater cat in Alice in Wonderland. But, he didn't say anything more which, I knew by now, meant I was supposed to keep learning something. It was a weird experience because I suddenly felt embarrassed and brilliant. I felt like I was standing on the edge, on the periscope (as Louis always said), just about ready to jump off and find out, once and for all, was I gonna crash and burn, or was I gonna fly.

"So, when you guys are talking about all this spiritual and intellectual stuff, if I just sit around and soak it all in, one day I'll be able to think up this crap for myself...right?"

There it was—that awful moment of complete silence when you're thinking, "Damn, it was crash and burn after all."

Then, he laughed. Big and loud, all head back and shoulders jumping up and down. When he calmed down, he just smiled at me and said, *"Right."*

The Shape of Healing

It was one of those great times when hymnandme were laughing our heads off about some stupid thing. When I look back on it now, it seems that there's a lot of times when you're laughing your head off and then something happens that makes you wanna die. A lot of the time they just seem to go together. Why is that?

Anyway, we were headed up the stairs and Louis was standing there on the landing. Louis didn't start laughing with us but I didn't think anything of it since, as you know, Louis only chuckles. By the time we got to the landing, I could see that Louis wasn't even chuckling, but it still didn't make me wanna worry because I knew he didn't like it when we were being all what he called "frivolous." Louis had a lot of serious thinking to do and he wanted everybody in the whole universe to do it with him, or, at least, stop and watch *him* do it. Yeah—joy.

But when I started to put my key in the lock he yelled, "Wait!" It was so loud and sudden that it scared the crap out of me.

"What the hell, Louis?" I was kinda pissed to get all scared in front of hymn and my heart was beating like a madman. I took one of those real long times that happens in just a second to search Louis' eyes. They were almost watery, which normally wouldn't mean anything—I mean, he's always sneezing, "Smog, y'know"—but there was fear behind the tears and my heart started beating just a little faster. "What?"

"Nana." He just said her name like that and then stopped. I could tell he was fighting with himself inside. I knew that fight. I had it all the time when I didn't wanna show any emotions in front of other guys.

"Nana. She had a stroke."

Bernard wasn't home to drive us and he would of cried the whole way there anyway so we got a cab, and on our way to the hospital I was filled with these two opposite feelings. I was feeling a lot of dread. I was scared my Nana would die and I'd be all alone in the world and there'd be nobody to be a before-me anymore. When you're born, everybody you know is a before-you. Then, they start dying off, and pretty soon, there's just you and the last before-you. The before-you-people are the ones who protect you from death. And, as long as I had Nana, I never worried about my own dying.

The other feeling was even more weirder. I was kinda doing a daydreaming thing, about hymnandme walking down the hallway of the hospital and all these people were popping up out of their beds and throwing down their crutches and jumping out of their wheelchairs and stopping the doctors from making that first cut—all just because JC was walking by, just kinda whistling down the hall. It was a great little movie running in my head and it made me so happy for all those healed-up folks that I didn't realize the movie was running *outside* of my head until Louis kinda nudged me and said, all surprised and all, "What the hell are you smiling about?"

That made me nervous because I didn't know before that just how much of my dreaming leaked out onto my face, so I started a long made-up explanation about how I had some medical problem that made me smile when I was sad and cry when I was happy. Well, that only made Louis mad and he just kinda groaned, shook his head, and started looking out the window again. Louis was always saying how I never took anything serious but I was taking this serious—I just couldn't help it if this little fantasy popped into my head like that.

So, with a lot of worry about how goofy that had all seemed to hymn, I turned around to try to guess JC's take on it. He was looking at me, but he wasn't mad looking and he wasn't laughing. That was my least favorite face because I couldn't tell what he was thinking.

He must of been reading my mind though—about everybody being healed just by hymn walking by—because all he said was, "You read too many stories."

It was a real quiet ride after that.

By the time we got to the hospital, they had Nana kinda half-sitting up in bed. Her left side looked like all the air had been let out of it. But when she saw hymn, she flashed one of those big Nana smiles and he sat on the edge of her bed and talked real low with her. It wasn't until a long time later that I realized her *smile* was full. I mean, it wasn't lopsided or anything. Shouldn't her smile have been lopsided too?

After the doctors had talked to hymn and Louis (even the medical profession knows better than to trust me with details) and they all decided that Nana had to go live in a nursing home, we called for another cab to take us home—Louis' treat. Anything that cost anything had to be Louis' treat because I didn't have any money, and hymn…well, I already told you what he did with bread.

We were standing in front of the hospital waiting for the cab. I was so upset I was practically pissing myself. It wasn't just that Nana was so sick that was bugging me. It was that she was *still* so sick that was bugging me. Here we were, with the *Messiah*, for Christ's sake, and she's up there in some nightgown thingy that doesn't even close in the back, drooling, and about to get shipped out like a UPS package to go live at Hopeless Central.

I decided it was time to talk to the elephant in the living room, like Louis was always saying.

"So, why didn't you heal her?"

Both Louis and hymn just looked at me and they both seemed surprised I'd asked that. But nobody said anything back to me so I just plowed ahead.

"You heal people, right? Like in the Bible and all. You did that. Right?" I was desperate for an answer.

"No." He said it calm and quiet, which just pissed me off more.

"NO?" I shouted it and Louis kinda jumped. "Whaddaya mean, 'No'?"

"I mean no. I didn't heal them." I could tell he was hurting for me, like he had to tell his kid that their favorite pet had died. "They healed themselves."

That was his explanation for all the centuries of folks praying their heads off to hymn.

"Great!" I practically barked it at hymn. "Y'know, we don't need messiahs that don't DO anything. Don't heal anybody or teach us…." I stopped. I knew that wasn't true. He *had* taught us. And not by rubbing our noses in it or being all strict or above us or anything. He taught us by *being* the lesson.

Now I really felt like crap because I still felt mad, and now I also felt bad for saying that. I turned my back on hymn, fast and furious. I could feel hymn reaching a hand out to my shoulder and I took a few steps away so he couldn't reach. Why do we do that? I felt bad for making hymn feel bad so I acted like I was still mad at hymn. Man, I can be an ass sometimes.

Somehow that ride home took about a year longer than the ride *there* and everybody seemed "off." I didn't know if it was because of what I'd said outside the hospital or what. Louis was winding and unwinding the string on my backpack and I sat between him and hymn, fidgeting, feeling hot and cold, and getting myself all worked up again.

I started worrying about Nana and dying and Nana dying and me dying and I started feeling like I couldn't breathe so I turned to hymn and just all of a sudden blurted out, "Haven't you ever been afraid to die? I mean, so bad you couldn't breathe?"

I think everybody in the whole world would wanna know JC's answer to that and right then, that night, it was just heavy on my mind. And my lungs. I wanted to know he understood what I was feeling. How scared I was. And if he wasn't gonna heal Nana, if he was just gonna turn it all back on us and tell us to heal ourselves, I at least wanted to know he really *got* it about the fear. But nothing, not anything, could of prepared me for his answer.

"Yes."

That was it. One word. Even Louis looked shocked. We just kept staring at hymn and he just kept staring out the window. It wasn't like hymn and then his leg started bouncing like all of a sudden he could hear some great jazz combo that we couldn't.

After a real long time he turned and saw me and Louis still staring at hymn. His face looked funny, but in a bad way, and he was sweating and his hands were all moving and wringing like he had an invisible napkin or something. It was weird, like some kinda panic had suddenly taken hymn over and was just eating hymn up. And I guess he felt like he needed to explain because he added, "Once. But it was a really long time ago." Then he just turned and stared out the window again.

I couldn't believe what I was seeing—he was afraid! To die! Hymn!

When we got home, JC asked me for the key to our apartment and then said goodnight. Me and Louis were still kinda freaked out about the whole night and I knew I wouldn't be able to sleep so I walked Louis home and asked him what he thought happened to JC in the cab.

"I'm relatively sure it was some kind of displaced reincarnational experiential loop."

Yeah. Right outta my mouth.

"No, Louis, I think it was a flashback and he was reliving that Garden of Sesame crap."

He just rolled his eyes and we went into his place for some wine and to sorta hash it all out. While Louis tried to find two clean glasses, I started thinking that if he, HYMN, was afraid, how could we *not* be afraid too? How safe were we?

"It's easy for immortals to talk about death," Louis said, as he sat down with a couple of boxes of wine and a handful of fast-food straws (guess he couldn't find any glasses), "There's no fear or *sting* because they know where they're going, so to speak."

He took his glasses off and rubbed his eyes. He looked as tired as I felt. And then he kinda shook his head, just a little, and almost whispered, "Yeah...it's the sublime possibility of eternity."

I knew Louis didn't like the way sheeple had to always "toe some imaginary line" in order to get a little "pie in the sky when we die," as he always said. And I think he was bitter about death because he was always saying he thought "the greatest evil ever perpetrated against the human race was the belief in *life after life*."

"Louis, why didn't he just throw down that death cup everybody's always yapping about?" Me and my box of wine were both getting a little sloppy...and soggy. "Why didn't JC just refuse to drink from it and not die?"

"Another cup would have appeared in its place," Louis said. "And another and another and another..." He was getting sloppy too, but in a real dignified, Louis kinda way.

"Why, Louis? Why would those stupid death cups just keep appearing?"

"Because..." Louis kinda laid back and closed his eyes and then almost whispered, "He brought the cup with him."

I didn't understand that at all. I kinda remembered what they had told us in Sunday School, that Jesus had to die so the "profits would be refilled," but that didn't make sense either. It just kept bugging me—if JC knew where he was going, why was he afraid to go?

But it also made me love hymn more, in a buddy-macho-GUY kinda love, of course. Or, maybe like the love you have for a kid when he takes that first step—all proud and sad and scared for what he's gonna face. Like that.

I snuck into our place after I left Louis, because I thought JC might be sleeping. I really should of known better. He was just sitting there but he wasn't watching The Box or writing his pages and he'd turned his chair around to face the window. He just kept sitting there, staring out the window, trying to see stars through the smog and streetlamps, I guess. I know it was stupid now, but at the time, I just had to ask hymn.

"I'm not gonna ask you again about being afraid of

dying," I said it as soft as I could and he looked up and smiled at me. But there was no smile in his eyes at all and that really spooked me.

"And I get that we're all supposed to just heal ourselves and not bother you with that or anything." His smile disappeared and he kinda looked at his lap. I wasn't sure what that meant so I just went on.

"But, my Nana told me what she wanted to happen...you know, if she ever died or anything and I was just wondering..."

I couldn't finish so, like the true friend he always was, he finished for me.

"When the time comes," he was almost whispering and I had to lean forward to hear hymn. His face looked a little wet or shiny, but I didn't wanna pry. "Just let me join with the earth I love," he continued, "and let the world leave us both alone."

JC was super quiet for a few days and even though he said all kinds of nice and encouraging things about Nana, he didn't really have that spark like he usually did. I was worried because it was almost Thanksgiving and, with me missing Nana and hymn being all scared and quiet and stuff, I knew I wouldn't be able to do it right or cheer hymn up. I talked to Louis about it and he said he thought he might just have "the prescription" and that I should just play along and leave it to him.

So, a few days later, Louis comes down and says that instead of Thanksgiving and turkey and pie and all the good crap Nana used to make for us, he'd planned something completely different—a whole evening of what he called a "Con-Silly-Nation." The name made me think of a bunch of goofy prisoners who'd got together to become some Indian tribe. But Louis said it was to get all his own heritage sides harmonized or something and then winked at me.

I was kinda pissed that Louis had wasted all that time and the best he could come up with was this real stupid and boring-sounding idea instead of something helpful. I wasn't very interested in it at all but JC was (which was the point). JC didn't know what Thanksgiving was anyway so he wasn't gonna miss it (like I was…it's always been my favorite holiday), so we booked it on up to Louis'. I mean, hey, it was free food so, what the hell.

What I didn't know was that Louis' "heritage sides" were Dutch-Jewish and German so all the food was kosher and all the music was torture. I didn't think I was gonna like the food—there was some real weird looking stuff that I didn't even try—but there were these little round hash brown things made out of some orange potato, for crying out loud, and I had about a million of them and, believe me, that caught up with me later, if you know what I mean. The only problem was that Louis didn't have any butter and wanted us to use apple-sauce on them instead, for Christ's sake.

But the big "treat" of the night was that we had to listen to a bunch of loud and boring music while Louis almost cried and made all these whispered comments, like it was a golf game on TV. "Now, listen to this glitter hondo" or "This a-daddy-o is particularly moving." You know, crap like that.

Now you gotta understand, Louis "couldn't carry a tune in a bucket," like Nana always said. He was tone deaf (like *he* always says), so why he was lecturing hymn on the inside scoop of music was beyond me. Though, I do gotta say, nobody could whistle like Louis. He could whistle anything, even jazz, and all on key. Ty and him would even "jam" (Ty's word)—he was that good. Go figure.

Anyway, I was about to get a headache or toothache or—unfortunately true—stomachache, so I could get out of there when Louis says, "Just one more. This is the piece of resistance." But he said it in some stupid accent and I laughed right out loud. Louis could be so full of Louis sometimes that there wasn't hardly any room for anybody else, if you catch my drift. And, it was kinda annoying that he was trying to teach hymn all about music since the beginning of time and on top of that it was German music, which could be interesting when the helicopter movie stuff came on but most of which was boring. And some of it even had people singing—NOT in English—and I started to figure out this is how they got people to confess to crimes they didn't commit.

So, Louis told us this last one was by this cat Beethoven, which I was sure translated to "You're not gonna need a 'lude tonight." But I was in for a shock.

I can't even think of any words to describe it. It was fast and slow and people were all yelling their heads off—NOT in English—but for some real weird reason, it didn't seem to matter. It was amazing. It made me get all lost somewhere. Not in my head, but in the music. It wasn't a scary kinda lost. It was like being washed over by it, like a wave that was rinsing you off, inside and out. At one point I got chills—not the sick kind or the fear kind. It was strange to have a feeling that usually means you're about to puke or crap yourself but this time, all of a sudden, made you think you could fly. I felt almost drunk or stoned but I hadn't had anything like that, not even any of Louis' kosher wine (Yep, he really served *kosher* wine—man oh man oh!).

This music was so good that Louis didn't even talk through the whole thing. Not a word. We all just sat there on the floor, three grownup guys, facing the stereo, with tears running down our cheeks. It was the most beautiful thing I'd ever heard. I thought that maybe, if there is a heaven and there are angels, this is what it sounds like.

When it was done, we all just sat there in silence. I was afraid to say anything. I didn't want it to end. And as long as we had that silence, we were still in the experience. You know what I mean?

Anyway, it was hymn who finally spoke. And again, it was just one word.

"Joy."

New Christiment

So, December is always a funky time at The Ark. I mean, with all the different kinds of ways to be religious, we really look like the United Nations or something. Since Louis and Jimmy and Jimmy's mom are all Jewish, they're always practically burning the place down, for Christ's sake, with all the candles and light and everything. And get this—they keep it up for over a week, like to show off their holiday stamina, I guess.

Charlie is Catholic, so he had to hang up all these gory crosses that were like this 3-D snapshot of Jesus dying—like anybody would wanna look at that for very long. Talk about "violence in media." But Charlie didn't want us to forget what a big thrill it was to see all that blood and suffering and stuff like that so he also wore about a million of those gold, 3-D crosses around his neck all year long. Yeah. Thanks, buddy.

He also had to open his presents on Christmas Eve, but I'm not sure if that was because he's Catholic or because Charlie always likes to try to get to the good stuff first, if you know what I mean (and what I mean is he kept flirting with Angela and it pissed me off).

Like I told you before, Mr. and Mrs. Yin are Buddhists but, even though they don't have a God or anything, they still have a religion—and that means that, just like most of the rest of the world, they gotta waste a bunch of time celebrating things they weren't even there for in the first place. I mean, I can kinda understand getting all excited about somebody coming back from the dead, even if it was 2,000 years ago and even if, no matter how much those religion guys promise you, *nobody else has ever done since.* But I've always thought that celebrating all the other crap, like somebody, *anybody* being born or having a dinner or getting pregnant (which guys don't hardly ever wanna celebrate anyway) was just some way for those same religion guys to drum up business. You know?

Anyway, I can't pronounce most of what the Yins were celebrating but it was always real nice and they put on a lot of colorful clothes and put up these wild looking posters and banners and ate some weird (but real good) food. They also had some sorta ceremony with light but I couldn't understand what it meant (they like have different words for every word we have so I get a little confused). But I've always liked the Yins a lot, so I don't mind.

Bernard is Catholic too and very religious, like I told you, and real emotional about it. He's always blubbering more than usual around the holidays but he says it's just "happy tears." Louis says it's some sorta "guilt-laden reversed edible complex," like anybody would ever understand what that meant. I usually can't understand Louis any better than I can understand the Yins, except I can tell he's speaking English—most of the time.

Bernard's place was always decorated "to the hilt" with inside and outside decorations and trains that moved and about a million stockings (for his cats, for Christ's sake, with catnip mice and real tuna for the special occasion), and this giant gold and white circle thing on his door that wasn't made out of anything real but was supposed to be a wreath and must of been left over from some other holiday I've never heard of.

Old Bernard would walk through the halls with bells on (really—I mean, he was actually wearing bells!) and singing at the top of his lungs. You knew he was coming when you could hear "*Ground-Round Version, Mother and Child*" ringing through the hallways. He was "filled with joy, my boy" and then, he'd laugh out loud, thinking that was funny because it rhymed. And then he'd burst into tears.

"I'm just going through the change, my boy," he confided to me once, and he real gentle-like tapped away his tears with his kleenex made out of real cloth! Louis told me once that Mrs. T was going through this change thing too, so I guess we're all gonna get old and grumpy and laugh and cry practically all at the same time some day.

Louis is already old and grumpy and whenever Bernard went to singing in the halls, Louis would yell down the stairs, "Merry Humbug, Bernard!" and slam his door. I don't know what a humbug is but Louis sure didn't seem to like them, the way he acted.

Ty was "raised Baptist, Brother!" and was always saying "Amen!" around this time of year, like he all of a sudden remembered he believed in something. Once, before you-know-who came along, I asked Ty if he believed in God and he got all serious and kinda misty and called God "The Man Upstairs" (which would of really been Charlie or Mr. Yin, for Christ's sake) and he talked about how "it's bigger than all of us," but unless he was talking about the world or the Universe or some of those Walmart Superstores, I'm not exactly sure what he meant by that.

So, I guess what I'm trying to say is that Ty was kinda old-fashioned, in a jazzy sorta way, and he always had a decorated tree with little white lights and angels and a star and some other girly stuff like that, but all of it was white, which was kinda weird and sorta plain and boring considering how cool he was the rest of the year. I asked him about his decorations once and he said it had something to do with his Mama and "childrens" and some kinda bread and shorts or something but when Ty went to (what he called) "rapping" about his past he joined the Louis-Yin-What-The-Hell-Are-They-Talking-About Club, if you know what I mean. Ty didn't decorate anything but the tree because I don't think Baptists are really supposed to enjoy anything sinful like colors.

The Earth Ladies were almost as nuts as Bernard when it came to decorating. They were always hauling a whole damn forest into their apartment and draping branches all over everything and singing weird songs (you guessed it—in another friggin' language!) and wearing these like real long ponchos with beads and shiny things all over them. They'd also take to wearing branches in their hair, for Christ's sake, and having their big celebration days before the real one (and Louis and Jimmy and his mom had their celebrations on different days each year so there was no way to predict when we'd have to haul out the fire extinguishers!).

The Earth Ladies called their big day the "soul-stitch" and nobody—I mean nobody—understood one damn thing they were talking about. They even had something called a "You All Log," but no fireplace! But it made them happy and I know that's what's supposed to count, but jeez, they didn't even put any decorations on their trees. Why the hell bring a ton of trees into your house if you're not gonna decorate them? I mean, unless it's one of those lacey kinda trees that's supposed to make your place look like you live in a jungle or something—but that's for all year long, right?

Mrs. T had this special shiny paper that she would cut out stars and snowflakes and stuff like that. She'd string them up all over the place and then she'd cry, so I'm not sure what religion that was supposed to be for. I always liked those stars though. I mean, she put a lot of work into them and they were kinda pretty, even though Louis said it was because she was poor (like the rest of us) and had lost all her real decorations in a fire her husband set to try to kill her and burn down the house and make it look like an accident. But he got drunk and fell asleep so he was the one who died and she just got all weird and started watching preachers on TV all day and night. I think maybe she just liked stars and snowflakes but they did make her cry so maybe Louis was right.

Me and Nana used to have a Santa face to hang on the door but Louis was always painting the beard black and calling it Rabbi Claus whenever he walked by so when Nana had to move to the dollhouse, I didn't put it out anymore. I kept it though, and I'd hang it up on a nail in the bathroom every year and ask Rabbi Claus to bring me some money so I could stop being so poor. I mean, sometimes you just can't make things any better, no matter how hard you try. I just wanted it to get better.

I always used to get a little tree and decorate it—for my Nana, of course—but once she moved, there were times I didn't even have enough "bread for bread" as Ty would say, so Bernard took to "borrowing" branches that were waiting to go into the Earth Ladies' apartment and bringing them down to me, all decorated to hell (by The Ark's Chief Elf Bernard). Yeah, he was one sweet guy. Bernard was always "clucking," as he called it, but I think it meant taking care of us all.

Sometimes I'd go down and cut out stars and snowflakes with Mrs. T. But this year, The Year of Hymn, she had run out of that special shiny paper, so I took up a collection from Charlie, Ty, and me, and I sat there and helped her cut stars and snowflakes out of the linings of our cigarette packs. This time, they were much smaller, but she seemed to like them a lot, except she'd start crying every once in a while and have to go take her medicine. When Mrs. T started taking her medicine, she'd start getting happier and smelling like old booze, so I knew I had to finish up as fast as I could and get out of there before she started preaching at me.

So this year, JC shows up and stays around for the holidays and I couldn't wait to see how he'd react to all the fuss about his birthday ("Christmas and other Catastrophes," Louis always called it). We walked by every apartment and I really don't think he knew what to make of it all. He looked kinda surprised and I was starting to hope he wasn't gonna freak out about all the home-made commercials.

So one night, after me and my girlfriend, Angela, had gone to visit Nana in that nursing home place (she was doing a little bit better) and then my girlfriend, Angela, had to go to *her* grandma's house with Zoe, I decided to take hymn visiting all The Ark folks so he could see, inside and out, all the crazy stuff we do in December.

We started at Louis' because I thought that would be better since it wasn't about hymn. Well, I was friggin' blown away that JC knew all about this Hanukkah thing! He and Louis started blabbering about some *other* Judas (not the Bible one) named Mack-A-Bee (which, I think, was the idea for a combo restaurant that never worked out) and getting all excited because some candle burned longer than it was supposed to. Jeez.

Louis gave us some leftover Kosher wine (yeah, delicious) and hymn and Louis even sang a few lines together that sounded like an orchestra tuning up but at least JC didn't freak out, so that was good. But after about a year of that crap, I was getting all bored and all, and wanted to get going since I was hoping to visit the whole building before sunrise, so we headed one floor down to Bernard and the Earth Ladies, or "dueling wreaths" as Louis called them.

Louis had decided to come along with us and I thought we'd better stop by the Ladies' place first since they were less likely to scare or offend anybody. I don't think JC'd ever heard of having a whole forest in a city apartment, but he said he knew all about this soul-stitch thing so at least he didn't go into shock when he saw it. He even sang some stupid soul-stitch song with them though, where he learned that I can't imagine. The Ladies served some "herbal wine,"—give me a barf bag—and then decided to come along with us to Bernard's, and I started wondering if we were just gonna pick up everybody as we went along.

Bernard was like practically fainting he was so excited for this unexpected chance to entertain and he blurts out, "This just warms my cockles…."

Well, I about dropped my load. I mean, I couldn't believe Bernard would be yapping about his cockles, for Christ's sake—not in front of hymn. But, nobody else seemed to notice, so we went on in.

We all sat in Bernard's puffy hot-pink chairs (he has about a million of them), dodging the cats as we tried to sit, and had to drink some kinda spiked cider or something out of these tiny little cups. I was thinking that cider crap must of been sitting out of the fridge for about a year, it was so warm. Yuck!

So, at Bernard's everybody had to sing *another* song while he played his new piano but all I could think of was how the hell did he get a piano up to the fourth floor! And—you guessed it—when we started downstairs to go visit the Yins and Charlie, Bernard decided to come along.

When we were at the Yins' everybody all of a sudden got all quiet and acted like they were in the dentist's office or something, but JC asked a bunch of questions and was real polite and made everybody feel comfortable again, so we all relaxed and ate some weird food from the Yins' store and sang—yep—another friggin' song. (I realize now that JC had already known enough about Buddhism to ask the Yins all the right questions that seem, looking back, like they were more to teach *us* something about different cultures than for hymn to get information.)

While everybody was laughing and singing and celebrating whatever the hell they were all celebrating (with all the mixed up religions and beliefs and all), I snuck next door and nabbed Charlie. I asked him over and he came and I was just all relieved that JC wouldn't have to see all the crosses all over his walls and everything.

So, to be a good guest, I guess, Charlie brought the Yins some "mauled" wine or something like that that somebody in his family in Italy had sent him but he said they had to serve it hot—yeah, real tempting—and after a few cups of that, *Charlie* started singing. Well, at least I'd heard of this one, but the real weird thing was that JC hadn't. I mean, it was a Christmas song, for Christ's sake, and all religious as hell. It was that one about a holy night and it's real pretty but it was just freaking me out that this song—*all about hymn getting born*—he had never heard it.

I gotta tell you, I almost got all choked up at the end with all those high notes and everything, and even Louis was singing it, which completely shocked me. But JC just sat there and listened and at one point he looked over at me (I wasn't singing either) and gave me one of those half smiles, like he wasn't real sure what was going on. His eyes looked full of questions and I thought for a second that he was looking to me for an answer. But, then he kinda shook his head, real small and slow. It was almost like he still couldn't believe that people wrote all these songs and angel-filled high notes just for hymn. Or he didn't wanna believe it. He never was easy with that kind of attention. As he told Noman once, "It's all about the message, not the messenger."

Well, of course, EVERYBODY decided to come on down to Ty's. JC liked his tree a lot, now that he was starting to understand the whole tree thing, which he hadn't known about before. Ty led everybody in some gospel song—something about this little light that's all mine and I joined in too, even though I didn't know the words. It was super fun and I really liked the feeling it gave me. I was stomping and clapping and shaking my hands in the air and shouting "Amen," and so was JC and everybody else. It was great, and I almost started crying it made me feel so good.

By this time, Jimmy and his mom came up (because of all the stomping, I think) and they joined in too. Man, you would of thought we were all the Temptations or Ray Charles or something. We must of spent a good hour there and everybody—even the Yins, the Ladies, and the Jews—were rockin' and swingin' to that gospel beat! And, all of sudden, I realized it wasn't about religion or holidays anymore. Somehow, it had become about love and neighbors and that connection that feels like home.

When everybody was all collapsing and sweating and everything, I pulled Louis aside and asked him if we should try to go to Mrs. T's. He didn't think we should and I was about to tell everybody goodnight and head across the hall when JC pipes up and says why don't we all go down to Mrs.

T.'s. He was always doing stuff like that—like knowing what I was thinking about *not* doing or just plain trying to avoid and then saying we should do that exact thing.

Everybody just sat there for a second and was real quiet. All of us knew Mrs. T and how strange she was—or, I should say, none of us *really* knew Mrs. T but we did know how strange she was. I don't think anybody but hymnandme had been in her apartment in years. I didn't think she'd let all these half-drunk-on-wine-and-gospel people into her place. She might think we were there to hurt her or take her away. But JC insisted, so we all quietly got up and followed hymn down the stairs.

He knocked on the door and waited. No answer. Well, we all knew Mrs. T never went anywhere. Hell, she even had food delivered, so we knew she was there. He knocked again. Nothing. We were all squeezed into the hall and it was getting hot and uncomfortable. JC knocked a third time.

Bernard whispered, "Behold, I stand at the door and knock." It was kinda creepy, the way he said it, but it didn't make any sense since he was behind me and not at the door, for Christ's sake. I was thinking Mrs. T probably could hear us all breathing and panting in the hall and was just about as freaked out as she could be.

Then, all of a sudden, the door opened. Mrs. T stood there in her uniform of that loose dress and thin robe thing and her hair in curlers. Like I told you, her hair was always in curlers, and Louis and I had guessed that if she ever took them out the spring force alone would knock her into downtown L.A.! So I was waiting for her to freak out when she saw all of us standing there…I mean, it was the whole damn building! But she just stood there, looking at us. Finally, she said, "Won't you come in?"

You could've knocked me over with a feather.

We all crowded into her living room. For somebody who'd lost everything (including a husband) in a fire, she sure had a lot of stuff. We were all kinda looking for places to sit, but JC just plopped hymnself right down on the floor. So, of course, we all did too. It was funny, looking back. She must of thought she'd bowled a human strike or something.

Mrs. T sat down in her regular chair and it hit me that he, JC, was sitting on the floor at her feet. And, I gotta tell you, it bothered me a little until I realized just how much he respected people—all people—and how he had this great way of showing it.

JC looked around the apartment and complimented Mrs. T on the decorations—all the little cigarette pack stars and snowflakes. She got all kinda flustered and said how it was nothing and then she started turning all different shades of pink, kinda like Bernard's puffy chairs. You could tell she was embarrassed—embarrassed by her looks, her apartment, her condition. Even her little stars and snowflakes.

I guess he could sense how Mrs. T was feeling so, pointing to the closest little silver star he said, "Would you show us how to make these?"

Everything went silent. I mean scary silent. We could hear our own blood rushing in our ears. Mrs. T looked around at all our faces and, for a second, I thought I could feel that every single person in that room all of a sudden loved her. I could just tell that each one of us was trying to tell her, with just our faces, that we completely accepted her and really wanted to make her a part of this little community. It was so intense I wanted to cry. I think the Ladies and Bernard *were* crying.

Mrs. T stood up and said, "I'll have to get more scissors." She went to this giant sewing basket like my Nana used to have and she found enough scissors and "pinky shears" for all of us. She picked up the extra cigarette pack liners I'd left with her and passed them out. Then we all sat there, at her feet, as she patiently and gently taught us how to cut out stars and snowflakes. Everybody was busy and concentrating and smiling. One of the Ladies started humming *Silent Night*. We all joined in—no words, just the music. Everything just felt so good.

And then, a real Christmas miracle happened.

Mrs. T got up, shuffled over to her TV and clicked it off.

We all just sat there, suddenly silent. She turned back to see us all staring at her. She looked at each one of us in turn. Then she looked at hymn for a long time. Her face looked about 20 years younger.

"We don't need that now, do we?"

She shuffled back to her chair, picked up her scissors and a cigarette liner and, very quietly at first, like only to herself, she started humming.

One by one, we all joined in again, humming *Silent Night* and cutting out stars and snowflakes. He turned around and gave me a misty-eyed smile.

I knew what he meant.

Good News

So, I guess there's this whole other holiday about JC getting his nuts whacked off that Charlie said was called Epiphany. This real sorry excuse for a celebration was in January (like New Year's Eve wasn't enough of getting drunk and acting stupid)—okay, it was *me* who got drunk and acted stupid so me and my girlfriend, Angela, broke up on that night. She found out I wasn't as mature as I seem to be and I found out that, even the sweetest person in the whole world can sometimes get a little witchy…except with a B.

Anyway, Charlie said this Epiphany thing had been on New Year's too but getting drunk and celebrating JC's circumvention at the same time wasn't always a good idea, so they had to move the date. Autumn tried to straighten us out and said that actually there was some big Feast for the Circumvention and that Epiphany was really about some magic guys showing up to see baby Jesus. I guess they must of been like the entertainment or something, after JC and his mom opened all his birthday presents from the Wise Men. That all sounded kinda cool and a whole helluva lot better than…that other thing.

Now, Ty's guitar says Epiphone on it (yeah, Ty can play about a million instruments and, besides his violin he has a guitar, a bass, and a bunch of drums from Africa—but no sax) and he's always teasing me about the fact that I thought it said "Epiphany."

See, Louis and hymn were always yapping about (what I thought was spelt) "epiphones" and how they could really change the way you looked at crap so, since before that I'd never heard the word, and didn't know what it meant or how it was spelt, I just sounded out the name of Ty's guitar one day and everybody just started having conniptions all over the place. So now I guess there's this whole line of guitars named after JC and holidays about his private parts and magicians. Jeez.

So the Earth Ladies, even though they still had all that forest in their apartment, decided to have...yep...*another* party (a giant celebration that was kinda for this Epiphany jazz and also because those Magic guys were horoscopers too), and they invited all of The Ark, the Delaneys, the neighborhood, and a ton of folks I didn't even know. Even Karisma was there!

I wasn't sure JC was ready for being out in that much of the world, you know? I mean, talking to people, all at the same time like that, since up until then he'd only been around The Ark folks and just the closest neighborhood people. Yeah, he'd talked to people one-to-one on the bus or in a store, but not a whole group *all at once*. And even on the bus or in a store, me or somebody was with hymn and ready to jump in just in case he started that, *Hey, my name is Geez-Us* crap.

So, that night, hymnandme picked up Mrs. T to, what JC called, "escort" her to the party. I'd only ever heard of a different kind of escorting, but I knew that wasn't what he meant! He even suggested that I wear clean jeans and a not-too-wrinkled T-shirt. Man. I couldn't understand why he was picking on me like that, especially since I was still hurting pretty bad from breaking up with my girlfriend, Angela.

But, after some "pondering" in the head (both the bathroom and my brain), I figured out that he wasn't trying to change me or anything but just to teach me about respect. We forget about respect sometimes. It's easy to forget it when we get all wrapped up in our own "ego system," as Louis calls it, and we start feeling all separate.

JC was always yammering about how "we only feel truly agitated or fearful or angry when we feel separate from our Source," and how that makes us feel separate from each other.

Anyway, I think this was Mrs. T's first time out of her apartment since she'd moved in, so JC told me it was our "duty and great privilege as gentlemen to make sure she is at ease." He sure could be one flaky dude but, ya gotta love hymn. He was the only real "gentleman" I ever met.

So, we're at the party and we're getting Mrs. T all settled on this little squatty stool thing and making sure she has something to drink and gentleman-y things like that, but I'm also trying to scope out the situation to see if any of the Delaneys had showed up (and yeah, I mean I was looking for Angela) but I'm *also* trying to do it with all this respect stuff for Mrs. T, and I all of a sudden start to panic because I lose sight of hymn, and I'm not sure how ready he is to be completely on his own. So, I bowed to Mrs. T (that was the only gentleman thing I could think of to do) and I went searching for my crazy, lost messiah.

It was packed in that apartment (The Ark's places aren't that big so it's not hard to pack them, especially with a whole forest in there too, but there must of been about 50 people there, not including The Ark folks, and a lot of them were real "high end") so I had to squeeze and "excuse me" through a crapload of strangers and trees.

I walked and squeezed and excused me through the whole place for about a year with no sign of hymn and my panic was starting to make me feel a little choky. Finally I spot hymn, and he's sitting on the floor in the dining room (the Earth Ladies and Bernard have dining rooms), *right next to Mrs. T*, still sitting on her squatty stool thing exactly where I left her, *and* Angela and Zoe are sitting on the other side of hymn, with Angela practically sitting on his lap (not really but that was the way it *felt*, you know?).

Now I gotta problem. I'd gone through all that panic trying to take care of hymn and be a gentleman to Mrs. T and now here's my best friend—*hymn*—and my ex-girlfriend—*her*—practically sitting on each other and you know I just gotta feel jealous and pissed but...at who? I was "fuming" (Louis' word) for sure. I couldn't figure out what to do, and especially not right then with all the party and strangers and noise and crap, and on top of it all I knew I had some sorta duty or something to be paying attention to what JC was doing and saying and why he was here, for Christ's sake, so I tried like hell to put all the jealousy crap "on the back burner," as Louis always says, and just *not notice* anything between hymn and her but it still felt kinda like, "Gentleman, start your fuming!"

So, he had a pretty good-sized crowd around hymn and he really seemed to love it, like he was all of a sudden completely alive or "awake," as he would say. He was doing that almost whispering thing (like he had with Noman) and all these super cool people were leaning in so they wouldn't miss a drop of what he was saying and I figured he was explaining the History of the Universe or something with how everybody was all hanging on his every word. So I sat down too, on the floor, and just quiet-like tried to focus and stop and listen and really "hear," like he was always yapping about and tried like hell not to notice anything else...like Angela.

When I really started to tune in, though, I realized he wasn't talking about the Universe at all—he was talking about the logging industry, for Christ's sake. But, like he was always saying, you can't judge a book by its cover (even though I don't know how else you could judge it when you're trying to buy something on Amazon.com), so I thought I better try to hang in and see if anything started to make sense.

And then, I suddenly remembered I'd brought the tape recorder along, so I whipped it out (the recorder) and without all the aha's and hmmm's and stuff, here's what went down:

"So, if a man is blind, how would it be possible for another blind man to show him the way? Don't you think they'd both fall in a ditch?" (There was some laughter here). *"Right, so to be critical or judgmental of others is like noticing a splinter in your friend's eye, and overlooking the 12 foot 2x4 in your own!"* (Much more laughter). *"How can you say to your friend, 'Here, let me get that speck of sawdust out of your eye' when you have half a tree trunk in your own. That would make you a hypocrite. No, first you must clear the obstruction out of your own eye and then you'll be able to see well enough to help remove the speck from your friend's eye."*

So, all these hip people sitting on the floor in that dining room suddenly go all quiet and start reflecting and crap like that and I'm thinking, Man, he sure knows how to bring a party to a screeching halt but then, all of a sudden, he laughs. Right out loud. He just starts laughing and pretty soon everybody else is laughing but not in a "Psych!" sorta way or "Sorry, I was wrong" sorta way but in a "Yeah, that's *IT*" sorta way.

And everybody is just all happy and laughing and I realized I was like the only one who didn't get it but if it was about judging people, well, I did that all the time. Hell, I'd just *been* doing it about hymn and Angela. And since I was hanging around with hymn, I probably should be doing a helluva lot better job of it, and I was probably gonna disappoint hymn again.

Well, thinking that just made me even more miserable. I'd calmed down enough during his tree story to realize that I knew—*knew*—he wouldn't move in "on my turf" like I think Bogie would say. I knew he wouldn't try to steal Angela or take her attention like Charlie did. And I knew Angela, no matter how much of a sorry excuse for a boyfriend she thought I was, wouldn't do that to me either. But I still couldn't pull myself out of the misery trap and I really didn't wanna be a downer to anybody else so I thought I'd just leave the recorder with Louis and go home.

Just then, JC caught my eye and, like he almost always did, figured out what I was thinking and feeling and came up, right on the spot, with a way to make it a special message just for me—or, at least, that was the way it seemed.

"*I'm going to tell you the secret to the whole Universe,*" he said, with this kinda twinkle in his eye and a quick glance at me.

Everybody sat forward again, like when you watch the magician real hard to try to figure out the trick.

"*It's okay to be wherever and whoever you are—right now. It's okay to be joyful, sad, healthy, jealous, happy, fearful, successful, uncertain, angry, loving. It's all okay. Wherever you are, whatever point you're at in your life, whatever you're feeling, you are where you need to be, doing what you need to be doing, feeling what you need to be feeling. Right now.*"

Everybody looked like they weren't sure about that one—like nobody had ever told them it was okay to be who they really were. Warts and all.

"*Now, accept that. Accept who you are, exactly as you are—right now.*"

You could tell that one didn't go over real good, and there was a kinda gasp sound. I don't think anybody is ready to accept who they are—right now.

"*You must begin with self-acceptance or you'll never move forward. But this is important to know: ACCEPTANCE IS NOT AGREEMENT. You don't have to like it, want it, or agree with it. Just accept it.*"

I was glad he'd said that again, "Acceptance is not agreement," like he did with Noman. And, it wasn't that folks didn't wanna believe hymn. I think it was more like, well, how could they? It was like he was on the other side of the mirror, and all he could see was all the good stuff we tried to believe in everyday. But we were the ones who had to leave that mirror and go out into the world, the *real* world, and there just ain't no acceptance out there. A lot of times, not even for hymn.

"*Acceptance is the starting point, not the finish line. You* begin *with acceptance. You don't have to stay where you are, or keep doing what you're doing, or feeling what you're feeling. The future is unwritten for your personal expression; a blank canvas and you have the only paintbrush. But for now, right now, accept exactly who you are. And know that you are loved* and *accepted, just as you are, right this very moment—no matter what.*"

He gave me just the smallest smile, that kinda look of connection that only family members know and recognize, and I was suddenly just filled up with wanting hymn to be my dad. He probably wasn't old enough to be but I didn't care. Everybody wants that "you're okay and I love you, *no matter what*" feeling from their folks.

"*You are, right now, the sum of all of your choices. You are where you are because of choices you've made as you journeyed along this life-path. And all those choices combine*

139

and mix and blend and contradict and lead to exactly—now. Every moment holds every choice. Every moment is a crossroads. And you can change your direction, your job, your house, your intention, your lover, your friends, your mind at each crossroads. Do you want to use your precious energy defending past choices to accept an other-directed life? That's fine. All I'm saying is, you can also use and accept the power of the moment to choose a different direction, if you wish."

Well, he'd lost me and probably everybody else. I was glad the tape was running. I was starting to get a little pissed, in a real loving way, because just a minute before he'd said he was gonna tell us this big friggin' secret and then we'd had to do all that real hard accepting and crap and I was still "fuming" a little, just around the edges, about the whole Angela thing. Now it was sounding like we had to do even more work to get the prize.

"I have a good idea what you're thinking...that you can't just up and quit your job." (There was some nervous laughter and a lot of nodding and hmmm-ing.) *"Actually, you* can *just quit your job. You may not choose to, you may not want to, but you are able to. All I want is for you to recognize that you have the power. Not me. Not anyone else. You."*

"I can't just up and move." I felt so bad for Mrs. T when she said that. This was her first time out of her apartment to "party with the 'hood" and I think she was starting to regret it. She looked scared but he didn't even seem to notice. He just kept yapping about how we could choose this or choose that. I chose for this part of the night to end, but it didn't!

"Mrs. T, you can *just move, right now, and never look back. Chances are you don't* choose *to move or Autumn may not* choose *to quit her job right now, and that's okay too. But you* can. *You are able. You may not choose to do it—right now.*

"Can *simply means* able to. *And you* can *do anything, absolutely anything, you choose to do. But you have to choose, to decide. And therein lies the challenge. To choose means you take the responsibility. You take the credit* and the heat *for your own actions, thoughts, feelings, life.*"

He looked around at the faces and he must of seen the confusion and, in poor Mrs. T, the fear.

"*Now, I'm not saying you* should *quit your job, or leave your families, or just go on a permanent vacation.*" (There was some relieved laughter here.) "*I'm saying you are* able *to do anything you choose.*"

Mrs. T just didn't seem to get it. (Join the club!)

"*What about sickness and accidents and hurricanes,*" she sounded a little like her Christ guys, describing what's gonna happen to all us sinners in these Last Days. A few people kinda laughed, under their breaths, but most everybody else seemed to really want the answer to that one.

"*Oh, don't be afraid,*" he said it right at Mrs. T. His voice was gentle and sure, like he was talking her through a mine field but pretty certain he knew where the bombs were. "*Most people aren't aware of their own power.*"

He looked around real quick at the faces, all safe and sheep-y, and winked at me. I had no idea why and then he just exploded:

"*It's HUGE! It's tremendous!*"

Everybody sat right up straight all of a sudden and he busted out laughing. And, after a beat, so did everybody else. It reminded me of this old-time music guy Louis told me about who wrote this long, boring concert to kinda psych everybody into falling asleep and then put in these giant blasts to wake them all up! It made hymn seem funny and a little crazy, in a divine sorta way, but he got everybody's attention and I guess that's what he wanted.

"*Your own power is enormous,*" he went on, but in a normal loudness. "*Remember, you are exactly who and where you need to be. Right here, this very moment, is your starting point. When you find yourself in a difficult situation, whether you're able to realize the responsibility for getting yourself there or not, you always have one extraordinary power at your disposal—the power to choose* how you respond. *Even if you feel someone or something else* caused *the situation, you still have that choice. At any moment, in any situation, no matter the origin or cause, you have that power. You decide how you* feel. *You decide how you* act.

"*I know most people freak out when they think there's no one else to blame.*" (Soft laughter.) "*If you're unhappy and* you're *responsible for yourself, who do you turn to to cheer yourself up? Who do you blame for your depression? Who decides how to deal with it, where to go if you need help with it? Who decides how you feel?*"

He paused and then kinda stretched his arms out to us. "*YOU.*"

There was that sorta thing where everybody said it all at once—"*YOU*"—and he smiled like a father whose kid just caught the ball after about a millions tries. We all did that shift thing people do when there's just too much good energy in you to sit still. Everybody at the party was in there now—sitting and crouching and squeezing in and having this great lovefest.

"*The scariest thing in the world is self-responsibility, right?* (There was some laughter and "Right's" here.) *It's doing life without a net. It's not blaming anyone or anything else for where you are, what you do, or how you feel. It's being your own messiah, your own leader, your own conscience, your* own confessor. It's replacing blame with compassionate understanding. It's acceptance—whether you agree with the situation or not. And it's the most liberating thing you will ever do."

The feeling in the room was a lot lighter than I thought it would be. The Ladies were whispering and giggling and everybody seemed real happy that they had learned something important without too much homework. Everybody was all smiling and nodding and acting like all this stuff he was saying was real good news. Even Mrs. T seemed more relaxed now that she knew she didn't have to move and probably didn't cause any hurricanes.

But *I* didn't get it, any of it. I didn't see how being responsible for everything could be good news. I was still feeling kinda jealous and pissed and panicked and I was about to ask hymn how the hell you could turn all that around when, without any warning, my world kinda went into slow motion and, for just a second, I thought I'd been dosed. I kinda shook my head to clear it and, all of a sudden, I could *see* that everybody there, except me, was *choosing* this happiness crap. I didn't know a lot of those faces, but the ones I did, I knew their troubles too. And they were *choosing* to accept where they were and who they were, in that moment. Just in that one second, they were choosing to look at their worlds with a smile, and in those smiles, I could see *my* world as a little friendlier.

And, just in that one instant—like a flash of what Louis calls "insight"—I finally *got* what JC meant about perception and how I could *choose* to create a reality of misery or one of happiness, all based on how I *chose* to perceive what was right in front of me. I guess some of hymn and Louis' yapping *had* soaked in, just like he told me it would. And, no matter how hard it was—and, man, it was practically the hardest thing I've ever done—I chose happy.

I opened my mouth to tell hymn my own real good news that I'd finally "got" something when there was a voice from behind us, booming and scary, and everybody jumped. Everybody but hymn.

"*How can you say that to these poor people? Choice? They don't choose to be poor or sick or in pain. This is just so much New Age mumbo-jumbo.*"

Yep, you guessed it. Old John Noman was there, lurking in the shadows (talk about creepy) and I guess he thought it was his turn to spoil the evening.

Everybody whipped around as Noman came out of hiding from behind some of the trees and kinda waved his hand at hymn, like when you're a kid in school and you gotta go to the bathroom, (what a dork) and says, "*I don't want to spoil the festivities but I feel I must ask you about all the trouble and hatred and war and disease in the world. You seem to be saying that all we must do is be conscious of our own responsibilities and suddenly there will be epiphanies* (there it is again…epiphones!) *all over the world and we'll all wake up and the trouble will be gone. But, I just don't see how that's possible. You and I both know that the world is just not that simple. We both understand the need for a strong leader* (Anybody in mind, Noman?) *who can point the way for the millions of people who don't have your…unique comprehension. Can you speak to that?*"

Everybody was kinda groaning at Noman, since there weren't any twelve-year-olds there to appreciate *his* "unique comprehension." What a jackass! But they all turned back to hymn, with this "Tell us a story, Daddy" shine in their eyes. I definitely was ready and excited to watch hymn take this turkey down.

"*Hello, John. Won't you join us?*"

JC was the perfect host and you could tell Noman was turning about fifty shades of purple. And like the snake he is, he waved hymn off like, I'm too good to sit on the floor. No matter, JC was ready and I couldn't wait to hear what he had to say to Noman.

"*Let me tell you a story.*" There was that cool shifting and settling people do when they're all wound up and ready for a great story. "*Once there was a Perfect Kingdom. The King and Queen provided the people with everything they could ever want. In the Perfect Kingdom, everyone had beautiful, safe, warm homes and abundant food. The people were all healthy and free to go wherever they wished. There were no locks on the doors, no police, no firemen, because there was no need for them. Everyone lived forever, no one ever got old or sick. There was never any pain or sadness. And all the people were…*(He paused for just a second with one of those twinkles in his eye and everybody leaned in)…*BORED!*"

Everybody kinda jumped and laughed at that, nodding and smiling to each other. You could feel how jazzed they all were to hear the rest of this story.

"*One day, a little boy and a little girl were sitting by the perfect river, under a perfect tree, on a perfect, sunny day.*

"*The boy said, 'There's nothing to do.'*

"*'Let's play a game,' the girl suggested.*

"*Now, there were many games in the Perfect Kingdom, but the outcomes were all predictable and the games were only interesting for a short while.*

"*'Which game?' the boy sighed.*

"*'I have an idea,' the girl answered. 'I'll hide somewhere and you try to find me.'*

"*The boy had never heard of this game and he became very interested.*

" '*Where will you…hide?' He'd never heard of hiding and wasn't exactly sure what it was.*

" '*I can't tell you that,' the girl laughed. 'It will be a secret that you must discover.'*

"*After explaining what she meant by 'hide' and 'secret' and 'discover,' all new words to the boy, the children set about their game. The boy covered his perfect eyes and perfectly counted to the 100th digit of Pi!*"

There was a big laugh here but I couldn't figure out what the hell this story had to do with dessert. I was kinda hoping it was gonna pick up or get a little more exciting or blow Noman's mind all to hell but everybody else seemed to be enjoying it.

"*When the boy had finished counting, he opened his eyes and looked around but the girl wasn't there. He went to her perfect house but she wasn't there either.*

"*As he searched the kingdom for her, he began to understand the game. He was 'seeking,' something he'd never done, and he felt excited, and scared—feelings he'd never experienced. After a long time, the boy sat down to rest (he'd never really felt tired before, either) and all of a sudden, his face was wet (he didn't even know what tears were because he'd never cried before).*

"*Others came to him immediately, but they did nothing because they didn't know what to do. None of this had ever happened before.*

" '*What are you doing?' they asked the boy.*

" '*I don't know,' he said, 'but the little girl and I are playing a new game and I'm not able to find her. She's hiding.'*

"*The boy then explained—perfectly—the whole concept*

146

of the game and 'hiding' to the others, and they agreed to help him look."

I was hoping he'd start looking for a perfect *ending* to this long and, sorry to say, boring story.

"All through the night, more and more people joined the search, until finally, right before dawn, the entire kingdom was involved. Everyone was seeking (something they'd never had to do) and this new activity awakened unfamiliar feelings of excitement, and a little fear, in each of them.

"When they had searched the whole kingdom someone asked the boy where the game had begun. He led them to the perfect tree by the perfect river and there sat the perfect little girl.

" 'There you are!' she said to the boy, feeling excitement and relief for the first time. 'I've been wondering what happened to you.'

"After a lot of discussion, everyone sorted out the confusion. They found out that while the boy was counting, the girl had hidden behind the tree. She'd been right there, all along."

He stopped and smiled. Everybody just stared at hymn, waiting for the rest of the story. It sure wasn't his best story and I thought he might be losing his audience. When nobody said anything for like a year, I figured I better help hymn out. *"So, what happened next?"*

He looked right at me and the smile went away. His head kinda hung down for a second and I had that awful sinking feeling that I'd just made a big mistake and I couldn't take it back.

After a few more seconds he looked at me again, but this time with the "dad" smile, like he's gonna love you, even if you just flunked sandbox.

"*NEXT…*" he said it so loud we all kinda jumped, "*Next, all the people realized that they'd enjoyed themselves, even when they were a little scared. They all knew that in the Perfect Kingdom, nothing and no one could ever really be lost, but they'd enjoyed* pretending *as though it could be. And they discovered what had been missing, even though they had never known anything was missing.*"

We all kinda leaned forward.

"*FUN!*" he friggin' shouted it and everybody laughed. "*For when everything is perfect and there is no deviation from the conventional, things can get a little boring.*

"*So the King and Queen and all the people agreed that every day they would play a game of pretending. They would* pretend *they could lose or fail or get lost. They would allow their imaginations to embrace the illusion of 'less than' perfection. It was a great success and all the people were happy in their pretending. They finally could understand what 'different than' was. They could experience and admire things that weren't 'exactly like,' and appreciate all the great things they really had.*"

Nothing. Not a sound. We all just sat there and he sighed.

"*After a very, very long time, some of the younger people, who'd played the game so much and so long, began to forget that they had perfection at their beck and call. They began to* believe *in the game and they even forgot it* was *a game. They believed in the illusion of separation from the perfection that was their birthright. In their* world, *in their* minds, *the illusion that was the game had become their reality.*"

Well, it was a bomb. Nobody moved. We all just sat there, waiting for the punch line. But nobody said anything. Finally, it was Noman who broke the silence.

"*You have* got *to be kidding. That's your answer? It's all in our minds? Are you actually telling these poor people they have nothing to fear because it's all just a dream? That, you misguided soul, is the height of* irresponsibility. *These people look up to you. You must tell them the truth. Guide them with fear and respect for the horrors of the world, especially if they stray from God's Law."*

There was a real long silence here. Everybody at that party that I knew hated Noman. I was sure he wasn't invited. Nobody believed a word he said. But here he was, making points, like when the politician you *don't* like wins the debate. We all looked to hymn for an answer. I felt a little sorry for hymn—I mean, it was a lot of pressure.

All of a sudden JC stood up so quick I think he scared everybody. We were all sitting on the floor and kinda all leaned back at the same time, and made that whooshing sound.

There they were, the only two people standing, Noman and JC. I thought it looked like two gun-slingers in one of those old westerns, and the rest of us—we were just the dust and tumbleweeds on the street.

"*John, I understand you can't control people without fear.*" JC was calm, but his eyes looked a little like a storm about to blow. "*But that is not the way of the Creator. Hate is not the opposite of love, John. Fear is.*"

And then, JC walked away, not explaining the story and not making any sense. He didn't seem mad at all. In fact, he seemed peaceful. I popped up and followed hymn, not wanting hymn to get into any new discussions.

I found hymn in the kitchen, where all the food was. He was kinda studying some dip and turned around to face me before he could of known I was there.

"Do you wanna go?" I offered as a way out. He looked

surprised and put a hand on my shoulder.

"Of course not!" He was all happy and smiling and loving the dip.

By this time, Autumn was in there too, mothering and making sure all her guests were playing nice.

"I'm so sorry, "she was saying as she came in. "I didn't invite John and I know Raindrop didn't." We all knew Raindrop didn't because Raindrop never said anything to anybody.

He kinda waved his hand at her because his mouth was full of dip and chips. When he'd finished his mouthful he said, "There's nothing to be sorry about. John and I were just having one of our little debates." He gave her that big JC smile and she was all melting and stuff. He added, "Very stimulating. What's next?"

When the party started winding down like winter parties do, you know, around midnight, and people started drifting out, and only The Ark folks were left, Autumn and Raindrop decided to play *another* stupid game but this one was about *What Do You Want To Be.*

We were all back in the big room with the trees and Noman had finally decided to leave so everybody was in a good mood again. I was feeling better too because when Angela left with Zoe, she whispered to me that we should talk, so I finally felt like I could breathe. I was still wondering what the story meant, and I was gonna ask hymn but I'd run out of tapes and everybody else had moved on to this new bullcrap game.

So Autumn started and said she and Raindrop wanted to be at one with the earth so they were saving all their money from being observatory cops and bad writers so they could open a New Age health food store in the Wilshire District and make a lot of bread (the spending kind) so they could save trees and whales and dangerous squirrels and wet land, for Christ's sake.

Mrs. T wanted to be a missionary (one who never leaves her apartment, I guess) but not to eat tribes of cannibals or anything. She seemed to think she could just waltz on over to Africa or Austria or one of those "A" countries and make everybody believe just like she did, which was kinda like a Christian except a lot scarier. She still believed everything those Christ guys on TV told her and was always sending them all her money so there wasn't much danger of her taking off for some weird other place any time soon.

Ty said he was a musician and he'd always be one and all he wanted to do was play his "axe." I think he was talking about that violin that his grandpa left him but Ty evidently named it Axe.

Mr. and Mrs. Yin just wanted to understand English better and be good owners of their store and, except for the understanding and *speaking* English better, I think they already are what they wanna be.

Like you already know, Jimmy was gonna be a Rabbi—if he didn't have to study. Otherwise, he thought it would be cool to be a priest, if he didn't have to be Catholic. I think he was just afraid of girls.

Bernard wanted to be a concert piano player and I guess that's why he got the piano but he said the cats didn't like it when he played so he was content just to be their "Mommy." What a crackup!

So, Louis said he wanted to be a great thinker. A philosopher. And as you can tell, he's halfway there now. I mean, man, he thinks about everything.

Charlie said he wanted to "dream dreams for other people's entertainment." Now, Charlie's a good guy and all, even though I was still kinda pissed at him for flirting so much with Angela. But now that I wasn't dating her anymore he didn't seem all that interested in her. Weird. Come to think of it, I don't think I ever saw Charlie with his *own* date—he just seemed to want everybody else's.

Anyway, he's basically a good guy and he's sorta smart, in a hot-wiring-cable kinda way, but I'm absolutely sure he's never had such a complicated thought as that "dream dreams" idea. Ever. I didn't understand it at all but he was directing it to the Earth Ladies anyway (on to his latest challenge, I guess) and they were kinda whispering to each other and I know he thought that meant he was making time with them but I had some inside information so all I wanted to do was say, "Wrong tree, Charlie."

But, I didn't say anything and that caught Louis' attention, since I usually *am* saying things. So, Louis says "And what do you want to be?"

They were all looking at me and I thought it was kinda scary because I really didn't wanna be anything. I never wonder about it. I mean, what the hell kinda job am I gonna get with no education and no goals and no attitude for anything? Besides, a lot of people tell me I don't really always *get* what's going on and so I shouldn't try to reach for too high of a star. I flunked just about everything in school, before I quit, but the teachers and I disagreed on why that was. They thought it was because I was stupid, and I thought it was because they were boring.

It's just that I have a hard time staying tuned in to where I am. I seem to always be somewhere else when I'm supposed to be here. But I didn't wanna stop the flow of the conversation, so

I just pulled up the most likely idea for somebody like me:

"An astronaut!"

There was that usual beat of what Louis calls "stunned silence" and then they all just cracked up. I couldn't tell if they were laughing at me or if I'd just made a real cool joke. I looked at hymn, hoping the expression on his face would clue me in. But he wasn't laughing. I'd never seen such a look on hymn, not exactly like it. It wasn't one of those looks that makes everybody stop laughing and so it took a few seconds for everything to die down again.

Before I could think better of it, I turned to hymn and asked, "Whadda *you* wanna be?"

He looked away for a long moment, then he turned right to me with one of those looks that made me think he was trying to tell me something, without saying it.

"Quiet."

Look What They've Done to Your Song

For a few days after the big bash, I tried to make it "quiet" for hymn. He seemed in pretty good spirits, just not yakking his head off like usual. All the running around during the *holidaze* had left us both a little tired, I think, and he seemed all happy to just sit in front of The Box and write his pages. So, I gave hymn his "space," like the Earth Ladies were always saying, and decided it was a good time to go for a long visit with Nana.

It looked like Nana was gonna stay in that nursing home for longer than we thought but she took it with her regular Nana "grin and bear it" motto and started calling it her "retirement palace" and all the people there were her "staff." What a crackup!

Anyway, Angela decided to go with me and on the way there, we had a long talk and "decided to be friends"—yeah, like that's possible. But, I really love her and I don't wanna think of a life without her in it, squeaky voice and all. So, I'm gonna try.

So, me and Angela get to the nursing home and go up to Nana's room and after everybody got through kissing and hugging and stuff, Nana pipes up and says, "Where's your buddy?"

See, Nana called hymn my "buddy" right from the first time she met hymn. She wouldn't ever call hymn JC or Jesus or Your Christness or anything. When hymnandme visited her, he'd walk in the room and she'd smile bigger than all outdoors and say, "Now, how are YOU?" But, she never used his name or anything when he was there, and if he wasn't there, she'd say to me, "Where's your buddy?" like that.

So, I started filling Nana in on all the latest Ark gossip, which always cheered her up, and then I told her about the Epiphany Party and Noman and how JC just wanted to be quiet for a while. She took it all in and even laughed right out loud when I told her about Noman hiding in the trees.

Then, because I really believed she'd know, I got down to the most important question burning my brain—was he *HYMN*. I figured, if anybody would know, it was Nana. I mean, she could be a real hard nose about religion and "getting it right" and all. She took it serious and had spent about a million years studying and having faith and crap like that and I didn't think anybody knew more about religion than her— not even Louis. But, unlike a bunch of Mrs. T's Christ guys, Nana was always fair. She always looked at both sides and told me once, "If it's the truth, it doesn't matter who said it."

So, I asked her, "Nana, do you think he's for real? Do you think he's *HYMN*?"

She went all quiet for a long time and I actually thought she'd fallen asleep. When I kinda nudged her, she just looked up at me and smiled and said:

"Well, if he's not, he should be!"

When I got home it was pretty late but there were no lights on—not even The Box. JC was standing at the window, with only a candle burning. It was kinda creepy looking and I didn't like the feeling I was getting so I tried to lighten hymn up.

"Hey, man, it's January, not Halloween!" I laughed but when he turned around I could tell he wasn't in a mood to laugh. He was real serious-looking and avoided eye contact which scared the piss out of me.

He sat down real slow, like he'd gone into instant replay and somebody had the remote and wanted to see hymn sit down again. His face was dark and I couldn't read it and all of a sudden I was terrified. He didn't look like the hymn I knew, but more like all the pictures of hymn in museums and churches, that didn't really look like hymn at all, all suffering inside.

I sat down on the old beat-up red couch, close enough to hear hymn if he decided to talk but far enough away in case he exploded or something. I was scared but also, I can't exactly explain it, but looking at his face made me sad. It made me wanna cheer hymn up or make hymn laugh at me on purpose or just about anything that would put some light back in his eyes.

In a real short time I had to look away. It just hurt too bad, like watching somebody die who doesn't want to. And, the funny thing was, I knew he wasn't mad at me or I hadn't done anything to upset hymn or disappoint hymn (like I felt I did a lot of). And it wasn't that scary "desperate frustration" face either. It was just—I dunno—just terminally sad and I got worried that maybe he didn't know what he was gonna do next. And if *he* didn't know, who the hell was gonna come and save us now?

His face kept changing each time the candle flickered, making hymn look mad and sad and alone and far away and like he was just *getting* it, all of a sudden, all at once. Maybe he'd figured out that the world hadn't changed one bit in 2,000 years except we got noisier, bloodier, and more crowded. Maybe he was starting to think that, if he *had* died for every-body, our way of paying hymn back wasn't to "do unto others" but was to whack our neighbor before he could whack us.

I knew not to say anything. I knew he would take the lead and tell me what was bothering hymn when it was the right time. But just in that moment, just for that one second, I wanted to jump up and hug hymn. I wanted to take hymn away to that ocean place he was always yammering about and go fishing and watch hymn catch all those people in his spooky love-net and watch hymn laugh and teach and make everything okay again. Wasn't that what they were always saying? That he was coming back to make things okay?

Well, here he was and hardly anybody knew it and things had been sorta fun in an I-always-seem-to-be-the-butt-of-the-joke kinda way but now, well, he looked like somebody sitting outside that crematory place and waiting for the big oven to stop burning up his best friend.

It was getting quieter outside and in the room it was like church, I mean, it was *that* awful and gloomy and silent. When he did finally turn to me, I thought it was a trick of the light at first and I jumped when I realized he was looking at me.

I can't be sure—and don't get me wrong, I mean he was absolutely a real guy and macho and everything in a kind, gentle sorta way—but just for this one second I thought he was crying. I just didn't wanna think of hymn as crying, you know? I mean, he was all sensitive and everything but he was just about always laughing and smiling and telling these great stories and teaching you cool lessons without you even knowing you were learning or your head exploding from TMI.

And this didn't look like just a tear or two. This looked like he'd really had tears running down hymn and that just made me wanna bawl. I fought like hell, I really did, but tears started dropping out of my eyes too, for Christ's sake, and they hurt, like giant heavy fists with those iron knuckle things, crashing into my face and drowning my heart. I didn't know what was happening and I wanted more than anything for it to stop. Finally, he spoke:

"I was watching The Box earlier," he said, all quiet and soft and scary.

"Yeah?" I choked out.

He looked at me so hard I thought for a second I became invisible. Then he whispered, "Tell me about September 11."

Well, he got an extension on his Epiphany wish—there was nothing but quiet for a lot of days after I answered his questions. We didn't go out, or eat much, and hardly said a word to each other. It was like when you gotta tell somebody some real bad news and then you feel all guilty for it even though you had nothing to do with it.

That night—the night we had talked all night—it was like he'd finally realized that the world could be a real lousy place, like he hadn't known that people could be so awful to each other. I didn't get that at all, considering how he'd supposedly met his end. And he'd met Noman—I mean, if that doesn't just about kill any hope you had for humanity, I don't know what would. But I guess maybe he was figuring that we must of made some progress since he'd been here last. And here I had to tell hymn that we'd really just gotten worse.

So, he'd asked me to tell hymn about September 11 and I tried the best I could but the more I talked, the more he asked questions like why and how and I didn't have any answers at all.

And all the questions about September 11 just led to questions about the Holocaust, and that just led to questions about all the wars and all the cheating and lying and stealing and murdering and he started looking like he'd gone into shock—all pale and shaky.

I guess 2,000 years ago he mighta heard of a war here or an earthquake there, but it must of been easier to take it all in a little at a time. I mean, they probably had all the same troubles we do, they just didn't *know* about it all at once like now. Today, there's a steady stream of bad news in giant, flat-screen living color and, jeez, most days I'm ready to pull the plug on the whole human race myself.

We sure needed saving, that was obvious. But would he still be willing? I mean, he looked real shook up. And what about all his turning it back at us and being all responsible and our own deciders and accepting but not agreeing? How was that gonna work in a world just jam-packed with pointing out the worst in each other and blaming every *other* poor sucker for every last thing wrong with you?

I knew I was way over my head, so I booked it on up to Louis' and dragged the old philosopher downstairs to face a very sad messiah.

To his credit, Louis dropped everything and followed me back to the apartment. He sat down with hymn in the candle-light and I went to get everybody some wine. That's all we had, water and wine, and no, he didn't change it or anything. It was weird because everybody was always giving us wine. When I came back in, Louis was just finishing up his lesson in world religious politics.

"So, we were Goliath...and there was bound to be a David." I thought it was nice of Louis to put it in Bible terms for hymn. But, I had no idea what David and Goliath had to do with September 11 or the Holocaust.

"Here's the wine," I said. "Now, don't go changing it back into water!" I was kinda trying to lighten things up and I thought it was a pretty good joke but nobody was buying.

"How about some cheese and crackers?" Louis could be

such a jackass sometimes. I knew he just wanted to get rid of me so he could be all serious and explain the meaning of life to hymn. But he knew we didn't have crap like that.

I went back in the kitchen and found some peanut butter but nothing to put it on since we'd already gone through all our weekly bread. (I suddenly understood that "Give us our daily bread" line, although we would of been fine with just weekly). So, I dug out three spoons and decided we could just glom the PB on the spoon and eat out of the jar. I could hear Louis being all-knowing in the other room. He sure did like the sound of his own voice. But it made me wait—and think.

Here was this messiah, all sad and confused, because we'd screwed up his beautiful love affair with the world. Before hymn, Louis had always said that if Jesus came back today, he probably wouldn't be a Christian. That we'd just strayed too far away from what he, Jesus, would want.

So, what *did* Jesus want? What had he *died* for? Love? He was always yammering about love. And, when he talked about it, it didn't seem girly or commercial at all. It was like he really meant it.

The thing is, though, that nowadays, everybody says love, but almost nobody *does* love. Love is just a 4-letter word. Folks today say love to mean sex, lust, things they own, things they wanna own...even people they wanna own. Louis says "love is the most over-used and under-applied word there is."

But hymn, he actually believed love was a powerful force. He meant it as a whole way of living. He really meant we should LOVE each other. And he did it. He actually lived it. I guess that's what made hymn a good teacher. You could see the results before you even started. There really wasn't any risk involved. You could look at how he did it, what happened in his life, and decide if that was for you.

Great system, right? But, what kind of *love* nails people to crosses and drives planes into buildings and sets real live human beings at 350° for an hour? And what kinda God lets all this crap go on and on and keeps saying, "Just wait... Another century or two...It's coming...The big prize is on the way"? Why are we supposed to believe that there's all this suffering and death and pain and it's all so we get this big reward in the *next* life? Well, I don't know about you but I want my reward *NOW*.

If this God Almighty is gonna condemn us, then we can condemn God. If we're supposed to grow up and take it like a man, then it's time for God to grow up too. Why should God get away with crap we'd *never take from anybody else?* Why doesn't God have to explain Himself? Why do we always, *always* forgive God?

I just wanna understand why some God would let all this crap go on. Like why my mom died and why I never knew my dad. What kinda crappy Big-Dad-in-the-Sky-God is gonna let people not even get to know who their folks are?

And this whole 9/11 thing had just reminded me of why I hate sports. I know that sounds stupid, but I hate sports because there's all these guys running around *thanking God.* They thank Him when they win or score or get the goal or the home run or the touchdown. It's always bothered me because, well, what about the guy on the other team? What about *his* God? He asleep?

Well, it's the same thing with September 11. All those terrorist guys were yapping about God and thanking Him for giving them this great career op and setting them all up to be martyrs, and over on the other side, all the good Christians and Jews are all thanking God that they're so much better than those guys because they'd never do anything like that, even though they've all had wars and slaves and cheated and stolen and every other kinda crap you can think of in their pasts too.

It doesn't matter what they're thanking God for, really. The fact that both sides, *all* sides, never seem to realize that it's all the same God. I'd even asked hymn once about what shape he thought God would be if He was a shape. Without even thinking about it he said, "Circle." When I asked hymn why, he just grinned at me and said, "No sides!"

So, when it comes right down to it, I guess I just want *my* God back—the one I had in Sunday School. I just wanna believe—in something. Anything.

And it might as well be hymn.

When I finally got back to the living room, Louis was saying, "....but isn't turning the other cheek surrender?" I knew it was time to switch on the tape.

"Surrender is not defeat. It's just not wasting energy fighting the inevitable. It's using that same energy for change."

I decided to dive right in, *"So, how can we stop them from blowing us all to hell? What do you do when the other cheek is a friggin' H-bomb?"*

I'd gotten real worked up in the kitchen, and I was still pretty pissed about God and everything. Louis was fishing a spoon out of the peanut butter with a look like it was worms or magnets or something and I could tell he was about to say something mean to me, but JC jumped in.

"When you extend the hand of tolerance, even if it is repeatedly slapped away, you are working in spirit. Eventually, that other soul will recognize that your gesture comes from love and will return the gesture. We only feel agitated or fearful or hateful or resentful or angry or threatened when we feel separate and separated. Once we all

feel loved and know that we are part of Love, the entire world will be transformed."

"Do you really think that's ever gonna happen? How long is that gonna take?" I can be pretty impatient sometimes. Louis says I'm like that because I live in the past and so the future seems even longer away.

I never saw the problem with living in the past.

You can't die in the past.

But JC seemed to of come out of his sadness long enough to believe in love again and he had what I thought was a pretty cool answer.

"Yes, I really do think that will happen. How long it takes depends on two things."

"What two things?" I leaned way in to see hymn better because the candle was almost out and he seemed to be fading away into the darkness.

"First, you must decide how you want to live your life. Do you want to use steps or slides?"

"Huh?" I was glad he seemed to be feeling better but he wasn't making any sense.

"Do you want to live your life using steps or slides? If you choose steps, it will take a lot longer and be a lot harder."

"Then I choose slides," I blurted out. Louis chuckled—naturally.

But JC turned square to me and got all quiet and kind. *"Yes, but slides can only go down."*

Louis chuckled again. It pissed me off and since I was still pretty ticked off with God too, my next question came out loud and fast, *"Okay, what's the second thing?"*

JC smiled, but it looked a little sad around the edges and I felt bad for acting like I needed my other cheek smacked.

"The second thing might be a little harder. You have to

remember that you are one with everything and everyone. We all are."

He paused a second, like he did sometimes, to let it sink in. I wanted so much to make hymn proud of me. I wanted not to be pissed at Louis and God, so I tried harder than I ever had to understand what he was talking about. I wanted to be one *with hymn*, not just everybody. I closed my eyes and tried to get quiet inside, like he taught me (and not fall asleep). And, suddenly, the most amazing thing happened. It was like a flash of light and energy and I knew, without a doubt, that I had it.

"*I get it! You mean like at one ment, right?*"

"*What?!*" Louis didn't even know what that meant! I felt kinda special that I had a handle on this big spiritual idea and old knows-it-all didn't.

"You *know*," I was kinda baiting Louis, "*AT ONE MENT.*"

Louis looked surprised for a second but then, creeping across his bony old face, he got that self-righting look he always gets when I really mess up. He pushed his glasses up his nose and glared right through me. A terrible storm of damn-I-think-I-got-it-wrong ran up me like a chill.

"*I think you mean atonement. A-TONE-ment?*" That was all Louis said. And then he chuckled—hard. Again. It was like he was real careful to just kinda come to the brink of a laugh and pull back into a chuckle.

Damn. I could really hate that chuckle sometimes.

I was about to try to explain that I'd only seen the word in writing and I thought it meant being all one with everything like JC was always yammering about. But, like usual, I didn't have to. I was saved, again, by hymn.

"*I think that's a very creative way to look at it. Getting right with the Spirit is a kind of at-one-ment. Wonderful concept.*"

Take that, Louis.

I know, I shouldn't of gloated and it was time to get back on track but that was the first time ever I think that I kinda "won" a mental debate with Louis.

"Yes, we are all at-one with everyone and everything," JC continued. *"Now, try to imagine that we're all walking a spiritual tightrope between the* perception *of good and bad, light and dark, love and hate. Sometimes we are master tightrope walkers. Sometimes it's easy. But sometimes we lose our balance. In the circus, that's when things get interesting. When the master leans, the crowd gasps, and he gets their attention.*

"When we're first learning to walk that tightrope, we don't mean to wobble. Our lack of balance is unintentional. But we learn valuable spiritual lessons when we lose our balance. As we gain skill and understanding, there are fewer and fewer things that can throw us off balance.

"Ultimately, our feelings inform our stability. When we are angry, we lean toward hate. When we are inspired, we lean toward light. When we feel separate, we might lean toward dark. And, when we know we are one with all, we lean toward love."

I must of looked as confused as I felt so he tried to break it down for me.

"Remember, leaning is not just an angle; it can mean supported and sustained by, inclination, propensity, or preference. So, when we 'lean' toward love, eventually we realize that the whole universe will rise to encourage, sustain, and nourish our spirits with a vast and indestructible foundation. It will appear to the rest of the world that we are still walking that tightrope, just like everyone else. The illusion holds fast for those who choose it—and most do. But, as spiritual masters,

we *will know, and experience, the Infinite upholding us and our loving intentions.*"

I was thinking that maybe that's what messiahs were here to do, like Noman said—to explain it all for us and tell us which way to walk on that spooky tightrope. But, JC was getting real good at that mind-reading trick and I was getting nervous and thought maybe I better start thinking about baseball or something.

"*Beware of those claiming to know* your *path. No one with such a claim is a messenger from God. No one frolicking in darkness is representing the Creator. Do you think that the Father is limited in His ability or desire to provide ALL for His children?*"

The storm in his eyes at the mention, *in my mind*, of those false profits passed, and his kind face came back.

"*Love is ALL. Love gives us a flash of golden under-standing, a glimpse behind the veil of illusion of separation from Perfection. Love is a powerful experience of The Real—a communion with the unlimited Mind of God. Love smoothes any path, heals any wound, fulfills any dream.*"

He saw the question in my mind and answered before I could even form it in my mouth.

"*Yes, any dream. If it is a dream* born in love, *anything is possible.*

"*Unfortunately, most of us become satisfied to live lives of only occasional equilibrium. We willingly accept and even pursue the drama. Some thrive on the appearance of danger, risk, and vulnerability, courting disaster by leaning out too far over the tightrope,* intentionally *putting their balance in peril.*

"*And, now, with September 11, there appears to be a continuing, world-wide agreement to embrace the idea of terror. When terror approaches, we close our eyes—and our hearts.*

We can no longer even peek at the promise of a life of never-ending possibility. We settle for the occasional hint. And, most souls believe that is all they can hope for.

"But, when we become masters—and we all do eventually —just to make things interesting, we sometimes appear to lean, intentionally. It's a choice. The people in our lives might gasp. We have their attention. The peril they imagine, the cross they believe we will bear, we know to be an everlasting foundation of love.

"For the master, the illusion of the tightrope has disappeared. And the rope has become a wide field of fortune and support. There's no longer any need for a net.

"And, as masters, in that moment, it is our duty to use our lives to illustrate the highest human potential."

He paused a minute and I knew he could tell that I still wasn't getting the story. So, he leaned all the way over the dying candle, just like Autumn's spooky "post-JC" drawing of the lady with the mirror, and he finished the evening with a strange, from-the-inside-out light in his eye.

"Keep leaning toward love."

Social Leopards

It was one of those spooky nights with no moon, and all the street lights look kinda yellowy and all the noise from the street suddenly goes quiet. I never understood that. Usually you can hear traffic and horns and kids crying and people fighting and just this kinda city hum all the time. After a while, you don't even hear it anymore because you're so used to it. Then, all of a sudden, it all stops and goes quiet. And that quiet is loud. It makes you notice it. People always say that happens right before earthquakes, but as you can probably tell by now, I don't pay attention real good so I never noticed if that really happens. It's pretty rare I notice anything at all, so it creeps me out when I do.

It was a hot night for early February, what I think they call Indian Winter, stuffy and sticky inside since there's no way to turn off the heat before the middle of March, so we were all sitting out in front of the building on the steps, smoking and just kinda talking about stuff. I'd been *leaning toward love* all over the place so I couldn't understand why it still hurt so bad about Angela. The only way I found to kinda keep the pain away was not to see her—but that hurt too. Man, love sure can suck while you're waiting for it to do all that healing and smoothing and fulfilling.

So Autumn and the Yins were yapping about how Chinese horoscopes were different from English-speaking ones and how the Yins had just celebrated their own New

169

Year's, for Christ's sake, so I tuned out of that and started telling Mrs. T—yeah, Mrs. T was out there too—all about Angela and the breakup and how I was feeling until she started looking like she was kinda sorry she'd ever joined our little Ark family.

Anyway, while I was yakking Mrs. T's head off was when I noticed there was no moon and I noticed there was that kinda eerie light coming out of the street lamps and I noticed it all went quiet. And all of a sudden I could hear that quiet. I shushed everybody and we all just sat there, kinda holding our breaths. There was nothing—no wind, no traffic, no people talking or fighting or crying in any of all the open windows. Then, in a prickly little way, I could hear it. The quiet got thick and something was snaking through it. I was still lost in this jungle of not-sound when Louis snapped to attention with a glance in the alley.

"What's that?" He whispered it and only later I would realize he'd said what, not who. (Alley Guy moved to the shelter for the winter and the alley was like his summer home.) It was usually too cold for any of the other "visitors" to the alley but you could see the little orange burn from their smokes or pipes if they were there. So, except for the roaches and broken bottles and trash cans, there really shouldn't of been anything else in there we didn't recognize.

By now we were all standing and leaning over the rail and looking and squinting and trying to figure out what it was. I mean, when you're used to something a certain way it becomes like the sound of the city—you start to *not* notice it— so, anything that changes it makes you wonder.

Charlie started down the stairs and we all followed, single file. We were all kinda tip-toeing, for Christ's sake, toward this black lump in the middle of the alley which wasn't there that morning. At first, I thought it was one of those trash bags that falls off the garbage trucks all the time. I think we all thought that. Right up until it moved. We all jumped about a mile and *Raindrop* screamed, which made everybody else scream.

The not-trash bag changed shape and got longer, like a pool of blood on a hill. Then it stopped moving and we heard just this real soft moan. It was a who, and as we got closer we could tell it was a real bad beat up who.

Finally, Louis leaned over this lump of human and stood back up real fast. He turned to us and the yellowy street lights let us see that his eyes were wide and wild, like he was in a real bad horror movie.

"Oh, my God," he whispered. "Bernard."

It took Bernard a real long time to come home. Alley Guy was even back before him, yelling "Facts aren't Truth!" or "New Message" every time anybody walked by. And the bastards that beat the crap out of Bernard, they were back on the streets before he was even out of the hospital because they got some kinda friggin' flea bargain.

Bernard was in the hospital in a coma for a couple of weeks and then in some kinda rehab to learn how to walk and talk and eat and not crap in his pants, for crying out loud. I mean, it wasn't his fault, but it was weird that anybody could get that far away from being themselves and still be alive. He was there a long time because I guess it's hard to remember who you are and how to do all those everyday things all at once and not crap yourself.

Everybody in The Ark had pitched in by cleaning Bernard's apartment and doing his laundry and making and freezing meals and taking care of his bills. Angela even knitted some little blanket kinda thing for him. And me and Louis and the Earth Ladies took turns feeding his cats, but Louis and the Earth Ladies kept "forgetting" to clean the cats' crappy litter boxes so that became my job. Yeah, I was top of the heap...so to speak.

And because of this whole mess, we found out that Bernard didn't have any family. Nobody. Us and the cats were all he had. And that just made me sadder than hopeless hope.

So, it was way at the end of March by the time we got him back, but he was definitely *not* Bernard. He looked sorta like him, in a scarred all to hell kinda way. He still sounded like him, straight from downtown Hollyweird, just a lot softer and inside. But his eyes were far away and he just sat and looked out the window and didn't play with his cats or bang on his piano and he didn't flirt or fluster Louis or anything. He didn't say any of the old Bernard things and we all got worried and started pronouncing his name the way he wanted, you know, just to show our support. Until then, not one of us had ever said Burr-nerd—except hymn, of course.

By the time he'd been home only a day or two, the buzz around the Bernard Beating had died down and everybody kinda moved on to their own problems. Louis said that was because Bernard was a *social* leopard and that's the way it always was with leopards. As usual, I didn't have any idea what Louis was yapping about but the whole thing had brought up a ton of new questions for me.

I'd come back from watching Bernard slurp some soup the Earth Ladies had made for him and helping him to the "powder room" and all which was *not* a big thrill and kinda made me wanna puke. JC was sitting in his purple chair, with The Box blaring, writing his pages. He'd been more quiet than usual since Bernard got the crap beat out of him. I think he was afraid we all had expected for hymn to heal Bernard, but really, we knew where he stood on that—you know, with the Nana thing and all. I think that it was more that we expected hymn to have *prevented* the whole thing in the first place. I mean, what the hell good is it to have Jesus living in your building if you're not gonna be safe?

"So, you wanna go check in on Bernard?"

He just smiled at me.

"Or, you wanna go get some oranges? We are the Orange Men, y'know."

"No thanks. You go."

That was it. He said it nice but that was all he said.

"Or, how about visiting Bernard?" I can be real stubborn sometimes.

"No thanks."

Man, I couldn't figure hymn out.

I kept trying to get hymn to talk to me about it but he wouldn't. He just went on being his Epiphany quiet self, smiling these real tolerant smiles at me, and that just pissed me off, to tell you the truth.

So, I booked it on up to Louis' and after listening to a long and boring lecture on not getting involved and not being his brother's keeper (even though when it was his brother *Jesus*, he dropped everything—shouldn't he *keep* his brother Bernard, too? The one who really needs the help.), we decided to get everybody together, at my place, to decide what we could do to help Bernard.

That night (after sunset, of course), all The Ark folks plopped down on the floor in my living room for the Bernard Beating Meeting. Now, I have exactly the same size living room as Mrs. T but there's a helluva lot more room in mine because I don't really *have* anything. We all made sure that

Mrs. T and the Yins and Jimmy's mom got to sit on the red couch. JC was trying to offer his old purple chair to the Ladies but they just wanted to sit on the floor.

So, there was a lot of talk about what *should* be done but nobody actually wanted to *do* any of it. The Earth Ladies said they were feeding Bernard and that's all the time they had to offer. The Yins offered something, I think, but nobody could make out what. I went up every day and took him to the "powder room," for Christ's sake, and cleaned the cats' crap box.

That was it. That was the total of help he was getting from the folks of The Ark.

But what really got to me was that Bernard was always the first one to jump in and help whenever anybody else needed something. We were his family, his *only* family. And now, everybody was all of a sudden too busy in their own lives to help out a real friend and practically family member in need. It pissed me off.

We'd all gotten a lot closer in the last six months, since hymn, so I was surprised and angry that the people I thought were all friends—all this big Ark Family—had suddenly turned back into these barely-know-you strangers. When I kinda said that, everybody jumped all over me and started yelling at me. All except hymn. He just sat there, looking at the floor.

I guess there was a lot of crap under my skin because all of them yelling at me just made me furious. Why was *I* always friggin' wrong? I was just trying to stand up for this poor schmuck who had the crap beat out of him for just being... well, for just *being*. We all had to be careful these days because we all could get in real trouble just being ourselves.

So, why didn't these, my friends, understand that? I get that we gotta be careful not to piss off strangers, especially on freeways in L.A. But, you should be able to be yourself with your friends, right?

And why the hell didn't JC say anything when they yelled at me? Why didn't he stand up for me? Me, his best friend, was being trashed, and Bernard had been *left* for trash in the alley. Me and Bernard had been wronged and I wanted hymn and the whole lousy world to know it. So I just exploded.

"At some point you just want the Universe to stand up and say, 'You're right!' and tell you it was you who was wronged. Like when you're at the bus stop and waiting in the rain and the goddamn bus driver just ignores you and drives right by. Or people make fun of you or curse you or you really *do* know the answers but just because you studied for a change, you get accused of cheating. Or you clean cat crap up all day and nobody even thinks to thank you. Or you're friggin' *gay* and a bunch of idiots beat you to death and all your so-called, God-fearing, self-righting, good Christian, Jewish, Pagan or whatever friends turn their back like they can't even see you."

It was just this bubble of pure frustration and I was kinda sorry I'd said it before I even finished. JC didn't even look up at me and he seemed real far away. All of a sudden my stomach jumped into my throat and a shiver went through me. I started having one of those epiphones again like had happened a lot in the last few months. It felt magical, like if you threw a jigsaw puzzle in the air and somehow, when it landed, all the pieces fell into place. But this wasn't fun magic and I realized what a jerk I can be sometimes. That puzzle picture just snapped into focus and I could see my petty little problems didn't even begin to compare to what he'd gone through. For a minute I thought about not saying anything at all but I wanted hymn to know I understood.

"Or they nail you to a cross." I choked it out because my mouth was all of a sudden drier than the Santa Ana's—something that had reminded hymn of his own desert winds.

The room went dead. Everybody looked to hymn in an I'm-not-really-looking-at-you-in-case-you-don't-wanna-be-seen way.

JC still didn't look up, but I knew he'd heard me. One single tear fell out of his face and crashed on the floor. It was the longest and loudest silence I've ever heard.

Everything stopped. Nobody moved. I don't think anybody breathed. We must of looked like those poor schmucks, just doing their everyday crap and getting all frozen in those positions when they got covered with a volcano.

After about a year he turned right to me and I had the feeling that it was real important for me to focus and try like hell to understand hymn.

"You can't change *them*," JC said, all gentle and kind. "Whatever forces you believe are acting against you, whomever you believe to be your enemy, you can't change *them*. Setting a good example will sometimes influence others, but even the best examples won't change them. Forgiving them doesn't change them. Loving them doesn't change them. It changes *you*. That's why you do it."

He went on and started talking about loving everything—again. I mean, he was always talking about love! But I was getting all quiet inside and it was like a movie when they do that cool camera trick and everything around you gets bigger or smaller and you stay the same.

It changes *you*. It changes me. It changes *me*.

I was torn between listening to hymn in my living room and listening to hymn in my head. I chose head.

His words just kept repeating, over and over again in my

mind. I wanted more than anything to *get* it.

It CHANGES me. IT changes me. It changes ME.

I was trying so hard it hurt, and that's the truth. Really. But that wasn't working very well so I started trying all these different scenes in my head, since I was in that weird camera trick movie and all.

So, scene one: If some messed up bully comes along and smacks me and I turn around and let him hit me again, that changes me? Well, of course it changes me. Now I gotta big bruise and three loose teeth on that side. What the hell?

Okay, okay. I'm pretty sure that's not what JC meant. Let me try something else. Oh, wait. Check in, check in.

"...and if you stand at a door and knock..."

Yep, got that one. Okay, scene two. So what about if some guy robs me and takes my brand new iPhone (not that I could ever afford an iPhone, but for the sake of my movie). Yeah, that's a good one. What should I do then? Forgive him and give him my iPad too?

My mind went blank. This was impossible. How could I forgive the guy *and* give him all the rest of my crap *and* feel real good about it all at the same time? Yeah, I'd change alright, because now I'd have a lot less stuff to worry about, I guess. And I'd be lighter. And I'd be colder. (And I'd be real pissed!)

And by forgiving this guy, I let him have all my crap *and* he gets away with it. *He* doesn't have to pay me back. *He* doesn't have to say he's sorry. He just gets everything *and* gets my blessing! Yeah, that works well.

I was getting so frustrated I almost started yelling again. And suddenly, in that urge to yell, I was back in the room and everybody was still there, but something had changed. And since I hadn't been paying attention, I had no idea what was going on but every single eye in that room was locked on *me*.

I felt that choking panic rising up in my chest and I wanted to run but I hadn't been paying attention, so I didn't even know from what. The eyes didn't look angry, which was a relief, so I shot a quick glance at hymn and searched his face for the answer. I could tell he expected me to say something so I pulled up my very best cover-your-ass comment.

"Huh?"

Okay, so it wasn't my very best, but at least it got the words moving again. JC paused a second, and I could tell by the light in his eyes that he knew exactly what was going on and he knew I was lost. And like the good sheepherder he always was, he saved me once again by somehow making me the joker, and not the joke.

He laughed. Big and wide and filled with love and teeth. And everybody laughed, real sincere laughs, like they got this great joke I supposedly had just told.

And when he caught enough breath to speak, he uttered just one word to pull it all together and make it seem like I knew what was going on and, in fact, should probably start a new career as a stand-up comic.

"Exactly!"

Later, after everybody left, I wanted to ask hymn about it. I wanted to thank hymn. But before I could even say a word he turned to me and said, "I know. You were thinking it over. Right?" Damn, how'd he do that? He was always doing that.

Anyway, I know I should of been feeling better than I did since everybody had agreed to do at least something for Bernard before they left the meeting. Everybody but hymn. I don't think anybody expected hymn to schlep soup up or clean boxes of cat crap or anything like that. But I know there was this kinda underneath it all expectation that, since he was *hymn*, there might be a little extra something in the way of a miracle or raising from the dead (well, not dead but from the leftovers of the beating) or some cool "from above" tip on how to win enough money to move Bernard out of this neighborhood he didn't feel safe in anymore.

It was getting late and I knew I should leave it all alone but I just couldn't. It really bugged me:

"So, what are *you* gonna do about Bernard?"

I was just trying to get hymn to see that it was kinda expected that he do *something*, you know, since he had that inside track with his Dad and all. I knew he wasn't gonna heal him (I still thought he'd had enough practice healing all those leopards in the Bible, even though he said it was *them* that did all the work and healed themselves). But something.

He looked up from his pages, put down his pen, and gave me the hugest Jesus smile I'd ever seen:

"What are *you* going to do about it?"

That was it. He just kept smiling at me and then went back to his writing and watching The Box.

I was so tired, I couldn't even speak. I just kept staring at hymn. He glanced over again and smiled, but it was real clear he wasn't gonna say any more. Yeah, he meant it was up to me.

I just groaned and fell back on the red couch to try to think and figure out what was going on. He just didn't get it. It was like he didn't wanna accept any responsibility for anybody else. But, wasn't that what a good sheepherder did? Wasn't that what that Good Sumerian was all about? Or even that "brother's keeper" crap Louis had been yapping about?

Here I was, just some schmuck, running up and down stairs all day and dealing with Bernard's crap and his cats' crap (and nobody thanking me) and trying to stick up for Bernard and get everybody to help out taking care of him and he, *hymn*, does nothing. And, I knew that no matter how much I begged hymn he'd just turn it back to me.

I was starting to get pissed again.

"Y'know," I sat up straight, "sometimes we all need help. Sometimes, no matter how kind our religions are, or how good we try to be, we need somebody else to help us."

He nodded, so I went on.

"It's like if I was drowning and I reached out for help and you showed up but you wouldn't throw me a lifeline. You know?" I was trying not to yell or cry. I wanted hymn to *get* it.

"You already know how to swim," he said. "You just have to remember."

Big help, huh?

"WHY?" I stood up and kinda shouted it, and immediately sat back down and tried to stay calm. "Why do *I* gotta understand and you don't? I swear, man, I *don't* know how to swim."

"You'll get it." He stood up and started to the kitchen.

"No!" I stood up again and then almost laughed, because this picture flashed in my head of what we must of looked like, just popping up and down like that.

He stopped and turned to me, kind and sorta like a dad.

"Everyone heals themselves. Everyone. And they save themselves. And they make themselves whole. Just like Bernard is doing right now. He may not realize it. He may choose to perceive that his power is in others; in those who are taking care of him. In you. I promise you, though, *he* is doing the healing."

"I don't think so, man. If we already know how to fix every damn thing wrong with us, why don't we do it?"

He smiled real big.

"You do 'do it.' You just don't know it yet."

And that was it.

He went to the kitchen and I just stood there. By the time he was back in his chair, I'd gone to bed. We didn't say another word to each other.

Even though I didn't understand a lot of what he was saying, as I was drifting off to sleep, I decided I would trust that he knew the truth and everything was gonna turn out great.

But that night, things started going down a scary road that I really didn't wanna walk.

Nightmare

The only time I ever saw hymn sleeping was after a whole lot of nights of me trying to stay up and see if he *did* sleep. I mean, he was always awake. If I'd get up in the night to hit the head or the fridge, he'd be sitting there, reading or writing or watching The Box. It felt like when I was a little kid and I tried like hell to stay awake to see Santa, to see if he really flew across the sky, or got stuck in the smog. I'd been told, of course, that Santa tried to come to our apartment, but without a fireplace, he had to land on the roof and leave our stuff outside the door. But, in this neighborhood, that could mean you never knew you got anything from Santa for years.

When I was about 8 or 9, they started trying to build the greenhouse, which really cut down on sleigh parking space, but by then, I didn't believe in anything anymore.

But here I was again, trying to stay up to see if he slept. I bombed at that every night until the night of the Bernard Beating Meeting.

It must of been about three in the morning but it was hard to tell because my eyes wouldn't quite focus to see the clock and L.A. always sounds awake. I'd fallen asleep, again, but I woke up because Alley Guy was yelling, "It's coming, it's coming" over and over. When he suddenly stopped, everything went quiet and I had one of those weird feelings like I was the only one awake. I knew there were other people awake in the building—I mean, there always were—but right there, in the apartment, my awakeness felt alone. I could tell the light in the living room wasn't on, and there was no alien-blue light from The Box, bouncing and changing shadows under the door.

I was real quiet and kinda tiptoed out to the living room. He was lying on his back on the red couch, with one of those square little pillows Nanas always throw everywhere, wrapped in his arms on his chest. He looked like he was hugging it and it made me kinda sad. Like he was drifting, and the pillow was a life preserver, and was all that was keeping hymn from drowning in this sea of human troubles.

Or maybe it was just that he looked lonely, like he was hugging that little pillow because he didn't have any person to hug. And I knew, in some strange way, that he'd never have anybody to love like that. Nope, he'd chosen the world—and you can't have both.

So that night I caught hymn sleeping, and I stood there for a long time and watched hymn. I don't know what I was looking for but it was that same trying-to-see-Santa feeling— like maybe I'd see something that would prove he was real.

I didn't though, and I was about to go take a leak and get back in bed when he started mumbling. It was real weird but I started getting all excited, like I was gonna hear something that nobody in the world had ever heard. So, I creeped closer, holding my breath, with my heart practically pounding out of my chest. But as I got nearer, I realized it was all in some other language. I couldn't understand a word.

He started moving around like he couldn't get comfortable and mumbling a little louder and I thought that maybe he could sense that somebody was there, even in his sleep. I decided to call it quits and let hymn be when, all of a sudden, it hit me that maybe I should record whatever he was saying.

So, I got the tape player and crouched down on my haunches and tried to catch the tail end of this fit he seemed to be having. After a few minutes though, I started getting more and more worried because he was thrashing around and sweating and not looking like hymnself anymore. I could tell he was saying the same thing over and over, but it sounded more like Mrs. T's yapping "in tongues" than any talking I'd ever heard. Finally, I just couldn't stand it and I put my hand on his shoulder.

Without even a second of adjusting, he went all quiet and still, and for one panic-filled minute, I thought he'd died. But then I could see that his breathing was normal and strong again and it was like nothing had happened. I sat there and watched hymn for a few more minutes, but he stayed all calm, and I was tired, so I decided to go back to bed.

I grabbed his blanket off the floor (where he'd kicked it off when he was thrashing around), and did my best to tuck hymn in. It wasn't a hug exactly, but if we really are all one, I hoped maybe he'd take it as the world kinda saying 'sleep well' and 'thank you.'

I headed to bed and, almost as a second thought, I went back and got the recorder and kept hold of it all night, to remind me this hadn't been a dream.

When I woke up again that morning, I headed on up to Louis'. I played the tape for him because I thought if anybody might know what it said, it would be Louis. Well, about two seconds into the tape, Louis looked like I'd hit him with a brick. He played it over and over and I was getting boreder each time he played it.

"C'mon, Louis, what the hell. What does it mean?"

He stopped and held the tape for a long time, like he was

Indiana Louis and he'd just discovered that Holy Grill.

"Do you know what language this is?"

He was serious.

"Of course I don't, Louis, that's why I brought it to you. Do *you* know?"

He stared at me like I had two or three heads. And I thought he looked a little pissed off at me, too. Finally he said, "It's Aramaic."

"So?"

"Aramaic is an ancient Semitic dialect that's almost completely extinct today."

"SO?"

"*So?*" He looked real upset with me and I thought I'd better act more interested.

"What does it mean, Louis? What's he saying?"

"He's saying, 'Eli, Eli, lama sabachthani.' It means, 'My God, my God, why have you abandoned me?' "

I felt like I'd just been punched in the stomach. I couldn't stand to think of hymn, or anybody, feeling so all alone and lost and rejected they'd say that to God. Especially a God they believed in so much and called "Father" and all. And what kind of God—what kind of *father*—leaves his own children …his own son? I sure could relate to that. It made me so sad and upset that I didn't realize why Louis was so freaked out, until he said:

"It's what Jesus said on the cross."

How Many Here Are the Messiah?

"Who?"

Well, I'm gonna guess that everybody in Tinseltown could of heard the whoosh sound of all the heads snapping around to stare at hymn when he asked that.

The whole Ark was in Mrs. T's tiny living room again, but this time because she'd asked us all over for an "Easter-Slash-Passover Party." I guess that meant she'd decided to recognize the fact that not everybody in the world was as Christian as she was—even though she thought they *should* be. And Louis had told her that that "Last Supper" she was always yapping about was really a Passover dinner.

But, it all started heading south when Autumn decided to rile things up by explaining how Easter was *really* named after some chick who lived about a million years ago and went around making sure everybody was having fun making babies…or something like that. Well, Mrs. T's eyes just kept getting bigger and bigger and she actually started backing away from Autumn.

It was Louis who saved the day by saying, "Actually, everyone in the world has some sort of celebration this time of year."

Anyway, we're at the Party and Jimmy, who was studying the *New* Tenement now, asked hymn about what he thought Paul would think of this combo-party idea and JC had shocked the socks off everybody when he answered:

"Who?"

"You know...Paul."

He just stared at us.

"*You* know...Paul...the guy who took your religion to the Gentiles."

Nothing.

"I think maybe you knew him as Saul?"

Nope.

"On the road to Damascus?"

Nada.

"You blinded him and then healed him and then he went to the Gentiles?"

He shook his head.

"Well, there goes 2,000 years of propaganda!" Louis was almost beside himself with what he'd call "glee."

Mrs. T broke into tears and it was hymn who went over and tried to comfort her. I didn't really know what a Gentle was or why Paul or Saul wanted to go to them but the whole thing sure did seem to upset Mrs. T.

But Louis had found a crack in what he called "the self-righting religious armor" or something like that and he was going in for the kill. He stood up and took a big, kinda chuckle-y, breath so I knew it was a good time to switch on the tape.

"*That's a good point, JC. Paul who?...indeed. Paul was the Apostle to the Gentiles, but he became a follower only after your...uh...after the cross. His ideas contradict yours, in spirit and letter. Basically, Paul turned an obscure monotheistic cult of your followers into a highly successful polytheist,* Pagan *world religion! Even Thomas Jefferson called him the '...first corrupter of the doctrines of Jesus.' What we know from the New Testament, except for three of the Gospels, is primarily*" *the doctrine of Paul."*

All I could think of was how much Louis suddenly reminded me of Noman.

"When will the Christians get back to Jesus?" Louis turned from JC and started delivering his I'm-smarter-than-everybody lecture to all the Christians in the room. *"As things are now, you shouldn't call yourselves Christians but Paulians. Yes! Paulianity!*

"How is it that you accept everything Paul says as gospel even when it contradicts what Jesus said and did? If you believe Paul was entirely inspired by the Almighty, who do you assume directed Jesus' path? In fact, if you take just what Jesus said as the only true Gospel, you'll have an entirely different New Testament and a radically new religion."

Yep, Noman's twin brother.

I didn't know what the hell was going on because I hardly knew who this Paul guy was either but I guess it was pretty weird for hymn not to know, at least to the folks there.

That made me start thinking again—JC sure didn't know a lot of Bible stuff. Oh, hymn and Louis were always yammering about that old part of the Bible and he knew that stuff like the back of his hand. But the crap you'd think he should know, all the stuff about hymn, a lot of the time he didn't. It seemed to me that if he was the real JC, he would know all the stuff that was so damn important to all these people.

Mrs. T finally calmed down after JC talked to her real nice and Louis gave her and the Christians a kinda fake apology, and we all had a great feast and everybody laughed and sang and seemed to have a good time. But I guess, maybe, I was being too quiet because a couple of times Autumn asked if I was okay and Louis told me it was selfish for me to act all depressed on such a great occasion but I was just trying to sort things out, for Christ's sake, not commit suicide.

I just kept wishing Nana could of been there. Nana could get down and party with the best of 'em and I thought she'd be jazzed to see The Ark folks all getting along. But, the doctors now said she wasn't ever gonna come home, not even to her dollhouse. I dunno…I just missed her, in a real macho kinda way, of course, and that made me start thinking and doubting things all over again.

I mean, having hymn around should of been just about all the proof anybody would need to say there is definitely a God. But the real weird thing was that since he showed up, I'd never questioned or doubted more. The truth is, I really never even thought about it before hymn. I was just this happy-because-I-didn't-know-any-better kinda guy who was told there was a "big man in the sky" who took care of you and, if the other poor schmuck got creamed by the cross-town bus, well, that was his karma and none of my business.

I never doubted anything because I never thought about anything. I mean, Louis was always trying to get me to think, but I was more into daydreaming than thinking. I'd always been a dedicated daydreamer. Daydreaming was a helluva lot more fun and a ton less work. And, hell, daydreaming could be about anything and anybody and anywhere. *Thinking* had to be about facts and philosophy and science and religion and all that stuff just bored me to tears.

Or, like with politics, it was something I just saw as stupid and not worth using up a lot of brain cells on. I mean, what was the point, right? There were politicians, who were all these super rich guys (who, I guess, kinda had it rough because they were evidently born with silverware in their mouths which probably hurt and made them pissed off right from the beginning), and there was us, who were born with just the regular stuff like tongues and teeth in our mouths and so we didn't need to make all that money for some expensive surgery to remove all the hardware old mom must of been scarfing while she was pregnant.

Like Louis was always saying, there really were only two classes in this country, and all the folks who thought they were in the middle class and the majority, were just some suckers who had bought into the commercial about the American Dream and were too lazy to do their own dreaming. When you think about it, which I usually didn't, us poor folks were a lot better off since we *knew* we were poor. We couldn't afford to believe the commercials, so really, we were kinda more awake than the rest of the country.

So anyway, that's why I didn't much think about things and that's why it was real weird when I started asking all these questions and doubting there was any kind of God anywhere looking out for me. With Nana not ever coming home, I figured all I could really count on was me and I better start paying attention before it all ran out and I came to the end of my life facing the Big Nothing or that Grim Weeper guy and wondering why the hell I'd ever believed in fairy tales.

And, I know it's weird but, I'd never felt more lonely. Before hymn, I had my Nana and Louis and I knew most of the people in the neighborhood, even if I wouldn't call them a friend, and I had my Big Ernie (which was what Louis liked to call God in front of people who were real religious), and even though that was about it, I didn't feel alone at all.

It was like a dream, my life was. Before hymn, I just went along, never really thinking about anything.

And I was happy.

I didn't have any money or a car or anything worth anything.

And I was happy.

I never thought about the future, I never thought about the world.

And I was happy.

Before hymn, life was all a great, big, slippery slide, easy and free, and I guess that means it was only downhill, like JC said. But I didn't *know* it was only downhill. And if I had somehow jumped off that slide and climbed onto JC's crazy tightrope without even knowing it, I must of been leaning toward love, just like he told me to, because I was all happier than hell.

But hymn and Louis were always yapping about balance. So, if you're on that tightrope and you're trying to lean toward love like you're supposed to, wouldn't you, sooner or later, wanna lean the other way—just to get your, what Louis calls equal-liberty, so you don't fall off? I mean, it's instinct, right?

So now, my thinking time had gone up a lot more than was comfortable, and I was kinda aware I didn't have a car and that that was a hassle and I worried about the future and I knew the folks in the neighborhood a helluva lot more than I ever wanted to and I "fretted," as my Nana would say, about the state of the world and I wasn't sure there *was* a God or Big Ernie or anybody or anything watching out for me and I was hanging out with some crazy but loveable profit who thought he was Jesus Christ and I never was more lonely and I was never more unhappy.

And, according to Mrs. T, for this I should be all grateful and blessed and jumping up and down and wetting myself because, jeez, wasn't this just about the greatest thing that ever happened to anybody?

And, on top of all that, JC was always doing things that made me like hymn, and the more I liked hymn, the less magical he was. And the less magical he was, the less I thought he was Jesus—the *real* Jesus.

I mean, we were all taught that Jesus was this guy who walked on water (hymnandme had gone swimming in the ocean so I know that wasn't true), and changed water into wine (he always drank water, everywhere we went, and never once did it become wine. Damn!), and raised the dead (nope—walked by a ton of cemeteries and even went to this one memorial place to see a "coliseum" or something like that and not one dead person popped up to say "Hey"—thank God). And, you already know about all the healing that never happened.

No, he never did any of those things and there were a lot of times I just thought he was this great guy who told real cool stories and knew a lot of crap and was kind and sad. The longer I knew hymn, the less different from me he was. But here's the real weird part—the more I liked hymn, and the less magical *he* became, the more magical *I* became! It's hard to explain, but it turns out he wasn't becoming more like me and that's what made us less different. In a weird and very spooky way, I was becoming more like *hymn*. Jeez! I mean, I sure didn't know stuff like he did and, as you can probably tell, I'm no great storyteller. But in some strange inside way, I was becoming a better person—and not even on purpose.

And just as I was thinking that, I was suddenly shocked out of my "brooding," as Nana used to call it, and back into the "Easter-Slash-Passover Party." JC was all hunkered down, right in front of me, and I could tell by the look on his face that he was waiting for an answer—to a question I hadn't heard.

"Huh?"

He looked real deep into my eyes, kinda patted me on the arm, and smiled. "Do you want to see the card we all made for

Nana?" he repeated.

Yeah, while I'd been all wrapped up in feeling lonely and sad and sorry for myself, the whole entire Ark had scissored and pasted and colored a "We Miss You" card for my Nana. There they all stood, smiling at me, and holding up this giant card that they'd all kept as a secret from me so I'd be surprised too. Here, in Mrs. T's tiny living room, was The Ark's United Nations of religions and races and beliefs, that had all gathered together around one simple idea—kindness.

And there, in that moment, I found something I'd been missing.

Home.

So, right before Easter, Noman had disappeared for a few days. Jeez, that guy was completely whacked. Even *I* got what dropping out of sight right before Easter was supposed to mean and even I, who likes a good story and all, thought it was pathetic.

I know Noman didn't like the way things had gone at the Epiphany Party and he hadn't been around the 'hood as much as usual. But, I guess he'd stopped licking his wounds long enough to try for a fake resurrection.

The buzz on the streets was—nothing. Nobody even noticed he was gone. That didn't set well with old John Noman.

So once he surfaced out of his craphole and realized nobody cared if he died—let alone got resurrected—he decided to fight dirty and stir up a lot of nasty rumors about JC. For weeks he went around telling all his teenyboppers that *JC* was a false profit ("Pot, meet kettle," as Nana used to say). He said ridiculous stuff like JC was stealing from Louis, that JC was an undercover spy for Israel, and that JC was a terrorist and planning to blow hymnself up if he could get enough of us stupid believers together in one place.

But, the worst, nastiest, most find-the-worst-swear-word-you-can-think-of-and-fill-in-the-blank rumor was that JC might just be a pedicure. He started warning everybody to stay clear of hymn.

Well, everybody in the whole city knew it was bull, but it pissed us off to see Noman getting to think he was winning the Savior-Showdown.

It was a great day in May (and yeah, the Earth Ladies had already had a party about it being May, for Christ's sake, and were talking about having, yep—*another* party) and if you've lived in California long enough you can tell when the clearer blue skies of winter are about to get crowded out by the smogs of summer and you try to hang onto every last second of that breathable air.

Anyway, we were all hanging out on the roof, waiting for sunset (all except Charlie who had been around less and less ever since Easter and the Paul thing. I didn't even notice it at the time but hindsight is some news show on TV, or whatever that saying is).

So, we're all, except Charlie, on the roof waiting and we can hear old Alley Guy shouting, "It's coming!" (like he was what Nana used to call "a broken record"—whatever that is) and we're all laughing and having fun and Louis said Noman probably thought Alley Guy was talking about him! That made everybody laugh even more but it also brought up all the rumors Noman had been spreading about JC and everybody was kinda buzzing and looking to hymn to see his reaction.

True to form, JC had only real nice things to say about Noman. But, he listened to all our concerns about Noman and then, real kind and all, nailed it on the head.

"*John just needs to realize that he can't be anyone else's messiah. A true messiah is an example. That's all. The example says, "Wake up!" By example, you recognize that you are your own messiah. By example, you realize your own potential— not the potential of another messiah who says they know the way for you. No one can tell you which way your path leads. No one can walk your path for you. Enlightenment can't be bought or sold, lost or found, purchased with a chant or magic formula. Enlightenment is all from within and no one and nothing from outside your own spirit can show you how to reach it.*"

Mrs. T, who was right on the fence with this 'is he or isn't he' crap, kinda spoke for us all.

"*But...*" She looked troubled and he jumped right in to help her.

"*Because, BECAUSE, there is no outside of you. There is no enlightenment that has not already been reached. The only thing you have to do to recognize your own enlightenment is wake up. You are one with the Creator and therefore you are one with all.*" He smiled a kind, Jesus smile and turned to leave (in the last few days he'd taken to watching sunset on his own. Nobody knew why but everybody accepted it). But, he had something left to say, and he whipped around so fast we all kinda jumped.

"*No! You are not one with all.*"

Everybody gasped (you could hear it on the tape) and his eyes just twinkled with what Nana used to call "mischief."

"*You ARE all. Already. You are God, devil, love, hate, good, bad, black, white, straight, gay, left, right, up, down, me, you. You are IT. ALL of it. Everything. Now. And all you have to do to realize this simple and extraordinary truth is...wake up.*"

He'd been walking around, kinda punching his words with little looks at each of us. He ended up, crouched down on his haunches right in front of Mrs. T.

We all just waited for her to start spouting those Christ guy versions of the Bible or talking "in tongues," which was always real weird. But she didn't. She laughed. I couldn't believe it and if you knew Mrs. T, you'd realize what a miracle *that* was. Then, we all laughed and we could tell that something inside us all was growing.

"*I...please....I....*" Mrs. T had calmed down from laughing (probably for the first time in her life) but she had one more question. He was still right there, hunkered down in front of her.

"*...I don't want to give up the...feeling,*" she whispered. You could tell she was fighting off tears. He just kept looking at her, kinder than ever, willing her to have the strength to speak her mind. I guess it worked, because she suddenly had all this power and she grabbed both his hands with hers.

"*I don't want to give up the feeling I get, the sense of being safe, the sense of being loved...by God. I want to feel that love. I don't want to believe that the feeling isn't real.*"

We all just sat there, sorta reaching back to touch our own feelings we'd had to give up. It's hard, especially when you feel all alone, to give up the last good thing in your life, even if it's a fairy tale. Even if it's a lie.

"*That feeling* is *real,*" he was as kind as a person can be without bursting into angels. "*That feeling is God.*"

It was a silence, without being stunned. He'd just given Mrs. T the biggest prize of her life. He'd given it to all of us. I knew he didn't believe in those Christ guys she watched all day on TV. I knew he didn't believe in all the judgments and real strict rules she was always coming up with on how everybody *else* should live. I guess this would of been his chance to teach her a real hard but true lesson. But, he didn't. He took what she was saying, looked way down deep inside her for the real meaning, and found a way to make her feel good about it. I think we all kinda fell in love with hymn that day.

"*Let's try this,*" he was still in front of Mrs. T, looking her square in her eyes. "*Let's start a chain of love. Stop everything and for just one moment think of someone or something you love. Someone or something that makes you smile. For only one moment. Just that. Just love.*" He stopped and we all kinda closed our eyes and thought.

I thought about when I was a little kid and my mom and Nana took me to the Merry-go-Round at Griffith Park. It was the first time they let me ride alone. I must of been about four but I felt like a giant. I was high on the horse, wind in my face, waving a little victory wave to my two beautiful princesses who waved to me with nothing but love in their smiles.

When I came back to the reality of the roof, I looked around and saw that every single one of us was smiling—that inside kinda smile that's just too big to keep all hidden. JC was smiling biggest of all, like the teacher who watched his experiment work its magic. But, he wasn't done.

"*Now, go show one other person how to stop and love for only* two *moments. Ask them to show one other person...for* three *moments. Before you know it, the whole world will be transformed. And all before sunset.*" He turned and pointed west, to the most glorious red and purple and pink and gold sunset I'd ever seen.

It just felt like something very special had happened— some kinda magic that had no name. We all felt it. And we had all changed.

I was so full of love, I just couldn't help shouting, "*I think you should start your own religion!"*

Well, this one *was* that "stunned silence" Louis is always talking about. I felt like a fool and all that good feeling was starting to leak right out my feet. And Louis' good feeling must of been going south too, because he says, all sarcastic-like, *"And, would you call it…uh…Christianity?"*

Well, as you probably guessed, everybody just busted out laughing. They laughed real and hard and I kinda sank into the roof. It pissed me off, in an all-loving sorta way, because it was Louis and his Paul spiel at "Easter-Slash-Passover-add-in-Pagan-Chick" that got me started thinking about it.

I looked at hymn for rescue and, of course, he did.

"What would you call it?" Sometimes he could be so kind I wanted to cry. But, I had a good answer, one I'd been thinking about for a long time.

"Jesusism." Nobody was laughing now. They all were just staring at me and I felt like I should share what I'd been thinking. *"It would be just all the stuff* you *said, not what everybody thought you* should *of said."*

"I like it," he beamed. And with that, I found something I'd never had my whole life. Respect. Even though I was gonna screw up a lot more in my life, I knew from that moment on that I also wasn't gonna be the butt of *every* joke. It was a mighty feeling. And it was all because of hymn.

So, after the sunset, we all got the idea that it would be cool to find out what he had to say about all the stuff going on today. What wisdom did he have for the modern world and would it be the same as what he said before? So we decided to have a "coming out party" as Bernard would say.

At first it seemed like a friggin' great idea, like it was time the world knew he was back (I tried to get hymn to say, "I'll be bock" like Arnold but Louis made me stop). I mean, if this was the Second Coming, he had to start somewhere, right?

So, we decided to invite everybody in the neighborhood and the Earth Ladies wanted to invite some of their regular party people they thought should be in on all this. Well, that brought the total up to 60 or 70 people and the only place all of them would fit comfortably was through Louis' apartment to the roof. Everybody would pitch in with food or drinks or something but Louis said his contribution was letting everybody traipse through his apartment—yeah, hey big spender! The whole place came alive with excitement and everybody started talking and working together, even folks you wouldn't think would (like Bernard and Mrs. T). It was like graduation or something.

But, under all that new found love, I started getting a real bad feeling that this was not a good idea. You gotta understand that I knew some of us didn't believe he was Jesus, the *real* Jesus, but we really liked hymn and wanted to hear what he had to say.

Also, I think some people—like John Noman—wanted to catch hymn in something, like if he said non-Bible stuff or things that didn't jive with what we thought he *should* say. That's what I was most afraid of.

And, of course, that's exactly what happened.

Sermon on the Roof

So, practically everybody in the whole world was up there on our roof, traipsing through Louis' apartment and touching his books and looking at his stuff, and he was having a great time having conniptions and being all "irate." It made me wonder, though, how so many other folks (a helluva lot more than just "the 'hood" and Earth Ladies' party people we had invited) came to know about this little idea we had just hours before. There must of been over 200 people up there and they all seemed to know this guy was supposed to be the *real* Jesus. I was getting an ugly feeling some of them were gonna try to prove he wasn't.

I think Louis was a little nervous too because, as we stood there trying to take a head count, he leaned over to me and whispered, "It only takes one wrong word to turn a worshiping flock into a rioting mob."

The Earth Ladies had brought some chips and dip crap, all made of seaweed or something, and Ty and the Yins kicked in for a truckload of beer and soda. It looked like a lot to me, but Mrs. T and Bernard didn't think we'd have enough until Louis, of all people, reminded them of some breaded fish story from the Bible and for some reason that made everybody relax. Go figure.

Me, Ty, and the Earth Ladies had had to practically beg Bernard to come. He was still not real comfortable being around people he didn't know and he about had a stroke when he saw all the folks up there on the roof. He was wearing Angela's knitted thingy around his shoulders, like a security blanket, and he looked sorta like a little old lady who'd lost her rocking chair. When he saw all the people he started to turn and go back but it was Mrs. T who took his hand and guided him through the crowd. His eyes darted around and you could just tell that he was looking into every strange face to see if that was the face who'd attacked him.

There was a bunch of little old ladies there, all praying on their knees, with lacey things (what Mrs. T told me were "doilies") on their heads and beads that had JC on a cross hanging off the end—like he was bungee-jumping, for Christ's sake. Me and Ty and Louis checked around but nobody knew them or where they'd come from.

Old Alley Guy was there. I expected him to say, "It's coming" since that's all he'd been shouting for a couple of months but when he saw me he smiled a big, almost toothless grin and held up an orange, sorta like he was making a toast, and shouted, "Not your grandmother's Jesus!" and started laughing like a madman. I'm pretty sure he didn't mean *my* Nana but just nanas in general.

I found out later that Alley Guy was the only person JC had invited hymnself. Weird.

There was even a bunch of gang members that showed up. I didn't really know why they were there at all, to tell you the truth. I mean, they were all about fighting and being tough and loud and not sitting quiet and churchlike for anybody. But, believe it or not, it was Bernard who said, "All are welcome at the table of the Lord." We only had the one table, at the back of the roof, with all the drinks and food and crap on it, and it actually belonged to the Earth Ladies, but the gang guys were helping themselves to all the grub, so, I guess

202

Bernard was on the right track.

I knew the Delaneys wouldn't be there because they always went to camp at Lake Elizabeth for their family vacation this time of year. But, I was looking forward to all the great things I was gonna be able to tell Angela when she got back.

I was real surprised to see John Noman there. I couldn't believe he'd show his face after all the bullshine he'd been spreading around. And, since he kept saying JC was this terrorist who was gonna blow up all his believers, it didn't make a lot of sense for him to be "in range," if you know what I mean.

Noman actually brought a couple of teenybopper "surfer gals" with him (I guess to be *his* crowd of—two). He was dressed all in white and barefoot (the beach thing, dontcha know) and tossing his newly sun-streaked (outta the bottle) hair back and smiling like he'd just won the whole game. His teeth were bleached, to match his hair, and he definitely didn't look Middle Eastern anymore at all. I heard he'd been spending a lot more time down on Sunset and at the beach and I guess he needed to look the part. Yep, Noman was the real Hollyweird version of the Christ. Sunset Swami was in the house. Jackass.

So, here was practically everybody in L.A., all waiting for JC. And waiting. And waiting some more. And—well, what the hell could he be doing? I was kinda surprised he kept us all waiting like that, and I even started getting nervous that maybe he'd decided to split from all the pressure of finally having to *be* the real thing.

When he did come out, I was a little freaked to see hymn wearing the same stuff he'd worn when I first met hymn, stuff he hadn't ever worn since. That bad feeling came back but he caught my eye and gave me a wink, so I calmed down and tried to breathe.

Noman was sitting as far from hymn as he could get and not fall off the roof. He was making comments under his breath, making clucking noises, giggling with his posse of two—basically being a turd. I couldn't help thinking that this would be the final shutdown for Noman. Man, was I wrong.

So, JC finally came out and just kinda found this place to perch that was just perfect for hymn to see everybody and everybody to see hymn, and he just sorta started to talk so I flipped on the tape.

IN THE BEGINNING...

"*In the beginning was the Idea, and the Idea was with God, and the Idea was God. And the Idea was made Illusion and dwelt among us, and we beheld its fantasy. And as we beheld it we became it, and as we became it, we forgot it was just our imagination. And as we forgot our imagination, we forgot God. And as we forgot God, we forgot we* are *God, and so we fell from grace.*" He flashed a great big Jesus grin at everybody.

He didn't seem to get it but I could tell he was already bombing. It was like he'd been talking Chinese or something but the Yins didn't seem to understand hymn either. It was one of those uncomfortable moments when everybody shifts and coughs and looks at each other but they're too polite to actually tell hymn it was crap or just get up and leave.

I glanced at Noman. He raised his eyebrows like, "Is this what all the fireworks is about?"

Man, I could really hate that guy sometimes.

There was this real long pause with hymn just sitting

there grinning. All I could do was groan. I had no idea what the hell he was talking about or what he was doing. He just kept looking at everybody and grinning. Finally, after about a week, he decided to pick up the pace.

THE "BE" ATTITUDES

He looked at the Earth Ladies: "*You, who are unspoiled and natural and without pretension, who are open and inclusive and welcoming, you are really lucky, because you can,* and will, *connect with your true selves and there, within, you will find the Perfect Kingdom of God.*" They both sorta blinked real hard and gazed at hymn like he was that mirror in Snow White that had just told them they were the fairest of all.

He looked at Mrs. T: "*You who have known real loss, who have experienced great grieving and still managed to keep a small light shining in your darkest hour, you're really lucky, because that little light will lead you to true comfort, under-standing, and immeasurable laughter and joy.*" Mrs. T just looked back at hymn with the kindest face I'd ever seen on her. And then, without blinking, two giant tears just went falling right down her cheeks, and without any warning at all, she smiled. It was a real great moment.

He looked at Bernard: "*You, who are kind and gentle, who seek the deepest beauty in others, you are really lucky, for you shall always find true beauty, in your own precious heart, and in* all *those you encounter and, in this way, you shall know the secret mysteries of life and love.*" Bernard grabbed his hand and, real soft, put his cheek on it, like a kiss.

I started to choke up but just then I noticed Charlie kinda shifting and shaking his head. I don't think I would of picked it up at all except everybody else on the whole roof was sitting absolutely still.

He looked at Jimmy: "*You, who try to do the right thing, who seek truth, who struggle against your own bitterness and desire good for all, you are really lucky, because you will find the answers you have waited for and you will be filled with satisfaction.*" Jimmy looked like he'd won the lottery and Jimmy's mom was just beaming at hymn.

He looked at the Yins: "*You, who are compassionate, who demonstrate generosity and great humanity in all your dealings, you are really lucky, because you will find compassion and grace and blessings in all your endeavors.*" The Yins put their hands together, like in a prayer, and kinda bowed at hymn. Then they put their hands on each other's and smiled at each other. Louis always says the universal language is music. With JC, it was love.

He looked at Ty: "*You, who seek peace in everything you do, who offer genuine respect for those who cross your path, who turn away from violence and seek equality for all, you are really lucky, because you will always be known as a child of the Light.*" Ty stood up and grabbed hymn in one of those man-bear hugs. Then, he sat back down again real fast and kinda tried to hide the fact that he had to wipe his cheeks.

There was some quiet applause, like when you're in church and you're not sure if you're supposed to clap after the choir sings.

He looked at Louis: "*You, who have struggled with forgiveness and trying to be your best, and trying to see the best in others, and who are beginning to find that the true way to the divine is through happiness, you are really lucky, because you are discovering the Kingdom of Heaven is here...now.*" Louis put his head down, not like in shame, like in prayer. I started to choke a little again.

He looked at Charlie: "*And if you have been made fun of for your beliefs and you still stick to your deepest knowing, you will have your reward...and you will not have to wait. Some may tell you to try to live a good life in order to gain a reward at the end. But I tell you, living a good life IS the reward.*" Charlie just looked at hymn. He didn't look happy, but he hadn't ever since the Bernard thing. I couldn't figure it at all, but I had to stop worrying about it because it was my turn.

He looked at me, and I felt like I was gonna cry: "*And you, who are pure in heart, who are willing to* try *to see the best in everything, whose kindness and loyalty and love outshines the stars, you are the luckiest of all. Because kindness, loyalty, and love will be returned to you a thousand fold. You will see* and know *the best in everything. And that is God.*" I did cry, and I didn't even care that anybody saw.

There was a new energy on the roof and almost everybody seemed lighter and happier. It all felt real good.

"ILLUMINATED CONDIMENTS" — LOUIS

"*You all know that salt does not lose its flavor. Just so, once you know who you really are, once you know you already* are *in the Kingdom, you cannot lose that knowledge. No matter what you do or where you go, the certainty of your true self is always with you—you cannot lose your essence.*

"*And once you know who you really are, once you know you cannot lose your essence, a little light awakens within you. That kindled spark will grow and shine and will not only light your own path, but will also be an illumination and inspiration to others. You never need to preach. Simply let your own light shine, and do not try to hide it. When you try to hide the light, it will burn you, as any great fire will resist confinement.*

"You know, I'm not trying to change anyone's idea of right and wrong. I just came here to tell you that you never have to cheat yourself. Cheating yourself is really cheating others. And when you cheat others, you are doing irrevocable damage to yourself. There is no need for sacrifice or martyrdom. I just want you to know it is possible to live a life that truly fulfills the law of your heart. You can live a life of fulfillment."

He was on a roll now and I started to relax a little. The mood of the crowd was mellow, like a breeze, quiet and kind, and everybody seemed to be happy with what he was saying.

So, of course, Noman had to try to spoil it.

"THE PURITAN PENITENTIARY"—LOUIS
(WHATEVER THE HELL THAT MEANS—ME)

"*Is anger really the same as murder?*" Noman looked all pleased with himself, "smug" as Louis would say. I didn't know why, though, because it was a stupid question.

"*Well, it all depends on how you look at it, John. Anger, especially that irrational reaction from a threatened ego,*" (man, that was aimed right at Noman…yeah!), "*certainly damages the spirit. It kills, for that moment, the ability to shine. In the next moment, however, your spirit is whole and able to illuminate as always, and therein lies the immortal characteristic of spirit. But, do you want to waste one second, "murder" even one moment of opportunity to let your spirit soar? When you waste your precious spiritual energy on anger*" *and resentment, you experience a kind of hell.*

"Isn't it better to have a generous and loving flow of energy between you and all those you encounter? If you have a quarrel with someone, isn't it better to reconcile and let the communion between you continue unfettered? If you cannot concur, then it's better to agree to part ways, and wish each other well. Holding on to negative feelings can only drag down your energy level and restrict the ability to let your light shine."

Noman looked like he'd been slapped. I was totally jazzed, even though I knew I shouldn't be—being all pure in heart now, like he said. But, JC wasn't quite through with his speech, so I tried to let go of feeling good about Noman feeling bad!

"If, however, you feel you can't let go of this particular anger, accept it, and allow it to become an opportunity to empathize with those who take anger to its extreme. Before judging the murderer, use your own anger to look in your own heart, investigate your own soul. Have you ever been enraged? Can you see how others would act out in those moments and lose control?

"I am not telling you to excuse murder—any murder, any killing is the deepest wound to the spirit. What I am saying is that every negativity can be turned around and can become a kind of instruction for your own heart. Instead of judging others, you can use that same energy to understand them. The opportunity exists for you to see the worst murderer as your brother or sister. Once you realize that everyone is 'family,' you can move forward with an empathetic heart, understand the deep pain the rage has come from, and endeavor to see past the act to the actor. I challenge you to see beyond what upsets you, to the pure soul created by the Father. It's there. It may be hiding under the rubble of a broken life, but it's there.

Find it. Start there. And, while you are seeking the goodness in others, I promise you, you will find the goodness in your own heart."

The whole time JC said that last part, Noman just sat there looking at his fingernails. It was weird—Noman being quiet and listening—so I didn't trust that that was what was happening. I got the feeling he had a plan, and he was gonna push it forward no matter what JC said. Noman had to know by now that his "plans" didn't work with hymn. But, for some reason, he kept on, like he just couldn't get enough of having his nose rubbed in his own mess.

"Is lust really the same as adultery?" If anybody could figure out why Noman was asking such stupid questions, it wasn't me.

"Of course not. In the old days, this statement referred exclusively to a married woman and a man who was not her husband or her intended. Today, if we view this principle with deep understanding, John, we can see that what we're talking about is commitment. And the sacred bond of love. It's not something that would cause you to struggle or yearn. True love is a wonder and, as I've seen, a rarity. If you are blessed enough to find it, then nothing *could turn you from it. But, don't confuse sexual desire with love. So much agony has come into the world from that misunderstanding. Within the embrace of true love, sexual desire is holy. Without love, it is lust, a purely physical reaction to a pleasant stimulus. And although that might be very exciting, it isn't love. All broken hearts come from this confusion. If love is true, then it is always sacred. There is no error. There is no sin."*

"No sin....No SIN?" It was pretty clear that Noman thought he finally had his opening. *"How can you say there is no sin?"*

He'd jumped up and was shouting, waving his arms around to make sure everybody noticed him and was listening to him. It was pathetic. But it made me nervous.

THE ONLY COMMANDMENT

"*I think what you're calling sin is actually error or ignorance, John. There are errors in our bodies, and we call that dis-ease; in our minds, we call it mental illness; error or ignorance in our hearts, we call it hate or rage; and ignorance of our true spirits, we call that—ego. And ego is simply holding on to the illusion of separation from the Creator. These are not sins, right, John?*"

JC had been slowly making his way through the crowd toward Noman when Alley Guy shouted, "*There's sin in every blessing! B-l-e-s-S-I-N-g!*" And then he started laughing his crazy profit laugh. "*Sin in every b-l-e-s-S-I-N-g!*" JC smiled at him and put a hand on his head, like a blessing—without the sin.

Noman had been backing himself up, trying not to let anybody see that he was backing up, but now, there was no place else for him to go. JC got right up to him and went on talking.

"*When we see something as sinful, John, we try to avoid it, or fight it, or ignore it, or destroy it. But it always comes back. This* idea *of sin has become indestructible and has plagued generations of kind and devout people. It has outlived every single one of these lonely souls who have spent their entire lives attempting to outrun it.*

"*And societies continue to confuse the 'sinner' with the 'sin.' They endeavor to beat, torture, or burn sin out, destroying innocent, precious lives...and themselves.*

"On the other hand, John, if we see these same actions as errors or ignorance, we can learn from them, understand them, and correct them. Once this correction is sewn into the fabric of humanity, we never have to be troubled by that error again. It is eradicated. It is gone.

"If there is any evil or sin at all, it is fear. From fear comes all of what we call sin." He paused and looked around. Then he walked back to his perch.

You could tell who all the real religious folks were because they all looked pretty upset. I mean, sin is the "main product of religion and fear is its CEO," according to you-know-who (Louis).

But there were also a lot of folks, like the Earth Ladies and Bernard, who looked kinda relieved. Like they'd always thought they might be good under all the sinning they might be doing, and suddenly here was Jesus, seeing them for what they had always hoped they were—good, kind, loving people.

Noman wasn't having any of it, though. Noman couldn't be the Messiah if he didn't have people to scare into believing he could take away their sins. And here, JC had just given everybody the power to do that all by themselves, at least the way I understood it. That made Noman mad.

"What about murder, and rape, and stealing? You don't think those are sins?" Noman was hysterical.

"What has caused those things, John? Why did that person kill, or rape, or steal? Have you ever asked why? Remove anger, remove powerlessness, remove need, remove fear and these things are gone.

"Basically, all of what you call sin only comes from harming others or yourself. That's it. So, you've made it very easy for us, and we can solve it all with only one commandment:

Do No Harm. Do no harm, John, and you cannot sin."

It seemed simple enough to me…sorta like The Ten Commandments—downsized. I was gonna try to think of a reason why that wouldn't work, but, as you know, I don't much like thinking. I thought for sure Noman would start a big ruckus, but he suddenly sat down and got real quiet. Looking back now, I see he was actually trying to copy hymn, and the way he was always kinda quiet and calm.

THE MUSTARD SEED CHALLENGE

"*Okay, Great One,*" Noman said, with a lot of nasty sarcasm, "*speak to us of faith. Surely you don't disbelieve that by your faith you are saved, do you? By your faith* alone. *All Christians know that.*"

"*Faith, John, has to manifest in action. It is what you do and how you live. You can't just sit back and say you believe something and then not act on that belief. Those who profess to have faith and then act in error, knowing full well what they are doing, are hypocrites. You cannot have faith without action. You cannot commend your spirit to a loving Creator without good deeds. Action is the very foundation of any faith. By your works you shall be saved, John. By your actions.*"

Noman looked away from hymn, but you could tell he was still listening. JC turned and talked to the whole crowd.

"*Don't look for faith to change a bad situation you've created. Faith changes you. And, don't idly pray for the Creator to correct the error in others. Look to yourself first. Correct your own errors. Then, as you change* yourself, *you become a beacon of inspiration to others. That is how you* change things."

JC turned back to Noman and said, "*That is what faith is for, John…to ACT.*"

Noman was on his feet again, "*That's blasphemy!*"

JC sat down, "*That's truth.*"

There were a few shouts of "Blastfoamy" from the crowd and a couple of the scarier looking guys jumped up, like they were itching for a fight. Ty popped up too, and so did Louis. It made me laugh, even though it wasn't funny, but I can be very inappropriate sometimes. Ty can look scary too, when he tries, so everybody went quiet and sat down again. Ty stood there a few more seconds, just to make sure everybody understood this wasn't gonna be a rumble, and then he sat back down.

I got the biggest kick out of how Ty was always watching out for hymn. It was like one of those old gangster movies from the beginning of time. Ty was like Humphrey Bogart or Jimmy Cagney, watching out for his best pal.

WHAT'S GOD *REALLY* LIKE?

After waiting about a year for Noman to sit down too, Louis decided to "redirect" the conversation and I think everybody was glad he did. "*Why don't you talk to us about God? What, in your experience, is the nature of God?*"

There was one of those shifts, when everybody sits forward and it makes that "we're interested" sound.

"*God is power, not person. God is everything perceived and everything invisible. God is billions and billions of different expressions of the same Idea. God's mind is Creator; God's heart is Father.*"

"Why does God seem so different in the Old Testament than in the New?" Like I told you, Jimmy had read the new part of the Bible, which I hadn't. He was always checking out ideas from other people and I think that's what's gonna make him a good Rabbi.

"Because we *are different, Jimmy. Each generation creates an* image *of God to suit their needs. Each tells the story for their own time, in their own words and experiences. Because of this, God appears to grow in reverse and closer.*

"To Moses, God was an old patriarch, rigid, angry, and distant. Two thousand years ago, He was a father, loving and forgiving. Today, a youth, wild and unpredictable. Tomorrow, His birth, a flash of holy light and the perception of any distance between Creator and Creation will be shattered. Our understanding of God becomes complete and He becomes, in truth, everything. He becomes us."

Everybody was all nodding and looking like they were really digging this part of the story—everybody but Charlie.

"If God is on our side, why do all these terrible things keep happening?" It was almost like Charlie was baiting hymn, which wasn't like Charlie.

"God is not on our side, Charlie. There are no sides with God."

THE CHRIST-LIKES

Charlie stood up kinda quick, like to make a speech or something. I just can't tell you how unlike Charlie that was.

"What the hell do you mean?" he shouted. *"What about Christians?"*

All of a sudden it felt like our reality had somehow gotten

all mixed up with somebody else's or we'd suddenly switched to some other movie without any warning at all.

"*God's on the side of Christians, right?*" I just couldn't believe Charlie was acting like that. "*If God is the God of all, aren't Christians the ones who should be showing everyone else about 'the true religion,' as John calls it? Shouldn't Christians be at the head of it all, you know, like* in charge *of the world or something?*"

It wasn't until that very minute that I realized that Charlie even knew Noman. It got that bad feeling going again.

JC paused, for just a second. "*Let me ask you something, Charlie. What sort of Christian are you? Are you a noun or a verb?*"

Charlie looked confused and, after a glance to Noman, he sat back down. I thought it was a bad move, picking at Charlie. He'd been twitching and itching in his seat ever since things got off that main "dogma" highway, as Louis would say.

"*What I mean is this,*" JC continued. "*If you say of yourself, I am 'a' Christian, that would be a noun. 'A' Christian is a title, and doesn't require any action or interaction at all.*"

Nobody made a peep.

"*But Christian—the word Christian—means Christ-like. Louis tells me that's an adjective.*"

Not a sound.

"*Now, let's make it a verb. I believe it is within our power to make* Christian *an action word.*"

I think he could tell nobody could understand a thing he was saying, so, like the good teacher he was, he settled down on his haunches, right in front of Charlie, and tried like hell to put the final pieces in the puzzle.

"*So, let's use the word* Christian *to describe what you DO. Do you live your faith to help and serve others?*"

Well, yeah, there was that whole hot-wiring deal.

"*Do you accept all without judgment? Do you produce the fruits of love from your heart?*"

Charlie *was* a ladies' man.

"*Does your light shine before all? Do you recognize the right thing to do, and do it, no matter what the current social convention or fad? Do you stand with your brother and sister, even when that's not convenient for you? Do you rededicate your spirit, every day, to the joyous task of finding good in this weary world? Do you make it a daily intention to forgive others, and yourself, of all the errors and ignorance in your life?*"

I thought he was asking a lot. I mean, who does all that?

"*The Spirit of Christ is in us all. Every single soul is anointed in the eyes of God. Do you see yourself in each face you encounter, in the eyes of every homeless person who crosses your path? And do you treat that soul-family member accordingly?*"

I was starting to 'get' that JC meant we should act like hymn. *He* did all those things, every day. But, I had some serious doubts that just regular folks would even wanna try.

"*Do you ACT, Charlie? Do you ACT like Christ? You can be so much more than you've even dreamed. Don't be satisfied to be a card-carrying* noun. *Say 'I am* Christian.' *Be a verb, Charlie. Act.*"

JC smiled, but it wasn't the great big Jesus smile. It was the kinda smile you do when your kid has been lying to you and you know it but you love them and you don't wanna make them feel any worse than they already do.

ONWARD CHRISTIAN SOLDIERS

"*I don't know what the hell you're talking about.*" Charlie shot up again and was acting real upset. It was strange because I completely agreed with him. I mean, I didn't know what the hell JC was talking about either. But I wasn't pissed about it.

Everybody was like whispering to each other. I guess they were trying to decide what part of speech they were. But Charlie seemed all nervous, showing his jaw muscles, like a fighter doing that dance thing they do before they knock the other guy's block off.

"*What do you want from us? I don't get where you're coming from. What the hell do you want?*" Charlie sat down real quick, and I could tell from the catch in his voice that he was about to cry.

JC looked at Charlie with all the love I'd ever seen hymn look. "*I want you to excel, to be your very best self. I want you to grow up, spiritually, to equal my understanding, to surpass my achievements, to be your own messiah. You don't need me to tell you what to do, Charlie. You don't need anyone else. That little light in your soul knows the way. Let it shine. I want you to understand me, not praise me. I want you to emulate me, not worship me. I want your spirit to be free, free from error.*

"*Each person has their own spiritual path. Their very own. You cannot borrow or steal from another's spirit or path. But finding your own path can be hard work. Sometimes it will feel like it would just be easier to walk someone else's path. After all, if they're on a path already, it's perceivable. Stepping out in faith onto a path you cannot see can be a terrifying prospect. This is the hard work. Trusting the path is there and not looking around to see where everyone else is and which way they're going. Keeping your eyes on your own path is hard. Walking it is easy. Walking your own path is what you are here to do.*

"*Charlie, you must begin by loving yourself, as I love you. To love yourself is not to idolize some trait or quality or even personality but rather to cherish that mysterious core, that breath of life, that part of God within. It is to love your Self. There is no ego involved. It is worship of the highest order. It is direct communion with the Infinite. Knowing that, in truth, all selves are Self. In this way, love others as your Self.*"

That was all it took to get Noman back on his feet.

"*What do you mean all selves are Self?*" Noman asked, kinda loud. "*You're not even making any sense. In the Bible, you yourself said there is only one God, and He is in Heaven. There is only one Messiah, and He is the Way to God. There is no way we 'commune' with God without that Messiah to show us the Way.*"

Well, Noman sure did know the pecking order of God and stuff.

"*John,*" JC suddenly looked and sounded tired, like the last two thousand years just all of a sudden caught up with hymn. "*Every single one of God's children has a direct and imperishable connection to the Creator. They do not need you. And they do not need me.*"

There was a gasp from everybody, like we *were* all one and we all thought to inhale at the same time.

"*You must see…*" he shot a quick look at Louis. "*You must see* through *the messengers to perceive the message. Believe you have the power to help yourself—even all mankind—and as you believe, so it shall be. It's good for everyone to think of themselves as a son or daughter of God and as you believe, so it is. There is no need for anything, or* anyone, *else.*"

It just kept getting worse. I couldn't understand why he

was doing this—making hymnself sound more like Alley Guy than Bible Jesus.

SECOND STAR TO THE RIGHT...

"The Kingdom of God is like....like a radio." He lost about half of them with that. Eyes started rolling and folks started checking their watches. Some of the girls even started giggling. Noman was doing his own beaming now. But Mrs. T seemed like she liked it, I guess because she has one of those old radios that's as big as a house with about a million tubes and lights and crap.

"The radio's not always on, but the frequencies are always there, ready and waiting. The radio might not appear to be working until someone comes along and turns a knob, tunes in the station, and suddenly you become aware of the connection. It was there all along. Someone just had to tune it in. That's the only reason for a messiah, to help tune you in to what's already there."

Weird.

"Then, what's the difference between the Kingdom of God and the Kingdom of Heaven?" Raindrop hardly ever said anything so I was real happy she felt strong enough to ask the question in front of all those people.

"The Kingdom of God is within you. The Kingdom of Heaven is what you make of the Kingdom of God."

"Paul said to put away childish things but you said we had to be as little children. Can you explain this difference?" Mrs. T looked all worried, like she didn't want to offend hymn, but she was still harping on the Paul thing.

"Let go of childishness—not childhood." He smiled at her

220

and she smiled back.

Several hands popped up, like in school. JC looked at the ocean of questions and seemed a little sad.

"*The answers you seek you already know. The guidance you're looking for is, ultimately, all from within.*" The hands went down and, even though I think a lot of folks wanted real bad to ask hymn questions, everybody was still interested enough to sit still and listen…for a while.

"*When you hear the truth, something in you resonates. You feel it. Whether or not you agree with it, you cannot deny that it strikes a chord that produces an actual physical sensation. So when you ask for advice, if it feels right, you do it. If not, you probably don't. That feeling is your inner guide. If the feeling agrees with the advice, you do it. But without that feeling, that confirmation, it goes in one ear and out the other. The guidance is within. The guide is YOU.*

"*If I say something profound and you react, who has done the moving? Who has done the feeling? Who takes the action? YOU! Truth, wisdom, spiritual guidance are all useless without the receptor. That's you. You take what I give and you use it. You create, you act, you decide, you just sit and meditate. But it is all you. I have given you only a series of random words. You have created the feeling, the movement, the action. You have, indeed, even created the inspiration by setting up the interaction between us.*" He put his arms out, to include the whole roof. "*You did it. You are the receptor and the received. You recognize the truth and thereby bring it to life. You. Your own guide. Own messiah. Own God.*"

Well, he was losing 'em fast. He was doing okay until he got to that 'own God' part. Nobody wants to be their own God, for Christ's sake. What was he thinking?

Noman was about to have a seizure. "*How can you say*

that? These people need a messiah, a real leader, someone to tell them what to do." Yep, there was no more hinting. Old John Noman was in full campaign-mode for Messiah of the Day.

"Messiahs are not here to lead you back to a place you never left, John." I'd never seen hymn look so "bone weary," as my Nana used to say. *"Messiahs are here to gently nudge you and whisper, 'Wake Up! Remember who you really are.'"*

THE GOLDEN...SUGGESTION

Autumn, in what I think was her stab at trying to help and get things back on track, asked hymn, *"What about the Golden Rule? Should we do unto others as we would have them do unto us?"*

He looked almost angry or shocked or something and I couldn't figure out what was going on with hymn. *"How would they know! How do you know?*

"Here's this *century's 'Golden Rule' for you: We can only know what works for us. Therefore, we must let others know how to 'do unto us' without imposing our will on them. As far as how we treat others—'Do No Harm' is your guideline. Do not assume you know what others want or need. Let kindness and compassion dictate your interactions. When you treat each living thing with love and respect, you are consciously dwelling in the Heart of God. Only good can come from that."*

Everything was dead quiet. I couldn't even hear the traffic. Something was changing, and not in a good way. People were looking at each other like he'd suddenly started talking Greek. But he didn't seem to notice at all. This guy, this messiah, with all his understanding and love and crap like that, was in his own world and I started wondering if I was gonna be able to get hymn out of *this* world without a bruise or two.

THE "OH, LORD!" PRAYERS

Mrs. T must of taken some sorta pity on hymn and, sensing the mood, tried like hell to bring things back to earth.

"Won't you lead us in the Lord's Prayer?" she whispered —like her being quiet would somehow calm down the rest of the crowd.

He looked a little dazed for a minute, almost like he was gonna faint. I started to move closer, in case he was gonna fall. Then, he lowered the boom:

"Of course.

"By acknowledging that we have ALL been created in the Mind of God, we confess our Union and Kinship with every living being as we say,

Our Creator
Which dwells within us, around us, and through us,
everywhere and all at once
Glorious is Your Imagination
May every being awaken to Your Reality
May Your loving, perfect Ideal continue and flourish
In all Your billions of earthly hearts and minds
We thank You each day for providing all our spiritual needs
And we know forgiveness is a gift we give ourselves and others
as we learn the lessons of our errors
Lead us toward Your complete Understanding
And deliver us to Your Infinite Comprehension
For Yours is the Perfect Idea
And the Ultimate Perception

> *And the Glorious All-that-Is*
> *Forever*
> *Amen"*

It got worse. The roof looked like one of those old time photos of people in a movie theater, all with their mouths open because they couldn't believe what they were seeing.

"But, I prefer another prayer, Mrs. T, a prayer that is hidden from all those who don't know where to look for it. It was put in the Psalms and, when you know the secret, it is a complete instruction for total communion with God.

> *Be still and know that I AM God*
> *Be still and know that I AM*
> *Be still and know*
> *Be still*
> *Be."*

Well, he'd lost 'em all. Not one single person there was nodding or smiling or doing anything that would make you think they knew what the hell he was talking about. I felt so sorry for hymn, but I was also getting pissed. I mean, he *had* to know what he was doing. He had to know he was losing them. Couldn't he tell that nobody understood anything he was saying? But, he actually seemed all jazzed to be sharing these supposedly great ideas, even though he was like speaking *Braille!* Why did he do it? I just didn't know.

THE HARD PART ABOUT BEING GOD

"This prayer shows the way. This prayer will lead you to the very heart of God's Mind." He just plowed ahead, all excited, like he didn't know he was barreling right for the cliff.

"You see, at each step of the prayer, the Creator takes you

deeper and closer to your Source. 'I AM' is our ego's way to consciously identify with, and as, God. Therefore, when you say 'I AM' sick, you are essentially saying God is sick!

"When God gave His name to Moses, He said, 'I AM'. If society dictates that we, by tradition, take our earthly parent's name, then in spirit, by nature, we take our Heavenly parent's name every time we refer to ourselves. I AM...good. Kind. Loving. What might appear to be conceit or gratification of the ego, might just as easily be praise of God.

"Here is proof: When God said to Moses, 'Tell them I AM sent you,' he provided the way for each of us to realize our own divinity. When Pharaoh questioned, 'What God sent you? Who is this God?' Moses had to say 'I AM.' Just imagine the shock that must have caused! Who is God? I AM. This simple statement though, when understood as the conscious identification of the ego-self with God, sets into motion our realization of co-creation with the Divine and, therefore, our self-responsibility AS *the Divine."* He looked tired but satisfied, like he'd finally been able to explain trigonometry to a toddler.

It was like watching a terrible, bloody accident. You wanna stop it, but it has its own "momentum," as Louis would say. Everybody on that roof just looked dazed and confused. They couldn't understand hymn. I couldn't understand hymn. Not even Louis could understand hymn.

Not once in the whole time we'd been hanging out had he ever talked like this—like every time I say 'I am' I'm somehow being God and better be friggin' careful what I say. I mean, who the hell can be GOD? It was like a real clever suicide, one you can't predict because the person keeps smiling at you the whole time they're slitting their throat.

L. A.'S ROCKIN' COSMIC TIME MACHINE
—OR—
WHAT IF YOU COULD ASK JESUS ANYTHING?

I knew we had to get hymn back to this world—but how? I looked at Louis but he was just sitting there with his mouth open. I thought, what would bring all this New Age crap back around to something all these real religious folks would love and, like a flash, I had it.

"*What about Purgatory?*"

I didn't know what that even meant but I'd heard Charlie mention it about a million times so I knew it was something he really liked.

"*What's Purgatory?*" JC said.

I thought Charlie was gonna mess himself. Jesus didn't know. *HE* didn't seem to know any of this crap. And he was supposed to be the guy who invented it all.

There started to be this kinda restless movement, like right before a storm. And suddenly, questions started coming, fast and furious, one right on top of the other. JC barely had a chance to breathe, let alone think.

I was grateful, in a way, because it got hymn out of the Purgatory mess, but I was holding my breath every time he opened his mouth to answer.

Q: "*What about not getting into the Kingdom of Heaven if you're rich?*"

A: "*Find a way to serve spirit with your money, and you will create your own heaven right here on earth.*"

Q: "*2,000 years later, would you change any of your teachings to fit the day?*"

A: "*I've found that what was said so long ago has been altered and colored to fit the time, and the needs, of those in*

226

power. This is not truth. The truth is the same now as it was then. Love God. And love others as yourself. In the truest essence of reality, all are one and all are God. It's very simple. It's all about love."

Q: *"How accurate are the quotes attributed to you in the New Testament?"*

A: *"Not very."*

Q: *What about women…especially in the church? You can't believe they have the same rights as men.*

A: *Of course they do! The Creator sees no differences in any of the Children of God. Gender is simply the definition of reproductive organs, not status. I can tell you truly, that the Creator sees each soul as whole, complete, equal. The physical personification of these souls—whether skin color, facial features, or gender—matters not at all. All are precious, and equal, in the sight of God.*

Q: *"How do you feel about all the wars in your name or those who cheat, use, kill, or abuse others in your name?"*

A: *"I'm sure you know the answer to that. I am horrified that any life has been harmed in my name. No harm—ever—was for me. And, no one speaking* for me, *has ever asked for or condoned any harm. I have always been very clear. Love is the answer. Love is truth. Love is strength. No harm can come from that. Any war, anything that causes harm, cannot be from God. God does not take sides in a war. God is Love."*

Q: *"Do we have to face temptation in order to truly understand it?"*

A: *"Temptation is a part of learning. How you choose to learn from it is what determines if it is considered error. If you apply the idea of Do No Harm, you will not allow temptation to take you down any road that would harm yourself or others. It is very simple."*

Q: "*But weren't you tempted by Satan? Isn't there a real Devil?*"

A: "*When wrestling with moral concepts, occasionally they are easier to understand if we personify the polarity of the ideas. Some thoughts are easier to express when given a 'nature' to identify them. In our imagination, that thought-form can take hold. A devil is just another tool for blaming something or someone else. Having a Satan allows us to avoid responsibility.*"

Q: "*What does it mean to be good?*"

A: "*Good is simply the absence of error. Being good is being God.*"

Q: "*Why don't you answer all prayers?*"

A: "*I don't answer* any *prayers. You answer your own prayers. And sometimes the answer is no.*"

Q: "*Wait…what? I prayed for it and then told myself no? That makes no sense.*"

A: "*When you are asleep to your true identity, you feel there is some 'other' divinity answering your prayers, or denying you the desires of your heart. When you awaken to your authentic Self, you will discover that, based on your previous belief in an other-directed life, you have actually denied and sabotaged yourself. Based on this erroneous belief-system, you, indeed, told yourself 'No.' *"

Q: "*Is there really a hell?*"

A: "*We make our own hell, right here on earth.*"

Q: "*Why isn't grace for everyone?*"

A: "*Grace IS for everyone. Grace is not a power tool, used to control people. Grace is a state of love, to which everyone is born.*"

Q: "*Does it embarrass you to have your birthday so celebrated?*"

A: *"What my friends have shown me has so little to do with why I came—nothing to do with my message. I suggest, if you wish to honor me as your friend, take that day to love each other. Then take every day, to love each other. That would be the way to remember me."*

Q: *"What's next?"*

A: *"I have no idea."*

Q: *"Why do we fear death if we know where we're going?"*

A: *"We fear losing our ego. We have identified with these forms we use, these bodies, and we believe they are us. We fear losing our personalities. We forget who we are. We forget we are the ocean, not the wave."*

Q: *"Then, why did you fear it in the Garden of Gethsemane?"*

A: *"I, too, forgot."*

Q: *"How is it you're here at all?"*

A: *"I have no idea."*

Q: *"What do you think of the decree of celibacy?"*

A: *"It is not necessary in order to lead a spiritual life. In my time, all of my friends had wives and husbands. Some may feel that the choice of celibacy enhances their spiritual pursuits. It is up to the individual. But, it is not required."*

Q: *"What do you think of capitalism? Is it like Rome?"*

A: *"I don't know. I do know that it doesn't seem to serve everyone and therefore, is not the best system for all. The ultimate system will be when every citizen has what they need to live a life of happiness."*

Q: *"Will the world end?"*

A: *"Someday, I suppose."*

Q: *"Is global warming a punishment from God for us sinning or not praying enough?"*

A: *"The thoughtless destruction of our beautiful earth is*

not from God. It is the manifestation of greed and the thought process that perceives the self as separate. Our home is being 'punished' by a lack of care, not a lack of prayer."

Q: *"What about saying prayers in school?"*

A: *"Have you found a way to honor every holy child and their beliefs in your schools? Every question, thought, or doubt, when earnestly and truthfully presented, is a holy endeavor. Breathing is holy. Living is holy. There is no time, whether in school or out, that you are not allowed to live your holiness. You do not have to mandate a time to commune with your Creator. If your laws say you must separate church and government, so be it. You needn't make a show of your prayers. Prayers are not for demonstrating your great respect for the Creator. Prayers are not for public illustration of your faith. Prayer is between you and your Source. I promise you, God is not on a timetable. Your Creator knows your heart and does not need constant reminders. Prayer is not for you to tell God. Prayer is your silent, private opportunity to listen."*

Q: *"Do you think we will crucify you again?"*

A: *"Probably."*

Q: *"Can you explain about not worrying? How can we not worry?"*

A: *"No amount of worrying can make it better. No amount of happiness can make it worse."*

Q: *"I don't understand all this New Age, self-love talk. Didn't you say to love God first?"*

A: *"I said to love God with all your heart and all your soul and all your mind. Love God with your entire being, with everything you are, as a human child of the Universe—with your very essence. When you love God in this way, you create within yourself a force of love that cannot be diminished or overcome. Then, wake up to your true nature. Open your eyes* and mind and heart to the truth that you ARE Love. When you realize you are Love, you realize you are God."

Q: "Tell us just one thing we can do, something you said in the Bible, that will put us on the right path."

He looked heavy, like all the whole world was on his back. Nobody had gotten anything he'd tried to teach. But he didn't have to piss them off.

A: "Be perfect."

Everything stopped. Be perfect? Yeah. Well, he'd lost the politicians, the Catholics, the pagans, and the Jews. I didn't think he could do much more harm to hymnself.

"And," damn, he wasn't done yet, "turn the other cheek. Those two things, from the Bible, as you say, would put you on the right path. To be perfect is to recognize that you are one with God. To turn the other cheek forces those who oppose you to face their own spiritual identity, to recognize the divinity in all life. Life is what we all have in common. Life is sacred. Turning the other cheek dis-empowers a violent heart."

He'd gone completely bonkers. I didn't think we could bring hymn back.

PUTTING CHRIST BACK IN CHRISTIAN— THAT ONE ORIGINAL IDEA

Louis stood up and shouted over all the other questions. "If you could sum up all of your teachings in one sentence, what would it be?" I know Louis was trying to be helpful and "suck-sinked," or whatever that word is that means…whatever it means, but it hit me, all of a sudden, that we should be looking for escape routes, instead of getting hymn to talk more.

"Love your enemies."

Well, as you can probably guess that didn't go over very big with all the different fractions we had there. I mean, there were gang members, for Christ's sake. We had Christians and Jews and Muslims and Buddhists. We had the JC bungee-jumping, doilies-on-their-heads old ladies on their knees. And we had Alley Guy. We had folks from every kind of life, and most of them had never gotten along very well with each other. Ever. It was hard enough to love yourself. Then he adds neighbors, which even at The Ark could be real tough sometimes. But, to add enemies—it just didn't make any sense. What about Noman? He couldn't mean him too.

"What does that mean? You don't mean everyone..." Charlie looked a little funny and I was pretty sure he had an idea of who he thought were his hard-to-love enemies.

"Everyone."

"WHY?" Charlie jumped up and actually yelled at hymn. It was like he suddenly had to stretch his legs and check to see if his lungs still worked.

"Because it is truth."

"Yeah, well who decides the truth?" Charlie wasn't one for speaking up like that and I was kinda surprised he did. There were some real disrespectful comments from the crowd but I couldn't tell whose side they were on. It wasn't a good sign.

JC waited a second and everything went quiet. Looking back, I realize he stopped like that because he knew what was about to happen and he had to decide if he was gonna "drink from that cup"—again.

"You do. You decide the truth, Charlie, and you will know when you hear it. Too often, people won't listen to the truth, because they don't like the package."

"*So, love everyone?*" Charlie was real riled up. "ALL *our enemies?*" It seemed like he had somebody in mind, but I didn't know who. "*They all get a free pass no matter what they've—*"

"*Charlie,*" JC was quiet and loving. "*When you love your enemy, you won't have any enemies.*" He was so kind I didn't think it would be possible to stay mad at hymn. Charlie thought different.

5 SECONDS TO SELF-DESTRUCT

It got so quiet I actually thought I could hear the ocean. Then I realized it was the pounding of my own heart in my ears. I glanced around real quick but, I couldn't tell what anybody was thinking or feeling. Everybody had these kinda blank expressions that didn't tell you anything about what was going on inside. It should of made me feel better, I mean at least nobody was yelling or screaming or pulling out guns or killing or anything. But I still had this crazy, sick feeling like the end of the world was about to happen and I was the only poor schmuck who knew it.

JC just wouldn't shut up like would of been smart. He kept going on, trying to reach old Charlie, who was about as far away from loving everybody as anybody could be.

"*Charlie, the Creator wants all His children to love one another. Everyone is precious to Him. You can see that, can't you?*"

"*Are you saying God is okay with queers?*" Charlie had lost it now. And once Charlie blew, Noman pounced. He agreed, out loud, with every hateful thing Charlie was saying. He really egged him on.

"*Are you really trying to tell me that fairies and fags and dykes are going to heaven? That all these homos and queer pansy queens can just run around poking everybody and God doesn't think that's a sin?"* Well, Charlie sure knew a lot of words for gay.

"I'm telling you..." JC paused. He was real quiet now and I wasn't sure then but looking back I know this was the beginning of his "desperate frustration." I was surprised that it started from such a place of calm. *"I'm telling you, Charlie, that the Creator loves ALL of His children. I'm telling you that God looks at every heart and knows His sons and daughters by the contents of those hearts. I'm telling you that there is not one expression of real love that could ever offend the Creator."*

When JC said God loves everybody and couldn't be offended by real love, Charlie literally jumped up and down and Noman clucked, "No, no, no!"

Some of those big bad-ass guys started kinda hooting and catcalling, like they were gonna have some kinda word-rumble, if they couldn't have the real thing. Bernard started crying, which didn't really help the cause, and he looked like he wanted to disappear. His eyes started darting around the crowd again, I think trying to guess who was gonna be his next bad dream. Our neighborhood gathering had become what Louis calls "a crowd with a purpose" and what the police call "a mob."

SO LET IT BE WRITTEN

JC stood up and the place went dead. And that sudden silence felt dangerous. When he started talking again, it was the loudest I'd ever heard hymn. He was almost yelling. It was like there was something inside hymn, just straining to get out, and it was so big even his veins and skin couldn't hardly hold it. His eyes were black and scary. Kind, sad, soft-voiced Jesus was pissed.

"I'm telling you, Charlie—I'm telling all of you—that a day will come when the very Spirit of the Universe will ask you, 'What have you done for the poor today? How many homeless have you sheltered? Have you ministered to the sick? In what way did you care for those souls caged in a prison of loneliness? When did you visit those in jail? And what did you feed the hungry?'

"Do you really presume to point out the flaws in others without first correcting your own errors? How can you dare to throw the stone of judgment at any *other soul until you have perfected your own nature? No—you don't want to be perfect because then you will have to let go of blaming, criticizing, and judging.*

"Are you really going to say to your God that you were too busy judging others and criticizing others and worrying about what others were doing in bed to help your fellow human beings?"

He sat back down on the perch, reached out, put a hand on Charlie's shoulder, and blew the whole day to hell.

"I'm telling you, Charlie, you don't need to anguish about moral and ethical questions like these. Your life is an opportunity to love and serve others. So, if homosexuals really bother you—don't frequent gay bars."

All hell broke loose. Everybody was up on their feet. Half of them were mad at hymn and the other half were trying to defend hymn. And everybody was screaming.

Bernard was crying again and the Earth Ladies were trying to comfort him. Jimmy was praying "Hashish, Hashish," with his hands and face in the air, and the Yins looked just plain terrified. Ty had put himself between the mob and hymn and Louis was trying to hold Charlie back. Noman was laughing, like the asshole he is. But Mrs. T was the one I couldn't figure. She was sitting on the edge of the roof, just watching the sunset, like nothing was going on at all.

I looked at hymn across all this insanity. He suddenly seemed very small, like a lost little kid. When he looked back at me, I just shook my head. The feelings I was having weren't good. Did he know all this was gonna happen? Why did he keep at Charlie like that? Why didn't he just let it slide?

I made my way across the roof. A real rumble was breaking out between JC supporters and all the rest of the folks who, I guess, really didn't wanna love their enemies. All the boxes and crates we'd hauled up to the roof for people to sit on were being thrown around and I had to duck a few times. There were a lot of hateful things being shouted and some real threats being made. I even thought I saw the flash of a blade. The rest of the people were running away, down the stairs, into the street, screaming all the way. It was crazy.

But I kept my eyes on hymn. I had something to say, and I wanted to make sure he heard it.

The Point

"*Let's take a walk.*"

I couldn't believe how mad I was at hymn. He could of had all those people in the palm of his hands. But he *chose* to screw it all up. He had to know that saying all that stuff would upset everybody.

The roof had cleared, the rumble had moved somewhere else. I turned away from hymn and walked down the stairs to the street. I kept walking, knowing he was right behind me. After all the screaming on the roof, the street seemed quiet. I finally stopped in front of Delaney's. I didn't know it then, but the tape was still running in my pocket.

I turned around hard and fast, trying to make it clear how pissed I was. "*Frankly, man, you blew it. You made it too hard. Nobody can love his enemies. Nobody can be perfect. Nobody turns the other cheek or disembowels the violent heart. You were wrong, man. You misunderstood your audience. You thought you were talking to angels but we're just a bunch of lousy human beings.*"

Even after all this time he didn't get it. He'd taken his real annoying habit of always turning things back to you, and gone completely off the deep end. I couldn't even help myself now because I didn't have anything quiet to say so I just kept yelling at hymn.

"*All your New Age bullcrap backfired, man. And now I know that everything you ever said was bullcrap, and if you don't understand what I mean you can look it up for yourself because I'm goddamned tired of explaining every goddamned thing to you.*

"*What was all that sin talk about? What the* hell *did you think you'd prove by letting Noman look more like the Bible Jesus and you look like a New Age A...A....A-hole?*" I turned and walked a few steps away, struggling not to curse at hymn—I was that pissed.

"*NO,*" I practically screamed it as I whipped around to face hymn, "*I MEAN ASSHOLE.*" My eyes were stinging and my throat started choking. I couldn't believe I said that—not to hymn.

"*And no Devil? Are you friggin' insane? Most of us depend on that dude to try to make sense of all this CRAP! Look, I just want my dream-life back. I DON'T WANNA WAKE UP! How are we ever gonna get all those people back on the roof so you can explain it all to them or tell them you were just kidding?*" I could hardly catch my breath but I was getting madder and madder and I wanted to make sure he knew it.

"*Everybody says they wanna be in control, but, I swear to you, man, nobody wants to be in CHARGE. Especially of their own life. We all say we want freedom, but freedom's too hard. Absolutely nobody I know really wants to make a decision. NOBODY.*" I was just plain pissed off about hearing I already knew how to fix every damn thing wrong with me, when I didn't. I didn't at all! I couldn't understand why he'd said all those things he knew would piss everybody off.

"*How could you do that, man? Why should we believe you or listen to your BULLSHIT ever again?*" I yelled.

"*Don't,*" he was calm and kind, which just pissed me off more. "*Check it out for yourself. You will never find your* truth in someone else's story. You can't find out who you *are* by believing me or listening to me. I can't be your messiah. I'm not *your* messiah. You must find your way yourself."

"*Jesus Christ! I DON'T GET YOU!*" I screamed. "*I don't understand what the friggin' hell you're talking about! I NEVER understand what you're talking about.*"

He got down on his haunches, kinda leaning against the front of Delaney's store, and got all quiet, like he always did when things got a little crazy, "*You're guiding yourself by stars that have already burned out.*"

"*WHAT!?*"

"*Don't follow me. Follow your own truth, not mine.*"

I couldn't take it anymore. I exploded. I yelled and cursed and spit my awful words of anger and frustration at hymn with all the cuss I had in me. I even threw a rock against one of those metal doors people put all over their windows just to prove they don't trust you with rocks.

But I couldn't help it. I didn't even feel like me anymore. I started walking back to hymn, getting more pissed with every step. I got up so close to his face I could feel his breath. And then it all hit me.

"*Wait—*" I said it so loud and strong we both kinda jumped. My mind scrambled to make sense of this terrible, heart-crushing epiphone *I* was having.

"*You didn't even pick me, did you? I'm not special at all, am I? I was just the first stupid schmuck you saw when you came around that corner. All of this has been a friggin', lying, bullshit fairy tale, hasn't it?*"

It hurt me, deep, to say that to hymn. I didn't want to admit that he wasn't special because that would mean *I* wasn't special. But the truth of it all hit me like a brick wall. He wasn't a hymn. He was a nobody. And I was a nobody too. And the fact that I'd been suckered into this insane game for nine months made me absolutely nuts.

I completely lost it. I told hymn off and I told hymn to go away and leave me alone. I told hymn I didn't believe in hymn or his Father or God or any of this mumbo-jumbo New Age bullshit crap he'd been spewing all over everybody he met. I told hymn he did a lot of talking about love but all I could feel was hate. I saw red. I HATED hymn. And, I hated me for hating hymn.

Somehow, all of a sudden, every hurt, every war, every death filled me with hate. And I raged. I raged at the terrorists who took away my cocksure sense of being safe. I raged at all the stupid politicians who sat a million miles away with tons of their own money making decisions that just made rich people richer and me, and most of the rest of us, poorer every day. I raged that my asleep-self was gone forever and now I was stuck with having to *think* about things all the time.

I raged because my mom had died, my dad never showed up, my Nana was *never* coming home, Angela dumped me, and I was poorer than dirt. But most of all I raged at hymn— for not being Bible Jesus. For not walking on water. For not healing Nana and Bernard. For not bringing any guarantees. For not making it easy. For showing up and making *us* do all the work. For destroying the fairy tale we'd all believed in for 2,000 years.

What was the point, man? Why had he come? Why had I wasted nine months hanging around with this flake and buying into all his bullshit talk? Talk about *talk!* He'd just told Noman it was all about action. Yeah, well, where was *his* action? When was *he* gonna perform? Where *were* all the friggin' parlor tricks? What the hell good is it to have a messiah around who can't or won't DO anything but tell you you're

240

already there, already healed, already God?

I raged until I was hoarse and exhausted. And he just sat there. He didn't say a word. Then, he did the most amazing thing—he smiled at me. Not a show-off smile or a know-it-all smile. Not a fake love smile or a wink-and-nod smile. Not the great big Jesus smile. Just a regular smile—a sad smile—and I dropped to my knees and cried like a baby.

I cried for all the hurts and wars and deaths. I cried for all the times *I* had turned away and tried to forget I was a human being. I cried for every time I looked down on a homeless person and didn't help, or crossed the street at night when some black guys were coming along, or chuckled with the boys in the doorway when some sad lady waddled her 300 pounds by us just as quickly as she could. I cried for all the spirits *I'd* crushed, whether I meant to or not, with way too important TV shows I just had to watch, instead of listening to some boring story told to me, again and again, by the sweetest person I've ever known.

I cried because I couldn't understand how wonderful somebody gets just seconds after they die and how you'd give anything, *anything* in the whole world, to be pissed off by them just one more time. Or how you know you've got a chance to do something good, and for no reason whatsoever, you don't do it.

I cried so much I actually thought I might get dehydrated or something and I thought maybe I should try to collect some of these tears and keep them in a canteen, and carry it around for when I needed to drink down some humanity.

And this whole time, while I was crying and slobbering all over the street right in front of Delaney's, this whole time, this guy Jesus just sat there, quiet as death, with that smile on his face that said he understood—and loved me anyway. And

241

every time I looked at hymn I cried longer and harder...until I had nothing left. There was nothing in me. No more tears and no more pain, no more rage and no more hate. Nothing.

And with a sudden, awful, blinding flash of white-hot understanding, I knew that was exactly what he wanted for me. And it was exactly what I needed. I was emptied—so now I could be filled. With love.

It wasn't sappy or phony at all. It was just an unexpected knowing, like when you suddenly remember how great you felt the first time you could ride a bike without somebody holding on, or when your Nana baked you your favorite pie for your birthday. That memory was yours, it was you, but you'd forgotten it for a long time. And it was great to have it back.

He waited a long time. I was still just this mess of slobber and realizing, right there in front of God and Hollyweird. Finally, he got up and came over to me. He took me up in his arms and just held me for a long time. It wasn't uncomfortable, like you'd think it would be, out there in front of the whole world and all. It was just calm and safe. Tears were still coming out but the part where you can't breathe had stopped.

I couldn't think, not in my usual way. I just didn't have a single thought. All I did was feel. It was like somebody lighting a match in a huge, pitch-black building. You're there, surrounded by all that darkness, and none of it can stop you from seeing that little light. That one tiny spark is more powerful than all the darkness in the world.

I let out a sigh, long and lazy, and suddenly felt wonderful. I imagined it must be like a little kid feels, all fed and warm and tucked into bed and falling asleep listening to their folks talk low in the next room. Knowing, *knowing* they're safe and loved.

He looked at me, with those sad eyes filled to overflowing with love. He took my face in his hands, and kissed me, right on top of my head. It seemed like a long kiss, like he was passing something to me through my brain. I felt a flush run through my whole body and mind. It was a prayer. It was a blessing.

He looked at me once more. Sunset was gone. He hadn't even watched it. It was the only one he hadn't seen in the whole nine months I knew hymn. He'd given it up to teach me about love.

I opened my mouth but no words came out. He gave me that smile, the one that was kind and wise. The one that was love. And then, he turned and walked away.

I didn't know what he was doing. I tried to move but I was just too weak to take a step. He kept walking and walking, down the street, by hymnself. I kept watching hymn, loving hymn, thanking hymn for coming into my life.

I watched until I couldn't see hymn any longer.

And I watched a little longer still.

Be of Good Cheer

I leaned over and switched off the last tape. We'd been listening all day but it was like eating those little ice cream things covered in chocolate—you just can't stop. After the constant buzz of hearing me or hymn talk all day, the silence was sudden and loud.

Louis didn't say anything and I didn't feel like talking either. So we just sat there, staring out the window-walls, watching the sun inch down the rest of the sky in its slow race into the ocean. It reminded me of us, all of us, and how, no matter what we do, we're in that slow race to our end. JC probably wouldn't say it was "the end," not the real end anyway, but it still made me kinda wonder.

I felt a little dazed and it was a long time before I starting hearing the world creep back in. The shadows in Louis' room were getting a lot longer and darker. His sky-roof was filled up with all these colors of blue and purple and pink and I was thinking it would of been a great day to watch the sunset on the beach.

I glanced over at Louis and he was still sitting in the same position, all hunched down in his polished stick chair, staring out through the glass wall, like a fighter pilot with incredible focus about to crash into a mountain.

As the day got longer and darker, I started to feel over-whelmed. And all of a sudden, I started to cry. At first it was a real quiet cry, like when you're at the movies and you don't dare to speak or inhale because if you do, you'll get that noisy, slurpy sound and everybody will know you're crying. But then it got louder and more girly until, without any warning, I was in full mourning mode. I was wailing like I'd lost my best friend.

To his credit, Louis just sat there. He didn't try to say anything helpful or come over or give me a hug or anything that would of really made me crazy. He was in that same position and I could feel through all my tears that he wasn't moving.

After a real long time, I started to run out of tears, not grief. I was still leaking a little, but I could at least breathe again, so I forced out my most important question. "Louis, do you think we'll ever see hymn again?"

"Maybe," Louis' voice was so low I had to strain to hear and I wasn't sure but I thought I heard a little catch in his cords too.

Then he paused. It was long enough that it makes you realize there is a pause and it makes you look to see if it's your turn to start talking. I glanced at him, all wet and embarrassed, and there was still enough light for me to see just the round middle of his face.

"Maybe...in about 2,000 years."

I couldn't believe he'd said that. And then, right in the middle of all this grief and pain and disbelief, Louis did something I'd never seen him do. He smiled. Not a Louis-all-mature-and-chuckling-at-you smile. This smile was different. This smile was kind.

This smile was hymn.

I'd never looked at a man that long—right in the eyes. It was the kind of look that should of been uncomfortable considering how long it was. But it wasn't. It wasn't gay and it wasn't fatherly. It was the making of some new connection, like an off-ramp to a place you've always wanted to go but couldn't figure out how to get there.

The room was completely dark now. There were no more words to say. No more tears to fall. Just two friends, and a little comfort. I had this strange feeling I'd known Louis forever. I wondered if this is what a friend is.

I knew old JC would be telling us to keep "leaning toward love" and make sure we get the enemies in there too! And all of a sudden, he *was* there. I don't mean in the flesh, or even like a vision. He was just there. I could feel hymn. And, with no words, I knew Louis could too.

It was a moment that I wanted to last forever. I stayed in that moment as long as I could, memorizing it. I didn't wanna move or breathe, I was so afraid of losing hymn again.

And then, just like when my Nana used to sit by my bed after I'd had a bad dream, in this strange and wonderful communion with hymn, I finally fell asleep.

Dear God, Having a Wonderful Time, Wish You Were Here

Louis told me to "write it all down, everything you remember," and everything on the tapes. He told me to start writing and just to keep on writing until I couldn't write anymore. He said that would make it "visible" or something like that.

So, after that day and night at Louis', I went to my place and didn't come out for three days. I was still kinda shook up and I needed to get my head together.

I'd be way up and excited that I'd met this guy and had these adventures. Then I'd be way down and wondering if it really happened at all. Did I just dream all this? Was it some kinda hallucination?

Finally, after the three days, I went back up to Louis and asked him.

"He was real, wasn't he, Louis?"

"It doesn't matter. The lesson is more important than the credentials of the teacher."

"Louis, please."

"What do you think?" He was back to the frequently chuckling old Louis.

"I think he was, but I wanna know. I gotta know, Louis. Please…help me."

I felt like I was gonna start bawling again and I began to wonder if we'd really made this friend connection or not. I started to doubt it. I started to doubt hymn. I started to doubt my own mind.

"But you don't doubt your heart, do you?" Louis was looking at me with a weird face and I realized he must of been reading my mind or I'd been thinking out loud again.

"I don't know!" I felt like screaming it and my own words punched me hard in my gut. I hated when JC had said that. Now, I was getting a firsthand lesson of how he must of felt. And, all of a sudden, I was on my knees and crying again.

This time Louis did move. He got right down there with me, on his knees, and put one skinny old hand on my shoulder.

"He was real," he whispered. "He was real."

Back at my place I knew I had to start. So, I tore the place apart looking for paper. Every night since JC had showed up, I'd seen hymn writing, and now I couldn't find one lousy piece of paper.

I was really starting to get all panicked when suddenly, underneath a stack of dirty laundry (what I realized later were the clothes he'd got at Goodwill), I found a kinda folder.

It looked like when little kids try to make a book by stringing yarn through holes to bind it all up. It was upside down but I could tell there were a ton of handwritten pages. I flipped it over, and right in the middle, it fell open, like it had been opened there a million times before and the book knew the way to the part you loved best.

But, when I looked, the only words written on that page were:

Write your own story.

When I flipped the book to the front, I laughed and cried at the same time. Written there, in big, block red crayon letters was his last message to me:

STOP READING THIS BOOK

I laughed and laughed. There it was, plain as day. In those four words was everything he'd told us, for all those months.

Don't follow others.

Find your own way.

Be your own messiah.

I was filled right up with his love for me. And, in that moment, standing there all by myself, with his handwritten words in my hands, I grew up a little. I knew what I had to do.

I dug through the couch and the chair and every pocket and hiding place in the apartment. I finally scraped enough change together to buy…two oranges.

Walking into the alley for the first time without hymn was weird. But I found Alley Guy and gave him one of the oranges. We sat there a long time, eating and sucking our sunset-colored dinner in the sad, beautiful, and weary world.

All of a sudden Alley Guy says, "My name is Jack. Do you know why there's clouds and stars?"

I kinda blinked. I don't wanna sound ignorant or prejudiced or anything but finding out Alley Guy had a name made me feel suddenly—awake.

"No…uh…Jack, why are there clouds and stars?"

"So we won't ever be lonely!"

He said it like a profit and then cackled like a madman.

When I got home, I dug through every drawer until I found an old beat-up legal pad and a working pen. It didn't matter if anybody else believed me or not. I know what's in my heart:

So, I gotta tell you first off…

Epilogue
Communion

So, I was thinking that all of us at The Ark were living in a kind of lifeboat, standing on its end. Louis was like our captain, at the top of the boat, and the rest of us were just there to row like hell.

A lot of life is like that. There's always somebody on top and the rest of us are just rowing like hell. And JC didn't change that balance, didn't even try to. He just came in and watched and laughed and made us think and emptied us and filled us up and left. Just like I guess he always did, whenever he popped in for a cosmic visit.

After he left, Louis was still the captain of the building, Ty and Mr. Yin still played chess and argued because neither one of them could understand each other, Jimmy and his mom still bought lottery tickets, and Autumn and Raindrop still listened to Leonard Cohen, without the music.

Mrs. T still watched her TV all the time, but she didn't watch those Christ guys anymore. Bernard still cried at the drop of a hat but, little by little, he started relaxing just a bit and the old Mr. B showed up more often. He even took to playing something called Pee-Knuckle with Mrs. T most days. (Sounds like a bad bathroom experience to me!)

And Charlie, after he broke away from Noman and apologized to Bernard, still hot-wired the cable.

Angela and me stayed friends. She didn't understand

everything I told her about hymn but she was a great listener. And every time I went to visit Nana, she came with me.

Louis and me still hopped the 217 every week down to Canter's to sit at Rosie's table for some hot pastrami and tough love. And Jack—Formerly Known as Alley Guy—still yelled his crazy profit wisdom every time anybody walked by.

Everything was almost exactly the same—and never more different.

He had touched us. And we were all a little bit better for having known hymn. I think we were all kinder and more patient. We noticed more, reached out more, cared more.

The earth didn't open up, but our hearts did. The skies didn't split apart and show us some MGM Charleston Heston movie about some second or third or fourth "coming." I can't say for sure we wouldn't all of been a little better for knowing *any* real cool, kind person. I mean, we *are* better for knowing them, aren't we? I don't even know if he was the real thing. And, it doesn't matter. He was hymn.

The world didn't exactly get any easier to live in…there was still a lot of anger, and hunger, and death. But, in our little corner of the planet, once a week, a small handful of once stranger-friends, all got together on the roof—at sunset—and remembered hymn.

I think he'd like that.

Acknowledgments

My most profound thank you to:

- My beloved Amber, for giving me the reason to continue... and for worrying I'd need bodyguards!
- My *Nidoba* Marc, for being, without knowing, the model for many aspects of the narrator...and, most especially, for never doubting.
- Mrs. Joan Genofsky, my high school English teacher, who was the first to encourage me to write.
- Sam Hunneman, for editing, over and over, with an astonishing eagle-eye for detail...and for telling me the truth, even when I didn't want to hear it.
- Ann Miller, for the extraordinarily professional text formatting...and for the patience of a saint.
- Mary Ann Cucinatta, for tirelessly reading each draft... and for believing, from the very first.
- The lovely residents of OceanView at Falmouth for providing, with open and kind hearts, most of the questions for Sermon on the Roof

- And to Sarah, for making me laugh.

About the Author

Barbara Buck lives wherever her heart is. Most of her life has been spent in the grand-scale storytelling world of theatre. She is currently working on Book Two in the *hymnandme* trilogy: STOP READING THIS BOOK